Rogue Fleet

Thane Keller

ISBN: 0-9969224-8-2
ISBN-13: 978-0-9969224-8-7

Cover illustration and design by Sarah Keller
Ancient G Font from GenAris @ DAFont.com

www.thanekeller.com

OTHER TITLES BY THANE KELER

The Conquests of Brokk Series (Space Opera)
Fractal Space (Book 1)
Rogue Fleet (Book 2)
Doomsayer (Book 3)

Trials Series (Dystopian Science Fiction)
Trials (Book 1)

For short stories, rich content, and character deep dives go to
www.thanekeller.com

DEDICATION

To the brave men and women that have sacrificed everything to make the world a safer place. May your courage never be forgotten.

GALACTIC MAP

MATEEN / RODAM

TASSI

HESTOS

RAINBOW NEBULA

CHAROTH

DESPONA

CHARLON

JARK / CORIDAN

ᒣᑐᖷᐱ᙭ᑕᓵᖙᗝᖷᑐᒠᖷ ᑎᔆᗝᖷᖷᓵᒠᒠᓵᑎᗝᖷᓵ᙭ᗝ ᙭ᒠ ᖷᑑᖷᑎᓵᖷᖷᒥ ᖷᑑᗝᓵᖷᔆᗝᖷᖷᔆ ᑑ᙭ ᑎ᙭ᙏᙏ᙭ᗝ

ᔆᒠᗝᒦᑑᒣᒦᑑᖷ

(Authoritative Classification of Species: Translated to Common Language)

ᑑᒦᒠᔆᔆᑕᖷᗝᖷᔆ ᒦᑑ ᖷᗝᖷ ᔆ᙭ᒠᑐᔆ ᙭ᒠ ᖷᑎᑕᖷᗝᖷᑐᒠᑎ ᒠᒦᒠᒠᒦᑑᖷᒦ ᑐᒦᒠᔆᒠᑎᖷᑐ ᑎ᙭ᒠ᙭ᑎᑐᔆᒠ

ᒦᒦᒦᒦ ᑐᒦᒠᔆᒠᑎᖷᑐ ᑑᖷᑎ᙭ᙏᒦᖷᑐᖷᑐᖷ᙭ ᖷᑑᒠ

(Published by the Board of Scientific Affairs, Galactic Council, 1342 Galactic Recognition Era[1])

---

[1] Galactic Recognition Era (GRE) is defined as beginning at the Hestonian colonization of other planetary systems. For continuity, all planetary species have adapted GRE as a common dating method.

⸬ ꠅ꠰꠆ꠀꠇꠣꠞꠤ ꠘꠇꠢꠤ꠆ꠒꠤꠘꠥ (Awakened Intelligence)

  ꠀ꠆ Homeworld: N/A.

  ꠡ꠆ Controlled Territory: Fringe Space.

  ꠘ꠆ Physiology

    ī꠆ Average height: N/A.

    īī꠆ Skin color: N/A.

    īīī꠆ Communication: electronic.

    īꠖ꠆ Outstanding features: bodiless self-aware intelligence that take the form of complex computer systems.

  ꠖ꠆ Military and Security: unknown.

  ꠢ꠆ People and Society: unknown, culture is not suspected.

  ꠟ꠆ Economy: N/A.

  ꠥ꠆ Transgalactic Issues: The Great Rebellion (323 GRE) by Awakened Intelligence occurred by a core group of computers operating remotely piloted ships on behalf of Hestos. AI was formally defeated in 511 GRE. Upon detection, AI is destroyed by Galactic Council members. Partnering with Awakened Intelligence is illegal under galactic law. Many AI vessels are believed to have escaped and hidden in isolated areas of Fringe Space.

⸬ ꠖꠢꠢꠤ꠆ꠅꠀꠤꠖꠘ (Desponian)

  ꠀ꠆ Homeworld: Despona.

  ꠡ꠆ Controlled Territory: N/A.

  ꠘ꠆ Physiology

    ī꠆ Average height: 6 feet.

    īī꠆ Skin color: green.

    īīī꠆ Communication: verbal/written.

    īꠖ꠆ Outstanding features: thick bodied and rugged; adapted to the tropical climate of their homeworld.

  ꠖ꠆ Military and Security

    ī꠆ Small defense force.

ii⁻ Reliant upon alliance with Jark to receive anti-piracy benefits.

h⁻ People and Society: Despona operates a democratic socialist government with heavy reliance upon the nuclear family. Families are matriarchal resulting in one female being provided for by one alpha male and several other mates. This results in an abnormally small population compared to other galactic species. Desponians are untrusting of outsiders but warmly welcome visitors when security is not a concern.

J⁻ Economy: The Desponian economy is based on trade, particularly farming and livestock. Because of the tropical climate and smaller but efficient population, Despona is able to grow and sell food all year. While the economy is weak relative to other species, its non-reliance on other galactic members makes it a resilient and self-sustaining planetary system.

U⁻ Transgalactic Issues: Despona has traditionally allied itself with the more powerful Jark Empire.

⁻⁻ ꓵꞰꞰꞰꓘꓥꓕꓕꓥ (Hestonian)

ꓕ⁻ Homeworld: Hestos.

Σ⁻ Controlled Territory: various asteroid belts and mining colonies.

Π⁻ Physiology

i⁻ Average height: 5 to 6 feet.

ii⁻ Skin color: varied between pale and dark brown.

iii⁻ Communication: verbal/written.

JJ⁻ Outstanding Features: the most varied of species in both size, skin, and hair color. Hestonian genetic variety has led scientists to label them a "seed species." Many other races in the galaxy share aspects of Hestonian genetic code but lack the total diversity that Hestonian code possesses.

ꝺ⁻ Military and Security

i⁻ Powerful but aging space fleet.

ii⁻ Members of the Galactic Security and Anti-piracy Pact.

iiii Chair of the Galactic Council.

ͱ⁻ People and Society: Hestos is a democratic republic obsessed with free market and trade. Families are loosely affiliated and typically spread throughout the galaxy for economic reasons. This patriarchal society results in males frequently choosing one mate and children leaving the home early to seek employment.

॑⁻ Economy: Hestos is a wealthy economy with multiple mining operations on moons and in asteroid fields throughout the galaxy. In addition to mining and selling exotic material, Hestos is the chair of the Galactic Council and receives tourist and political revenue.

U⁻ Transgalactic Issues: Hestos has been known to lash out at economic competitors when they feel their interests are threatened. Deep-seated issues between the Hestonians and the Jark Empire date back to 467 GRE and the First Galactic War. Hestos has also fought to maintain a presence in its colonies on Charoth and Charlon, but ultimately failed to prevent them from gaining their independence. Hestos is currently the chair of the Galactic Council and seeks the council to resolve issues peacefully before resorting to armed conflict.

⁻⁻ ͱϡ℧ℓ (Jark)

Ⅎ⁻ Homeworld: Jark.

Ƨ⁻ Controlled Territory: Coridon and various mining operations.

Π⁻ Physiology

　i⁻ Average height: 7 to 8 feet.

　ii⁻ Skin color: red.

　iiii Communication: verbal and non-verbal body language; written.

　ii⁻ Outstanding Features: The Jark prefer to walk on all fours. They have large, thick arms and big shoulders to help support their bodies. Jark males have large protruding teeth that appear to have been used to ward off predators and tear through prey pre-civilization.

ℏ̤ People and Society: Lysops function in no known society and it is unclear how they are born or come to be. The highest concentration of Lysops can be found on Hestos, but they are dispersed throughout the galaxy. Lysops prefer separation from their own species for unknown reasons but have banded together in small groups for religious colonies. The largest Lysop religious cult is found on the southern-most continent of Hestos.

ٮ̤ Economy: unknown.

Ⴑ̤ Transgalactic Issues: Rumors follow wherever a Lysop has been. During times of war or unrest, armies that find Lysops will hunt and kill them to prevent their influence on the battle. Many are accused assassins, spies, and even witches and have been subjected to horrible treatment throughout history.

Ξ̤ Ⴘ⅂ḱḱḱⱭ Ⴖ⤬ϨϨḱⴖḱⵌⴊḱ (Mateen Collective)

Ϥ̤ Homeworld: Mateen.

Ϩ̤ Controlled Territory: Rodam and various mining operations.

Ⴖ̤ Physiology

ꙇ̤ Average height: 8 feet.

ꙇꙇ̤ Skin color: gray.

ꙇꙇꙇ̤ Communication: telepathic; verbal.

ꙇⴊ̤ Outstanding features: tall and thick, the Mateen have dark gray skin and a thick brow. Their hive nature enhanced by telepathic speech makes them unique in the galaxy.

Ꙅ̤ Military and Security

ꙇ̤ Isolationists.

ꙇꙇ̤ Large, powerful space fleet with significant technological investment and innovation.

ꙇꙇꙇ̤ Mateen infantry prefer stealth and utilize cloaking technology to mask their ground movements prior to attack.

ɪɪ꞉ Using telepathy, Mateen fleets are known for swarm tactics and dynamic maneuver that traditional tactics struggle to adapt against.

h꞉ People and Society: Mateen society is tightly knit. While the Mateen mate for life, they are born into a collective hive where all members have access to and are responsible for the other members of society. Non-conformist behavior results in social outcasts that are quickly labeled and permanently removed from the hive.

ɪ꞉ Economy: The Mateen operate a strong economy and have multiple mining interests in and outside of their own systems. They engage in exotic material trade, manufacturing, and defense/munitions sales with other members of the Galactic Council.

ʮ꞉ Transgalactic Issues: The Mateen have ongoing issues with a breakaway colony. More recently, the Mateen have experienced conflicts with the Jark Empire and occasionally with Hestos.

ɛ꞉ ꞮꞀHꞂ (Pisky)

ꓕ꞉ Homeworld: Pr'ioski.

Ƨ꞉ Controlled Territory: none.

ꓵ꞉ Physiology

ɪ꞉ Average height: 4 feet

ɪɪ꞉ Skin color: pink.

ɪɪɪ꞉ Communication: nonverbal with limited verbal expressions.

ɪɪ꞉ Outstanding features: This small and unassuming species are often mistaken for children by uninformed travelers. They rarely speak and instead prefer to use non-verbal cues. When they do speak, their language is broken and limited to few expressions. Only the severely studied have mastered any spoken language.

ɓ꞉ Military and Security: The Pisky are refugees on a galactic scale and rely almost entirely on the Galactic Council and member species to provide for them.

ᛡᚽ People and Society: The Pr'ioski people band together in tribal communities. Resulting natural disasters followed by opportunist groups on Pr'ioski has left their planet uninhabitable and most of the culture and knowledge of the Pisky were abandoned along with their planet. One male mates with multiple females, but relationships between males and females are not exclusive. Many times throughout a year, males and females will have multiple mates.

ᚵᚽ Economy: The Pisky have no economy but dedicate themselves to low skill labor and barter within small communities.

ᚢᚽ Transgalactic Issues: Permanent refugees.

ᛖᚽ ᚢᚱᛒᚱᛁᚻᚨᚱᚢ (Radaishar)

ᚻᚽ Homeworld: Mateen.

ᛋᚽ Controlled Territory: Fringe Space and deep space asteroid colonies.

ᚾᚽ Physiology

   ᛁᚽ Average height: 8 feet.

   ᛁᛁᚽ Skin color: reddish-gray.

   ᛁᛁᛁᚽ Communication: verbal.

   ᛁᛁᚽ Outstanding features: The Radaishar are an extremist group of Mateen that have removed the part of their brain that allows telepathic communication. Their bodies will look diseased as a result of these surgical interventions.

ᚦᚽ Military and Security: Radaishar have no known military and limited security forces.

ᛡᚽ People and Society: Believed to have been a lost Mateen colony, the Radaishar have quietly flourished in fringe space, an area of space at the very edges of the galaxy. Very little is known about current Radaishar society after their battle for independence in 613 GRE, however, it is believed to be similar to the Mateen.

ᚵᚽ Economy: Unknown, suspected piracy and black-market trade.

ⵏ꞉ Transgalactic Issues: Ongoing conflict with the Mateen collective. Minor security conflicts between Galactic Council member species as a result of piracy and black-market trade.

ⵣ꞉ ꞌꓭꓧꓧꓫꓞꓭ (Tassian)

ⵍ꞉ Homeworld: Tassi.

ⵢ꞉ Controlled Territory: N/A.

ⵑ꞉ Physiology

   ꟷ꞉ Average height: 5 to 6 feet.

   ꟷꟷ꞉ Skin color: pale skinned, sometimes described as reflective in sunlight.

   ꟷꟷꟷ꞉ Communication: verbal.

   ꟷꓘ꞉ Outstanding features: N/A.

ⵟ꞉ Military and Security

   ꟷ꞉ A small fleet is held for planetary defense.

   ꟷꟷ꞉ Infantry force was reduced to a planetary defense force in favor of corporate galactic security.

   ꟷꟷꟷ꞉ The Tassians have traditionally relied on a Galactic Council security pact for planetary defense, however, increased nationalism risks a future arms race.

ⵀ꞉ People and Society: Tassians live in a democratic society where the rule of law is honored. Tassians typically find one mate for life and embrace a small nuclear family. Their society still has remnants of a caste system and upward mobility is difficult without the right connections.

ⵏ꞉ Economy: Tassi has substantial wealth from tourism because of the continual daylight it receives from its dual-helium suns. While trade has waned recently between Tassi and Hestos, the Tassians still engage in significant trade between the Mateens and various mining colonies.

ⵏ꞉ Transgalactic Issues: The Tassians endure continued conflicts with the Jark Empire over land disputes.

BEFORE THE JUMP

"Look alive," called a red-headed, barrel-chested man wearing a gray tank top that used to be white. Red, a name he had picked up because of his fire red hair and pale white skin, sent shivers up the spine of anyone that dared to cross him. He was good at his job and he commanded his vessel with an iron fist. He kept them alive too, but when mercenaries complained about their leader they rarely considered the good. "We're crossing the border zone!" he bellowed, wandering from station to station to ensure his men were scanning their sector.

Three of them, one at the front and one on each side manned laser cannons that supposedly cut a ship in half in a matter of seconds if someone crossed him. None ever had but Tamara wasn't sad that she didn't get to see the show. It was a far better strategy to let a mercenary boast about the capabilities of his ship rather than be forced to show her what it could do in a dogfight.

Tamara glanced over at Red and smiled. She liked him. She always had. Red grabbed his handle bar mustache and gave her a wink, his pale white skin shining whiter than ever under the florescent lights in the cabin of the transport ship. He fancied himself more desirable than he really was. Another aspect of his shining personality.

"You gonna keep us safe up here, Red?" She asked.

Red stood for a moment and stared at her, rubbing his mustache the whole time. She suspected he wanted to say something deep and meaningful, but that just wasn't Red. The deeper he thought, the harder he rubbed his face until finally Red's foot, covered in a black leather boot, started tapping too. Somehow that mustache must have been hardwired into his brain because when he rubbed the hair on his mustache, the foot couldn't help but stomp. Finally, after what would be an awkward length of time for anyone else, Red conceded and threw the question back at her. "I should ask you the same thing."

"You know I don't work well up here in the void. Not much oxygen, Red." She looked around the cabin and out of the window before adding "not many elements to play with either."

"Yeah, yeah, I know. None of us want to die if you get out of sorts," he responded with a bit of disappointment in his deep brown eyes. "I had to ask though."

The burly man flexed his chest as he walked past Tamara and continued his checks in the cabin of the small vessel. Their trip was a relatively small one, only fifty parsecs to travel, or the equivalent distance between the planet Hestos and the moon of Charlon. Their ship, a small transport vessel carrying about sixty passengers, four marines, two pilots, and Tamara was a trading ship but had recently been contracted to supply workers to the ever-growing farming requirements on Charlon. The folks they carried were happy for the work and Tamara was happy for some fresh air away from the bustle of Hestos.

As they entered the border zone, their ship groaned and creaked. Tamara could see the steel bulkheads pressing inward but she knew they would hold. They always did. Gravity was distorted in the border zone and pressed on even the most well-constructed vessel in ways that nobody could guess. Not anybody on this ship at least.

As the ship entered, the once blackness of space was suddenly a soup of colors bombarding the small portholes evenly spaced in the crew compartment. Reds, yellows, greens, and blues penetrated every crack of the ship forcing the gray bulkheads and silver floors to reflect a magical array of rainbows throughout the cabin. There were more elements now, but still nowhere to run if she allowed herself to be tempted, if she allowed herself to reach out and seize the boiling gasses of the Rainbow Nebula. No, deep space and the center of a nebula were no place for her talents.

Suddenly Tamara heard laughing from the front of the cabin and saw a small Hestonian boy, no older than thirteen giggling and pointing. "His hair is purple, like a girls!" the boy exclaimed gleefully. Tamara found the source of their entertainment just in time to see Red storming out of the passenger cabin and towards his pilots. Suddenly, she realized his hair was purple from the blue light of the nebula inundating is features. Even his mustache was purple and hid the scowl of contempt he held for the workers that mocked him.

So space can humble even the most barbaric of men, she thought to herself, giggling a bit but suddenly feeling terrible for the man that was so easily angered. He wasn't a bad man, but he was demanding to work for and he relied far too readily on the false image that he sought to portray. Empathy was her strength and she felt it more for Red than she did anyone else. As a young girl, it was him and his team of mercenaries that saw worth in her. Where on Hestos, a place of logic and science she was an outcast, he took her in and made her his own. She clung to him like a father. *And what child isn't just a little embarrassed for their father?*

Tamara wasn't a marine, but she was a fighter and her worth to Red was more than just the company of a daughter. Tamara was a half-breed, a mix of Lysop and Hestonian that gave her certain gifts. Men who didn't understand feared her people, but those who did, men like Red, knew there was nothing mythical or magical about the things she could do; she simply had a greater understanding of nature. A greater sense of the form that elements took and the properties of those elements under certain conditions. That understanding gave her the chance to manipulate the natural world and create things entirely out of the ordinary.

Call her a witch or a wizard and you might be right, but Tamara didn't think so. To her, it was as natural as talking and as enjoyable too. There were constraints of course, but as she grew under his tutelage she learned to harness her understanding and had only once mistakenly seared his fire-red hair.

"Hit the thrusters!" She heard Red shout from the cockpit. Instantly, pressure increased on her chest as the ship pushed against the soupy nebula that exerted its own force against the small gray vessel. "Is that all you've got?" He shouted again, chastising the pilots for the lack of power in the nebula. "My mother can swim faster than this!"

He wasn't simply bellowing orders, however. Underneath the humor and the insults, Tamara suddenly sensed panic in his voice and climbed to her feet to rush towards the open cockpit.

"What is it?" she asked, reaching him as he left.

He ignored her, instead searching for his marines. "Lock and load, we've got pirates coming!" he hollered.

Gasps filled the cabin and scared passengers looked towards their fearless red-haired leader for guidance. The smile that once rested smugly on the young boy's face was now flat and fearful; his eyes wide with dread.

"What about the lasers?" She asked, watching as the men manning the guns pushed away and grabbed their personal rifles.

"Won't work in here," was his response. "Too dense, we'd ignite the whole cloud. Want to die?" he asked, looking at her before turning his attention to his men. "Jakk, put their heads down and take position behind that steel," he ordered. Tamara looked to see a man with hair as dark as coal and a black beard moving through the cabin with a rifle held high. He looked calm, but she could hear his heart beating fast in his chest. She could sense the blood pulsing beneath his veins supplying nutrients and adrenaline to his muscles.

The border zone was no place to get caught by pirates and made for an impossible rescue. If the enemy vessel breached their hull they would be burned alive by the scalding nebula. If their engines were damaged, they would sink to the core of the gaseous beast until all of their food and life support had been depleted and the gravity of the nebula itself crushed them all to death. Their only chance was to run to open space and hope they had enough power left to escape the pursuing ships.

Suddenly, Tamara felt thrusters fire, this time pressing upward on their bodies. The pilots were trying to evade the pursuing vessel and seek a way out of the cloud. Immense pressure attacked her lungs. Her breathing was short and her vision faded.

The cloud was too dense, too deep, and too thick to think. Colors continued to pour in through the window at a dizzying rate of speed. Green. Yellow. Blue. Red. Green. Orange. Then nothing. Blackness. They had escaped. The pressure on her chest disappeared. Sighs of relief filled the cabin but a jolt and a shriek brought Tamara back to reality.

A small spear the size of her fist ripped through the steel hull of their ship and anchored like a grappling hook into the rear wall. Oxygen rushed from the vessel but a second jolt pulled the hook tight against the frame and sealed the hole.

"They've got us!" shouted Red. "Suit up! Get your oxygen masks on!"

Panic ensued as frenzied passengers gripped for their belongings, desperately searching for their emergency kits in the event of a damaged hull or other disaster. Tamara too zipped her blue jumpsuit up to her throat and pulled a hooded mask up from behind. She could feel oxygen fill the suit, but there was something else as well. Complete silence. The ships engines had been dampened. They were fully in the grip of the enemy ship. Lights flickered and faded, replaced with the red emergency lights that came on when they were operating on auxiliary power, fueled by the batteries that contained who knew how many hours of life support before they were done for.

Tamara sensed Red's approach and spun around to see that he too had switched out his filthy tank top for a clean black jumpsuit. A clear mask covered his eyes and mouth. At first, he didn't speak, instead looking at her figure in her skin-tight space suit. In the midst of panic, Red always found a way to show people he simply didn't care. His interest in the carnal was paramount at all times and never once wavered in the realm of uncertainty.

"I can still make your blood boil from inside your suit," Tamara said.

"My blood is boiling just looking at you, girl," was his response. She didn't retort and he didn't give her the time to. "Can you sense anything up there?" He asked, suddenly with fearful dread coating his words. "Are you connected to them by the harpoon cable?"

Tamara tried, but she couldn't. "The void... they're too far still," she strained.

"It's okay, girl." He responded. "They'll be here soon, maybe you can feel them then."

He never accused her, never demanded anything of her. He was her comfort and her rock. He cared for her unconditionally, even in this moment where she felt helpless and desperate. At a time where she should be panicked and considering the past and her future and what might become of her, she instead looked up to the calmness of her captain and found peace.

The ship creaked and jolted as the larger vessel reeled them in like fish caught in the sea. The groaning of steel being pushed and contorted intensified until a sickening realization struck Tamara—they had docked. The enemy ship was directly above them. Suddenly, pounding could be heard and the pale shrieks of steel yielding to cutters filled the compartment. Marines fixed their weapons on the ceiling, waiting to extinguish the threat.

They wouldn't get their chance. The enemy was prepared. As soon as the ceiling of the ship had been cut, they simply let the ten-ton steel object fall into the cabin below. Passengers screamed as smoke filled the compartment. Guns erupted upwards shooting at anything that dared enter, but it was too late. The filter on her suit was never calibrated to remove the toxin emitted from the smoke grenades that now filled her lungs.

Losing control of her body, Tamara fell hard to the ground. As her vision faded she could see Red standing tall, firing his weapon. Then everything was black.

CHAPTER ONE

Fluffy white clouds drifted across a deep blue sky. The sun peaked out just long enough to expose the hundreds of workers below to its warmth and then dipped behind another meandering monster. It was midday and Tamara was starving, but she had not yet reached her quota and lunch was served proportionately to the amount of fruit an individual picked.

A breeze pushed inland from the south, carrying with it the scent of salt from an inland sea and kicking up dust into the faces of the slaves that labored against the elements for a few good greltins. The small bulbous fruit typically grew in clusters on tall orange vines but the drought had been vicious this year and Tamara and her companions were worked even harder to get every last ounce they could scavenge before the harvest season ended.

Tamara stepped through a series of wires holding the greltin vines to the wooden posts and examined the next section. They were bare. A second gust of wind hurled more dust into her face from the south and she grimaced, tucking her hazel green eyes deeper into the cloth that covered her mouth and nose.

The protective tuck brought a sharp pain to her skull and reminded her not to move too quickly. Even after five years, the metal crown she wore that was screwed into her skull at the corners of her head to stop her from escaping still hurt if she moved too quickly.

"It looks like we might finally get some rain," whispered a fellow slave over her shoulder. "Keep some of that dust down."

Tamara agreed but declined to respond and hated him for risking the attention of the overseer for such an obvious comment. As the other man worked, he eventually passed her by without another word. Feeling her hot breath venting up into her eyes, Tamara turned from the wind and dropped the cloth down to her neck, eager to breathe the unfiltered air.

It was a hot day, but not the hottest of days. She was grateful for the clouds to block the sun but dreamed of the mountains beyond their dusty farm on the outskirts of their town. The mountains, like an oasis in the desert, shot up from the north against the backdrop of a dust-filled horizon. More attractive than the mystery of the wild was their rich green color that promised clear water and dust free air. In the evenings after a long day's work, Tamara listened to slave tales of rivers flowing abundantly and more food than anyone could hope to eat.

It was nearly every day that Tamara considered escaping there, but she couldn't; not because of fear but because of the nagging question—*what then?* She wouldn't survive long with the crown blocking out her mind; certainly not if she was confronted by a pack of wild animals. In truth, she knew she was without options, and while she vaguely remembered the life she once lived, it was simply a memory, a ghost from the past, an inconsequential cluster of neurons that distracted her from her work.

Tamara turned back to the greltin vines just in time to notice the overseer was watching her. She had allowed her eyes to linger on the mountains too long and now her taskmaster had become suspicious.

Moving quickly from vine to vine, Tamara tried to look busy in her work, but he had already come down from his stoop and was walking towards her. Panic surged from within. A pit grew in her stomach and erupted upward towards her throat.

Tamara walked quickly to the next row, desperate to pass his gaze. Hopeful that he would see something else that dissatisfied him and forget about her. It didn't work and his hot breath was soon heavy on the back of her neck as he leaned in to spin her around.

The stench of garlic and onions carried a raspy voice with it. "What were you looking at, girl?" he asked, every word dripping with indignation and hatred for the slave he was forced to watch over.

Tamara tried to look innocent. She tried to speak but the pit that had moved to her throat clogged the words. She swallowed and tried again. "The vines," she said. "I'm searching for clusters of greltin."

He held her gaze for a moment, penetrating his brown eyes deep into hers. His leathered skin, darkened from years of laboring in the sun, glistened with fresh sweat that had drained from gaps in his dusty brown tunic. It was a heavy cloth for this time of year, burlap and cotton, catching the heat of the sun and torturing its wearer. Tamara's eyes darted over his large body. The burlap was tied at the waist with a leather belt. Attached to the belt and hanging off one hip was a whip, which he now reached for.

"I swear," she murmured. "I swear I wasn't looking at anything. Please believe me, I swear." She raised her hand to her face as he lifted his own to slap her, but instead, the large dark-haired man grabbed her by the wrist and threw her to the ground.

Dust splashed up as she sunk into the heavily traveled soil and her head rung in agony from the jostling of her slave collar that had been bolted into her skull. He would have known the pain such a throw would cause as he too held the scars of a former slave on his forehead; marks of a man who came from humble roots but now found his calling torturing those that were not as fortunate to buy their own freedom.

Tamara tried to scramble to her feet but her overseer had already unlatched his whip and rose it above his head to discipline the helpless woman. The first snap struck her forearm and she screamed in pain. Her vision blurred as tears welled in her eyes but she fought them from pouring to the surface, feeling a cold wet trickle of blood drain from her arm and drip to the dirt below. The whip sunk into flesh a second time, sending shooting pain up her back as she curled to protect herself.

From the corner of her eye, she could see him raise his arm for a third strike but stopped. In the distance, a voice called the cruel man to a halt and she recognized it. Her master. Her owner. Temporarily her protector. *Temporarily.* "Send her to me," the man shouted.

The overseer reached down and grabbed her arm, pulling her to her feet like she was a child throwing a tantrum. Dust kicked up against her open flesh as he drug her upwards, stinging the raw wound. Through tear-blurred eyes she could see her *temporary* savior clothed in white standing on the balcony of his stone villa, disappearing as he walked inside, but his status as savior wouldn't last. She knew it wouldn't. She had been there before, summoned by the one that owned her body and she instantly regretted ever looking at those mountains.

"Take my word for it, girl," the overseer said dragging her towards the villa. "You don't want anything to do with those mountains. If the cold doesn't get you, the beasts will. It's untamed; even the strongest warriors don't last more than a day." He looked her up and down as they walked before adding. "You wouldn't last more than a few hours."

Tamara didn't respond. Anything she said would surely earn her additional punishment. As the brute brought her closer to her master's house, she knew the night would bring greater pains than this man's aggression could have brought in a lifetime of beating. Where the overseer could only force the whip, her master owned her. All of her.

Tonight, he would make her wish she had never distracted him from his work and in the morning, try as she might to hate him, she would be forced to make amends for her captors and look forward to another day. If she didn't... if she refused to forgive them, the guilt and hatred would surely overcome her. Then where would she be? Depressed? Suicidal? No, Tamara would bide her time and keep herself healthy and one day, like the overseer that hit her, she might be free.

"When you get inside, you only refer to him as Master or Lord. Do you understand?" he growled, stopping to face her.

She nodded. "Yes, overseer."

"Good."

They had reached a brown front door made of darkened wood and bolted to the tan sandstone exterior. Two older women, the master's servants, waited in the lobby wearing tan burlap aprons stained from food and dust. Their dark hair was pulled back into a bun and at once they rushed out to grab the slave from the overseer's hands.

"Come," one of the women said. "Let's get you cleaned up so you are presentable to Master Orno. You remember how particular he is?" she asked, looking Tamara up and down before finally gasping in despair. "This just will not do," she said in a high-pitched squeal. "Jelna, get the medical kit, we've got to have her healed up. He won't like this at all, no, no, no," the woman muttered with an outstretched hand, gesturing for Tamara's.

Tamara accepted and suddenly the warm calloused hand of the housemaid had gripped her and was pulling her quickly through the home. It had only been a few months since her last encounter but the home had already been renovated. Sandstone tile was replaced with creamy marble and the light stone staircase that led up to the main dining hall had been cleaned and painted. Pots full of plants lined the hallways and the smell of flowers nearly overwhelmed her.

Despite the many changes, this was the same old villa and tortured memories of agonized nights fluttered back into her mind, tormenting her. The pit in her stomach that she so eagerly fought back down with the overseer outside suddenly ballooned upwards again and into her throat. Desperation engulfed her and she felt as if she would explode in nervous anxiety. Her face was hot and cold at the same time and each step, forced by the short fat woman felt weak under the weight of her body.

Fighting down the urge to throw up and pass out she tried to focus her mind elsewhere. It was hard with the collar and even the walls refused her ability to sense their texture. Her life was dark and without feeling, trapped within the fleshy walls of her skin, bones, and organs. Finally, upon passing a window at the back of the home, she set her mind to the mountain and all the solitude that it offered her. She *would* escape but first she had to survive. This was going to be a long night.

CHAPTER TWO

"A planet that doesn't rotate?" Brokk was on the bridge of his battleship receiving a brief from his staff. After narrowly escaping Tassi, they had arrived to Charoth, a planet of outlaws where he would rebuild his fleet and hopefully restock his crew. It was a big task that lay ahead of the now hunted battleship and her leader. He hoped they could succeed, but since Lago's death, doubt continually surfaced to the forefront of his thoughts.

"Yes, Commander," his pilot Terre responded. "The side we are currently facing is deathly cold and never exposed to the sun, but because of the planet's location and distance, the sun-facing side is able to maintain plenty of warmth without the overbearing effects on its plant and animal life."

"So this is why it's able to evade the prying eyes of our governments," Brokk thought out loud.

"Exactly. Charoth shouldn't exist. When scientists search for habitable planets, they look for ones that rotate because that is how a planet maintains its magnetic field, maintains its climate, and maintains its atmosphere. This one is truly an anomaly; making it the perfect place for us to regain our strength."

Brokk knew the last line wasn't a dig, but it still hurt. The scars of losing Lago and the Battle for Tassi were only a few weeks old and he could still taste the bitterness of their defeat fresh in his mouth. Defeat he could deal with, betrayal however, betrayal stung almost as bad as the loss of his best friend. His blood still boiled from the anger and an animalistic rage that brewed beneath his skin.

Brokk had been abandoned by his people and made to look like a fool in front of the Galactic Order. This very morning, Brokk woke to a nightmare, reliving Lago's death over and over again as if it was his own. He felt the bitter cold grip him, oxygen rush from his lungs. He would wake up gagging; gasping for the oxygen that he knew existed but was too distant to breathe. Try as he might, he couldn't get Lago's death out of his head. It was changing him, tormenting him, destroying him. Lago's death was his own near-death experience and for a reason he could not fathom, it terrified him beyond his limits.

Some days, Brokk wished it had been his own life that was sucked out into the abyss. His own eyes that exploded from the sudden change of pressure by being ripped into space. Lago would have dealt with this defeat far better, but it was Brokk who was left alive and for whatever the reason, he determined in his mind seize the opportunity to repay betrayal for betrayal, blood for blood, and death for death.

His crew waited patiently and Brokk suddenly realized he had been stewing for too long. He had done this a lot lately and Brokk worried that the men he led were beginning to notice. *Focus.* "How does it maintain those essential qualities with no rotation?"

Terre smiled. "I'm going to do a terrible job quoting our scientists, but what they tell me is that the planet is actually leaching a magnetic field from the nebula it orbits so closely to. In fact, it's likely that the star and the planet both were born to the nebula and are only recently drifting to a safe orbit where life can exist."

Brokk shrugged. "Whatever you say, Terre. Have you found us a place to land our ship?"

"We have," his top pilot answered, spinning a three-dimensional hologram of the planet until he had found the location he wanted. Zooming in, Terre pointed to a plot of farms near the mountains that divided the frozen wasteland from the habitable portion of the planet.

"Obviously, landing your battleship here is ill-advised, but we think building a base camp near this mountain range is a great option. We can keep the battleship functioning from above, using its scanners to search for threats while we conduct our operations from the surface. Our probes reveal the mountain itself is capable of sustaining a small outpost while you explore the city. If our food replication fails, there is wild game to hunt and grains and fruit in abundance."

Terre stepped back and allowed Brokk to examine the map more fully. Terre was full blood Jark but had perfected the ability to stand upright without slouching. His large frame and jet black hair complimented the confidence that he exhibited in his work. To be a fighter pilot, you had to be at the top of your game. To earn the title of Top Pilot, you had to be nothing short of remarkable.

"How far is it from the city and the main spaceport? We'll want to trade and hire crew to replace the ones we lost. I want to survey the ships and build a new fleet of planetary fighters to fill my empty hangars. Can I do all of that from the outpost?"

"I think you can. Even amongst outlaws, word travels fast. We don't want anyone saying Brokk and his fleet of renegades are here," Terre said with a chuckle through a mouthful of razor-sharp teeth. "Piracy is the main economy; we risk someone spilling information you want hidden if we take up residence near the port. Besides," Terre added, "the mountains are dark and shaded. We don't want to relive the constant sunlight from Tassi."

Another dig but Brokk let it pass. They had learned more than one lesson from Tassi. His crew had changed. Brokk had changed. They would dust themselves off and they would learn. If that meant a few misplaced insults had to be absorbed to avoid reliving past mistakes, Brokk would be happy to shoulder them. "Very well. Let's make it happen. Keep the Juggernaut on the far side of the planet. I'll take a shuttle with a company of marines while a second shuttle begins constructing the camp. Ensure we have sufficient defenses, to include ground to air. No mistakes; keep our fortress solid. Remember that we're in hostile territory. These aren't trained soldiers but they're gang leaders and mobsters with a business to run. They'll see us as a threat if we slip up before we're ready to take over."

Terre nodded and prepared to continue but Brokk wasn't ready and instead raised his finger for silence. "And who benefits from the trade?" Brokk asked, certain he knew the answer but eager to let his crew hear it from an unbiased mouth.

Terre hesitated to answer but seeing Brokk's silence he finally conceded. "The Jark Empire seems to benefit from most of the slavery. There are some Hestonian traders that buy slaves as well."

Brokk rubbed his chin but remained silent, letting the information soak in. Finally, after a few more moments Brokk addressed the group as a whole. "The same empire that betrayed us; that left us for dead after sending us to conquer the Tassians has been dealing in the slave trade and drug smuggling. We were trained in the honor of our ancestors," he scoffed, "this is a disgrace." He paused to let his speech soak in before making one final statement. "We already have operatives in the capital. The government is called the Iralene; they are merely a shadow government for the Jark Empire. Remember this. We strike the Iralene, we strike our betrayers."

Brokk spun the hologram around and zoomed in closer on one of the larger farms. While the landscape was speckled with homes, this one was larger than the others and had three other large structures that could house people hostile to his cause. "I want to see who's living on those farms. We're going to need to come to an agreement with them first. We don't need anyone alerting the city that there is a new group in town." He paused again choosing his next words carefully and making sure to address his entire staff. "We can't afford any mistakes. Our mind has to be on the goal. Everyone is our enemy. Everyone."

Brokk looked over to the chief of his army, a man who had served him honorably time and time again. On Tassi, he almost paid with his life. The scarred pure blood Jark, a thick-faced, red-skinned man, breathed heavily as he absorbed the map with his eyes and committed it to memory.

Of the two eyes that he started life with only one now remained; the other was missing completely, leaving only a stitched over flap of skin to remind everyone of his sacrifice. His left arm too rested higher than his right as a result of a broken shoulder that was still healing. Long black and silver hair contrasted sharply with his red skin and, noticing Brokk was staring, he rose to his feet.

"We will of course be ready, Commander."

"I know you will, Canis." Brokk said warmly, then deciding to add, "I'm glad to see you on your feet again. I've been hoping for your full recovery."

Canis didn't smile but instead took his seat again and returned his gaze to the holographic map. With the blue light from the hologram beaming against his face, Brokk could see the full extent of his injuries. Wide gashes covered his cheeks and forehead from his battle with the grootslang. On his temple was a puncture wound, starting above his ear and jutting backward from where a fang narrowly missed penetrating his skull.

Canis had been lucky; but upon learning of his attempted sacrifice, Brokk went into a fury. He gleefully executed the priests that survived the Mateen counter-attack, not just for Canis, but for Lago as well. The priests wrongly read and accepted the infant sacrifice as a symbol that the dead would give them victory. The dead did not, and in turn, Brokk executed their messengers. He decided he was done with their false religion. If the dead had no power in this world as indicated by their defeat and if the priests had no ability to discern that, he would either find new gods or abandon them altogether.

Now, they would rebuild and as his staff examined the map and made notes based on his instructions, Brokk went through his list again. The first order of business was to learn about Charoth, a planet of outlaws and vagrants. With the current information, Brokk believed that the fastest way to grow the fleet was to seize a sizable amount of illicit operations. If ships were being pirated he wanted to intercept the goods. If slaves were being sold, he wanted the first cut so the skilled wouldn't go to waste. If people were being killed, he would find a way to spin it against the current government. Brokk needed to put his hand in everything on this worthless planet, and then, when he was good and ready, he would make the Jark Empire pay for their betrayal until he had executed their king himself.

Climbing to his feet, the men in the command center of his ship snapped to attention. "I'll be ready in twenty minutes, Canis. I'll meet you at the launch bay."

Without waiting for a response, Brokk left the command center and walked down the main corridor towards his private quarters. He went to Tassi to be a chancellor and was betrayed. He would go to Charoth as a warlord and there would be no mercy for those that crossed him.

The three-minute walk from his command post to his quarters gave him enough time to switch mental gears. Remmel, the captured general from Tassi, waited outside the door with his hands and feet shackled. Two Jark guards bracketed him on each side. The pale-skinned general stood taller than his men, but he was frail and old. Wrinkles covered his worried face and his hair had grown long during the three weeks of imprisonment. The gray mop of hair on top of his head now draped over his forehead and rested messily on his shoulders.

He looked weak, but Brokk knew he was well fed. Brokk also knew not to trust appearances. This was the same man that confessed to killing his own kind just to survive. Brokk knew Remmel was a cutthroat leader and he wouldn't dare let his guard down around the man.

"We've stopped," the old man said spitefully, looking him in the eyes with indignation he had only gotten once before from the Tassian chancellor.

"Today is your lucky day," responded Brokk. "I'm going to sell you at the market down there." He paused to make a show of looking the man that hated him so much up and down. Brokk knew his fleet's defeat brought great joy to Remmel; he didn't want the man to see that it affected him at all. "I wonder if anyone will even buy an old man," Brokk mused. "I hear the labor is hard and you can't have more than a few good years left in you."

"I had hoped in the weeks following your embarrassing defeat at the hand of my army, you would have changed tactics," Remmel retorted, spite dripping from every word.

Brokk wanted to slap him but he abstained. Instead, he decided to continue past his captive to don his combat garb. "I hope they pay what you're worth," he muttered.

CHAPTER THREE

After shedding her cotton clothes and taking a bath, Tamara was dressed by the two handmaids in a flowing blue dress that shimmered in the ever-present sunlight. She felt beautiful, but she was just an object. A tool to be used for the outlet of a man's energy. Nothing more.

Tamara longed for the days of good old Red and his band of mercenaries. Red viewed her as a tool too, but he also treated her like family. She didn't mind being a tool if that meant she was useful and cared for, but an object without worth was a fate worse than death and she wished she had been given the chance to die fighting just like Red on that ship all those years ago. She thought about Red often, wondering if he'd made it. Wondering if someday, Red and his filthy white tank top would show up at Orno's door demanding Tamara back. A pipe dream, yes, but something worth holding on to.

It was dusk on the planet and despite the fact that Charoth didn't rotate, it did wobble. The north-south rocking of the planet shifted the sun in the sky between morning and night over a fifteen-hour span.

Thus, the sun would move to the top of the mountain after fifteen hours and then travel to the sea over the next fifteen hours.

As the handmaids fussed over the back of Tamara's dress, she gazed lazily out of the window towards the mountains where the sun presently hovered. Those beautiful mountains; the very ones that had thrust her into this present predicament. But they were worth staring at all the same; maybe even worth escaping to. *Bide your time,* she thought. *One day, you'll be free to explore those mountains.*

"Not like that," hissed one of the women. Tamara heard a slap of flesh against flesh as the two bickered back and forth.

"Stop being so childish," exclaimed the other. "I'll do it, just get me that pin."

The first woman sighed and Tamara could feel fingers gently running up and down her spine as they worked to tailor the dress to fit Tamara's slender figure. The wound on her back had been treated in mere minutes and her skin was entirely healed. *The benefits of modern medicine,* she thought. *He can destroy a body only to put it back together again.*

Her master was a man of peculiar tastes and instead of simply using the female slaves for his pleasure, he preferred to dine with them first. Tamara suspected he secretly abhorred himself and wanted the women to like him, not as their slave master but as a man they would like to befriend. Of course, none of the women did; instead, she and the others despised him all the more. He was too gutless to treat them like the objects they were and too dull for any of them to be interested in his friendship. Her master's loneliness, she suspected was well deserved, and instead of finding real friends or changing who he was, he surrounded himself with servants to tell him how great he was. A man to be pitied; a man to be hated.

"There," said one of the women from behind. "Don't you look beautiful? Master will be so pleased," she exclaimed with glee.

"Now if we can just fix this flower," said the other. Tamara could feel the woman gently tugging on her hair and she detected the scent of a tarib, a beautiful red flower with an orange stem and large petals. There was no mirror in her dressing room, only a window carved out of the tan stone that the rest of the home had been made of but she knew what was happening. The master didn't like to see the metallic crown that he had surgeons screw into her scalp. He liked the benefits but pretended to be blissfully ignorant of the fact that he kept her there against her will. His maids busily worked to cover it up by weaving and braiding her hair around it and then using flowers as an extra layer. He was a gutless and peculiar man indeed.

A gentle breeze pushed through the north-facing window and Tamara allowed herself to close her eyes as the gentle fingers continued to work on her hair. Footsteps alerted her to open them again but instead of a visitor, she realized that someone had left while the other continued her work. She had moved to Tamara's shoulders now, sewing the seams of her dress tight against her skin.

Tamara's eyes were heavy from the work and she wanted to drift again but something called to her from the window. Suddenly, a silver dart streaked across the northern sky and caught Tamara's attention. The spaceport was to the west and she would never be able to see ships taking off and landing at the spaceport out of her current window, especially not facing the mountains. As she watched, Tamara became certain it was a vessel because on several occasions it slowed and changed directions, only to accelerate again. *But why would a ship venture to the far end of the habitable zone?*

Eventually, the craft disappeared from view, hidden against the mountains to the north. Footsteps again came into the room. "Dinner is ready," said the woman. "The master will have you seated now."

* * *

The dining room in the master's villa was on the second floor of the stone structure and possessed its own private balcony that wrapped around the entirety of the villa. The room itself was open to the air and a gentle breeze on a warm night pushed past stone pillars that held the roof above their heads.

Tamara sat upright in her seat and waited for her master's arrival, at which point she would stand and bow, giving him the honor he believed he deserved. While she waited, she allowed herself to gaze out at the mountains, the barriers between civilization and chaos and the gates of her freedom. Instead of escape, she wondered what she had witnessed earlier. Curiosity drove her mad and she yearned for another day in space; for an opportunity to travel the cosmos with Red and his mercenaries.

Most of all, she yearned to sense the elements again. To be able to feel the atoms in the sandstone, the raw emotions of a friend, and to be able to manipulate the heat of the fire. To muzzle her senses with the metallic crown was like taking the gift of sight away from a person. It was cruel and painful, but what was she to do. *Bide your time, Tamara,* she could hear Red telling her. *Bide your time and strike when you're strong.*

Torn from her thoughts was the announcement of her master. She stood and the same shrewd man she had been with mere months before entered and provided a hand for her to kiss. "My lord," she said, bowing and pressing her lips to his hand. It was as soft and as feminine as the women that braided her hair. She suddenly felt scorn for the man welling up inside her; scorn and hatred.

"Ah, my beautiful Tamara," he exclaimed, looking her up and down. "It is a beautiful dress they picked for you tonight, is it not?"

"It is my lord," she replied, eager to sit down and be on with the evening. Her master was dressed in a long thin robe that opened to reveal an ornate green tunic with a high collar. She'd never seen such a thing and thought it looked ridiculous. Making his dress even more absurd were the clashing gray pants under his white robe that flared at the knees and hugged his ankles. Certainly not something a man with any sense would wear.

He paid no attention to her eyes and instead spun her around to look at her open back, touching her sun baked skin with his soft, unlabored hand. "A beautiful dress indeed," he said again.

At last, the greeting was over and her master seated himself across from her. The table had been decorated with two candles made of hoffo wax and a platter of bread and fruit was sprawled out in front of her. Her mouth salivated and her stomach growled but she couldn't touch a morsel until he had sampled all of the food first while her own hunger grew to an intolerable level.

He was in a talkative mood tonight and to her great dismay, pushed his empty plate from his chest and let out a sigh. "My dear Tamara," he started, pausing to look around at the extravagant food choices laid out before him. "Do you remember the day we first met?"

Did she remember? How could she forget standing on a pedestal for all of Charoth to gawk at? Men touched her and examined her features. Filthy slave buyers shoved their fingers into her mouth to examine her teeth while others knocked sticks against her knees to see if she was sturdy. For days she stood in that sun, only to be brought in after she had collapsed from exhaustion, rehabilitated by the modern medicine she wished didn't exist, and sent back out into the sun to bake for another twelve hours.

She certainly remembered. It is a strange sensation to realize that the fear of being bought by slavers has been conquered by the dread of standing any longer. That the desire for death outgrew the desire to continue living in the destitute world of Charoth. When she saw him, she knew he had picked her to purchase. He had returned to her three times previously, questioning the slaver and examining her records. She was relieved to move on with her sentence and into a home with someone that had spent money for her.

"Yes, lord," she responded, eyes cast to the table ensuring to never make eye contact with her master.

"I remember too. You were terrified in that market, but look how far you've come. I've always thought you were a great addition to the team," he said, gesturing beyond the open pillars towards the slave quarters below.

She knew where this was going and steeled herself for the catch. There was always a catch and she never knew why he felt the need to give motivational speeches to his slaves.

"But," he continued. "I can't have you looking towards that mountain. That's what Fielio told me you were doing. Were you looking towards that mountain? Were you thinking of escaping?"

"No, lord," was her reply, but sensing the need to elaborate she quickly did so. "The dust was in my eyes… and the wind. I was simply shielding myself. It was just a mistake, lord." She hoped he would accept her explanation.

He didn't. "We can't have you running off, Tamara." His words faked concern but dripped contempt. "You wouldn't survive out there, you know?" He paused and surveyed the food again. "Let's put this behind us and eat, shall we?"

Relief flooded into her body and her saliva ran wild inside her mouth. But she wouldn't get the chance to taste even one morsel. Rushing through the door came the buffoon that had whipped her earlier, red-faced and panting, but this time he carried a rifle. "Orno, visitors, warriors, they demand to see you at once."

Her master jumped to his feet. "What? Right now? Are they downstairs?"

Taking a breath, the man nodded. "Yes, lord. They're waiting downstairs."

"Well," he said, pausing to gather his thoughts. "Bring the guests up. There's plenty of food and I'm sure they'll appreciate the view as much as I do." He grinned and Tamara knew he meant her, sending shudders down her neck. "Put the girl in the corner," he hissed at one of his maids. "Make sure they can see her form."

Moments after being moved to the corner, Tamara's legs trembled as three very large men entered the dining hall. The first had light golden skin and towered over her master. His broad shoulders and square jaw were offset only by the size of the legs that carried him. He wore black clothes and a rifle of some sort hung at his fingertips, dangling on a sling off his shoulder. On either side stood two red-skinned men, nearly as large and just as wide. Hair covered their bodies and their jaws, the lower bigger than the upper, caused thick white teeth to be exposed beyond them. They too were clothed in black and armed with rifles.

Orno jumped to meet their guests. "I'm Orno, please, sit and relax. While I'm surprised by your visit, I'm grateful you've come so far from the city to meet with me."

The men ignored him, instead looking around the room. Tamara suspected they were searching for threats. Three of Orno's thugs were also in the room, but they looked tiny compared to the men that now occupied her former space. But there was something else. Something Tamara hadn't felt in a long time. As soon as she saw the golden man, her head throbbed and tingled, but it didn't hurt. Suddenly, she could sense everything around him. She felt and heard his heartbeat. She could explore his skin and the elements that composed the clothes covering his body.

She suddenly sensed the room around her too, not as she had with her eyes or her hands, but with her mind. All of it, down to the very elements that beamed and beckoned her to call them. A flood of relief filled her. She could sense again. She felt alive, rejuvenated, filled!

Finally, the golden man spoke and each word that flowed from his mouth formed a visible ladder for her to climb on and dance around as his voice sent sound waves up and out through the room. "Orno, it is nice to meet you. I'm Brokk." The man paused, but something on Orno's face led him to continue. Unalarmed, he moved forward and pulled out a chair. "I'm grateful for you providing the food on such short notice," he continued. "We're new here and looking for friends.

My ship crashed near the mountain, we had mechanical issues. Do you think you could lend us a hand?"

The golden man lied. Orno couldn't sense it, but Tamara could. Suddenly she was perplexed. The words that came from his mouth were red but were coated in blue and green as well. He lied, but she sensed it was for some unknown purpose. Some positioning or strategy that was yet to be learned. Orno took a seat as well and a pleased-looking grin coated his previously perplexed persona. "I'm grateful you've found me first. From where do you come?" he asked.

Tamara could suddenly sense Orno's words as well, as if the golden man amplified everything around her. His presence sent a tingling sensation down her spine and she could hardly contain herself, but she had to. She had to wait a little longer.

Brokk ignored him, instead shoveling a handful of greltins into his mouth. "These are your men?" Brokk asked, waving a sharp utensil around at the three overseers standing on the balcony.

"I have many more than just those three," Orno replied, "But yes, those are my men."

"How many more?" Brokk asked. The question worried Tamara. It was too forward, too probing, too carefree. The red disappeared and instead, his words were black, bloodthirsty, manipulative. This golden-skinned man wasn't here on accident. He was looking for something, but Tamara was too overjoyed to consider the danger. She felt as light as a feather, entirely sustained by the sudden return of her senses.

Orno again didn't notice Brokk's intentions. If only he hadn't thought so little of Tamara, she could have helped him. She had found a new master now, she would reach out to him. "Perhaps fifty," he said slyly as if the man that made his own men look small would shake. "Are these you came with, are they it?" Orno asked.

"Hardly," Brokk responded with a growl, once again looking around the room. His eyes met Tamara's and lingered for just a moment before moving on and eventually resting back on Orno. He noticed her, but not enough and a sudden urgency gripped her. Tamara knew she had her chance. She reached out with her mind and touched him gently, moving his chin back to her eyes.

Like a doll on strings, Brokk lifted his head and fixed his eyes on hers. *Good,* she thought, cupping his head in her hands. *Notice me and I am yours.* But she sensed tension. More than she had ever felt before and the man with the golden skin ripped his eyes from hers and returned his glare to Orno. *No!* She screamed in her mind. This was her chance. *Get him back.* She focused, grabbing him with her immaterial self but feeling only darkness.

"You trade slaves?" he asked, motioning with a knife he had picked up from the table towards Tamara.

"I buy them for work and sell them once they are no longer useful. But I don't trade them per-say. This farm provides the wine to most restaurants in the city. I need workers and occasional company at night. They do well."

Brokk scoffed but Orno pretended not to notice. His eyes were on making money. Tamara wasn't so certain these men had come to do business. She wondered how to be more forceful, how to get his attention. She might never get this chance again.

"You should do your research when you buy a slave," Brokk said.

Orno suddenly looked caught off guard. He looked around the room and stammered, trying to find the words. "Excuse me," he finally managed to say. "My slaves have all served me perfectly well. They even prepared this meal you are devouring."

Orno was simply too dull. Brokk had known immediately. As soon as she reached out and touched him he knew what she was. Her heart leapt in her chest. It had worked.

"How much for that one?" Brokk asked, pointing again at her.

"Oh, she isn't for sale." Her master responded. "She wouldn't serve you any purpose. It's only escape that she thinks about and she doesn't work very hard," Orno lied. He paused to examine her, staring into her eyes as if to teach her a lesson for her mistake earlier in the day. "I have some strong men that I would be happy to sell you. They work hard and would surely help on your journey."

Brokk pushed his chair back abruptly and rose to his feet, giving a nod to his guards. Tamara was startled, she hadn't sensed his sudden action like she should have. The man was masking himself from her. She watched as the two red-skinned guards he entered with faced Orno's slavers. They didn't raise their weapons but they startled the bodyguards and put them on edge. She was in the middle of a stand-off, if not announced, certainly spoken with their body language.

Brokk looked at Tamara, suddenly his own eyes flared and she could sense him again, all of him. She felt his hatred and his pain. She sensed his longing for something deep. She felt the power and energy in his body. But most of all, she knew what he was going to do, and she was suddenly terrified. Terrified, but excited. Excited and ready.

"You don't have fifty men, do you Orno?"

Orno rose to his feet as well, but before he could speak Brokk silenced him by raising his finger. Awestruck, Orno watched as Brokk walked over to Tamara and placed his hand on her shoulder. Instantly, her senses erupted. She not only could feel Brokk and the people in the room, but she could sense everyone on the farm. She heard and felt the beating hearts of dozens of slaves and she could not only feel them, she could hear and touch them too.

How the golden man knew, she did not know, but he squeezed her shoulder and whispered "focus" into her ear, bringing her back into the room. Then, Brokk addressed Orno.

"This one is special, you fool," he said, sending Orno's mouth to the floor and his eyes wide. "In a few seconds, you and the cowards in this room are going to feel extreme pain under your skin. It will be your blood boiling. Then, I am going to take your farm and your slaves with it."

Orno wanted to speak, he even tried to, but he couldn't. Not anymore. Tamara reached inside the hearts of Orno and his overseers and turned their blood from warm to hot and from hot to boiling. Orno screamed, but Tamara couldn't hear him; all she felt was joy. She could sense again and each high-pitched note that erupted from the men agonizing around her fluttered throughout the room like butterflies in an open field.

Turning up the heat, she allowed her spirit to climb each note until she was hovering not just above her body, but above the entire villa. From her new vantage point, she could feel dozens of hearts pounding below. She wanted all of them and she no longer had to ask permission. They were hers for the taking. As with the four in the room, musical waves burst upwards as she heated their blood, using their hearts as ovens and boiling the liquid through their skin. Their screams meant nothing to her, it was only her joy, her elation that mattered.

Then, there was silence and it was finished. A light breeze pushed in through the balcony and Tamara returned to the room with a newfound sense of freedom. Her slavers lay on the floor unmoving and she could no longer sense their life. Orno's mouth hung open, forever frozen in agony. *He deserved worse.*

Brokk spun her around to face him and she eagerly submitted herself to his grip. Gently, he pulled the flowers out of her hair and unbraided it to reveal the metallic crown embedded in her skull. Removing a tool from his belt, he unscrewed the contraption one bolt at a time. Tamara wanted to faint from the pain, but she dug deep, not in herself, but inside Brokk and once inside, she found all the strength she would ever need.

"You're going to be very happy with us," Brokk said with a smile. "Let's get you to your new home."

CHAPTER FOUR

Kostia Klavarnyk was sleeping soundly in his city high-rise when he was rudely roused from his slumber by the sound of fists pounding desperately on his door. Grumbling, Kostia swung his feet over the edge of his bed and scraped at the cold floor with his toes until he found his slippers. He despised being woken from his sleep, especially when he was having a dream where he was winning.

He wasn't winning in his dream yet, but he would have. In fact, there were two larger men from Hestos that were preparing to punch his head in over a woman he must have met that same night. He couldn't remember and cursed under his breath at how quickly the memory of a dream dissipated. He knew the tide would have turned though. He knew he was going to get the upper hand.

Reaching the door, Kostia grabbed the cylindrical handle and pulled it towards him. "This had better be good," he hissed through yellowed teeth at the man opposing him.

Wide-eyed and apologetic, the larger man, a dark-skinned local from Charoth apologized profusely. "I hate to bother you, Mr.

Klavarnyk, but we tried calling nearly a dozen times."

Kostia could see his face was flush with blood and his breath was heavy. His hands fidgeted nervously at his side, grabbing and releasing the gray duty pants that he was issued from the company. The man tried to hide the fact that he was out of breath, but very little got past Kostia and he assumed this man's message must be important. Still, he thought, what is the point of waking up in the middle of the night if you can't have some fun?

"It's the middle of the night," he said flatly. "Why would I pick up my phone in the middle of the night?" Kostia knew what he would have looked like to the man and had worked for years to perfect his image. He was green skinned with yellow and gray scales that started as his cheeks and covered the back of his neck. This alone would have been terrifying for anyone that hadn't grown up with his people.

Where most sentient beings had ears; Kostia did not. His hearing came through the sensing of vibrations that sound waves caused in the air. These vibrations were not captured by ears but by fluid that formed in his large eyes. Yes, this man would certainly be afraid.

Showing Kostia that he was right, the poor messenger responded to his question by gulping in fear and waiting silently for Kostia to continue. As he examined him, Kostia could see that the messenger had black marks that ran up his neck from brandings and the scars of slave bolts long removed from the corners of his forehead. He must have earned his freedom working for Kostia's company, but Kostia could not place the man's face as someone he knew.

"Get on with it," he said at last after letting the anxiety build in the former slave and growing tired of the taunting.

"A ship, sir," the man managed to stutter out of his mouth. Spit had already formed on the corners and instantly Kostia wished the conversation was already over. He wished that he had slammed the door in the man's face and told him to try calling again. "We detected a ship enter the atmosphere and land somewhere along the northern gates. Your instructions were to make sure you knew about every vessel that did not check into your port or attempted to bypass your protocols." The man shifted uneasily on his heels and rubbed his hands together now, unable to contain the nervous energy at his sides for any longer. Kostia could see beads of sweat forming on his lip as he anticipated anger, but Kostia would not be harsh.

"I know my instructions you fool!" Kostia blurted at him. "Who sent you here with instructions to tell me what my instructions to you were?" he yelled.

The man stiffened. "Horick sir, Horick sent me."

"Send the data on the ship to my personal device and get lost," Kostia hissed, slamming the door before allowing the messenger to respond in the affirmative.

A smart man wouldn't have waited long enough to say anything anyways, and, leaning against the inside of the door, Kostia listened to the footsteps echo down the hallway. Now wide awake and full of anger at the foolishness of the messenger, he wandered over to his kitchen, pressing a yellow pad on the wall to summon a cup of tarib leaf tea. Almost instantly, the sweet aroma of the tarib leaf filled his nostrils and left his mouth salivating. A soft beep indicated his drink was finished and he grabbed the steaming cup full of light orange liquid from the receiver and opened the shades in the living room.

Rays of light from a rising sun over the South Sea beamed into his window. While the natives to Charoth easily slept during the dusk and dawn hours, Kostia was not a native and found the rest to be extremely difficult. Still, with heavy shades and the right mattress, a man could sleep through nearly anything.

Setting his cup on a nearby table, he sunk down into his favorite chair. It was white and pod-shaped. An oval capsule with deep padding made from wild corelves hunted near the mountains at the outskirts of the habitable zone. Corelves were expensive beasts, not because they were rare, but because they were vicious. Hunting a pack of those wild fanged animals was risky, but their fur was soft and warm and desirable to anyone that had the cash.

Steam stopped rising from his cup just in time for a file to glow on the inside walls of his chair that doubled as a home office. Swiping his green hand to the left suddenly inundated him with blurred photos of a craft circling in the upper atmosphere and disappearing as it was dwarfed by the northern mountain ranges. Judging by the time stamp on the photos, he could tell his reconnaissance drones had waited dutifully for the craft to rise again, but it did not.

Kostia felt a sudden rage well up inside him that had nothing to do with the information or the blabbering messenger at his door. Who could possibly have the nerve to bypass his spaceport? Did they really think they would smuggle slaves or drugs onto his planet without him knowing? Did they really think they could avoid paying taxes on doing business in his territory?

Kostia waved his hand a second time and commanded the pod to call his office. One the first ring, his secretary answered the phone.

"Yes, Mr. Klavarnyk?" she asked.

"Have my chief of security meet me at my office in half an hour," he ordered. "Tell him it's about the craft that landed last night."

"Yes, Mr. Klavarnyk." she responded.

Kostia flew from his pod and towards his wardrobe. Nobody did business on his planet without him knowing about it. Nobody.

* * *

"More Tarib leaf tea," Kostia shouted to his startled secretary as he flew through the glass door of his top-floor office suite in the Iralene government building. Before she could respond, he was through the next set of double glass doors and finding his seat at a steel coated conference table. Across from him was his chief of security, a large man whose muscles had long turned into fat from the effects of both age and too much food. His white hair was shoulder length and an untrimmed beard covered his neck and fell past the collar of his white shirt. He wore a gray wool overcoat made from some sort of farm animal, of which Kostia couldn't ever tell, and a held wand he planned to use for pointing.

"I'm not interested in a brief, today," Kostia muttered. "So put your stupid wand down. I want you to get straight to the point. How did a ship get past our marauders without being detected and where is it now?"

Horick placed his wand gently on the table and leaned forward to address his grumpy boss. "We don't know. I've dispatched additional marauders in the skies above the city but so far they haven't found anything in the north. I've also asked the northern garrison to look into the alleged landing and maybe question the farms beyond the garrison for answers. At my request, they've agreed to allow a bounty hunter named Thilgod Furstil to investigate further. He can go where the garrison can't, he can find out if there has been smuggling under our noses better than the army."

"Yes, I know Thilgod," Kostia responded, rubbing a scale on this throat thoughtfully. "He's a good hunter and I trust him to get the job done; hasn't failed me yet." Kostia stared at his tea and let the warm steam rise from the cup while spinning a word that Horick had used around in his mind. "But alleged?" Kostia finally mocked. "I saw the photos of the ship. What do you mean, alleged?"

Horick wasn't startled as Kostia had wished. No, not much would get to the veteran soldier. He calmly continued his train of thought as if he wasn't mocked for his choice of words at all. "In the two decades the Iralene party has been in charge we've never had a dealer pass up our port. We've held this planet with an iron fist and men in taverns are afraid to even consider ripping you off." Horick shifted positions uncomfortably in his chair and unbuttoned his jacket. Years of management in a corner office had made him fat and slow. He might have still possessed the military mind, but his body couldn't kill a common rodent and he had been too lazy to buy a suit that didn't cut his circulation off at the waist each time he reclined in his chair. "It's possible this is a ship that took off from the port and had an emergency. Or," he continued to theorize, "simply a drone that was out of sorts. Either way, we'll canvas the taverns. I'm sure Thilgod will ask the local slavers as part of his investigation. I'm certain I'll be able to get you an answer by the end of the next solar cycle."

Kostia gazed into the table and watched his green reflection return his stare. He wanted to be angry but Horick was probably right. Nobody had bothered challenging him or his rules since they established themselves on the planet. He was impulsive, sure, but he also wanted to think that he was introspective enough to determine what was really bothering him about all of this. Why was he so angry and why did it bother him so much that another criminal organization would try to bypass his laws? Isn't that what he did twenty years ago?

His mind shot back to the dream where two men were pummeling him to death with their fists. It had been a long time since he dreamed as violently as he had last night. Maybe it was a sign. Maybe he was bored. Suddenly his reflection's eyes glowed with new life behind them; fueled by the power of a simple idea. "We need to give the men something good. It's been too long since they've tasted the true spoils of piracy. Far too long."

Horick looked at him inquisitively. "We take a new merchant ship nearly every day…"

"That's old news, Horick!" he shouted, cutting him off. "I'm talking about a raid. We need to raid a village, drag the women off to become slaves, execute the men. Sell the boys." His eyes were wide now and he felt himself uncontrollably pushing away from the table and standing to his feet. The idea excited him, rejuvenated him. "Find us a village far out of reach of the Galactic Order and its territory. We're going raiding."

CHAPTER FIVE

The return to their new camp in the mountainside was silent. Fear of detection by using noisier forms of transportation had led Brokk to walk his small element by foot to Orno's vineyard, but now, nearly complete with their four-hour trek, Brokk was regretting his decision. Sprawling farms and vast gullies were the only things between Orno's vineyard and his camp. To Brokk, it was an utter wasteland, but this wasteland was underutilized. Beneath the farms were rich mineral deposits and rare metals that he needed to fabricate weapons, munitions, and equipment. This was a wasteland just waiting to be exploited.

The sun had moved from the mountains and was now at their backs as it sunk slowly in the sky towards the southern pole of Charoth. Once it reached the pole, it would disappear for only a few hours before the planet began its slow rock southward, forcing the sun to restart its journey to his mountain hideaway. Even a few hours of darkness was preferable to the nightmare of Tassi, and despite Brokk's hatred for the white light compared to the red skies of Jark, he appreciated the untamed wild of the mountains and the vast expanse of the prairie.

There was something calming about this planet and the lack of people, something that he suspected he had needed for a long time. Three weeks ago, Brokk was on top of the galaxy. He was a conqueror and a self-made ruler. He believed he was the chosen one, but in the weeks following, he was no longer sure. It was time for Brokk to forge his own way, to throw off the old and put on a new form. Charoth was going to give him the opportunity to start over, and now, with an asset like Tamara by his side, he would have a smooth road ahead of him.

Brokk could finally see the base of the mountain, signified by tall reddish-brown trees with trunks wider than his arms could grasp. Though the forest was thick, he could see the outline of shapes that did not belong. His command center waited.

Entering the forest, Brokk saw the start of their defenses. Mines and sensors were attached to trees and buried under the brush to detect and deter personnel. These smart mines were harmless to a Jark, but an unwanted patrol would be silently vaporized from a blast of compressed hydrogen heated to several thousand degrees. Tamara, however, had nothing to worry about. The mines would not detonate if their targets were too close to a Jark patrol.

Beyond the mines, laser wire waited, threatening to silently slice an unknowing enemy to pieces while simultaneously alerting his command center of danger. Finally, beyond the laser wire were steel towers with feet that drove deep into the ground. On the towers were automatic weapons that continually scanned the landscape beyond. In the center of the triangular perimeter, an oval command post lay fully constructed, ready for Brokk to disseminate his orders and build his empire.

At the base of the nearest tower, Canis waited. With the sun in his face, Brokk was once again reminded of the old soldier's struggle with the grootslang. Deep scars and unhealed gashes ran the length of his face, lessened only in appearance by his dark red skin and black and gray hair that sprouted from his head, cheeks, and neck.

"This is a bad idea, Brokk," Canis said, as soon as Brokk was in earshot.

"What do you mean?" Brokk responded. "This is a perfect location."

Canis fixed his stone-faced gaze on the newcomer and pointed at her. "I mean her. Bringing her here is a bad idea."

Brokk stopped and looked at Tamara and then back to Canis. Canis' eyes were wrought with worry and refused to flutter in even the slightest uncertainty. "Let's talk somewhere alone."

* * *

"This is a bad idea, Brokk."

Canis was reclined against a rock gazing towards the south. The sun had just begun its climb over the inhabited side of the planet. Already he could feel its heat fighting back the cold that was creeping over the mountain during the sun's retreat. The dynamic of the north was unique and Canis admired the extraordinary desolation and beauty. The mountains, like a fortress, guarded the inhabited side from the bitter cold, acting as a thermal barrier that jutted up as high as the sky itself. The cold, the real enemy to the inhabitants of Charoth, tried each night to cross that barrier. Each night it failed.

Jarks, however, were a wild breed and the mountains called to him to explore their darkened landscape. Canis had to fight the urge to forsake his duty and felt enslaved, having to focus on his task at hand. The mountains did not stop, however, they merely settled in the back of his mind until a more convenient time. Another life perhaps.

Brokk stared at him coldly from against his own rock. The sun danced off Brokk's back and formed a golden aura around the man they had once believed to be their chosen one; the golden ruler who would thrust the Jark Empire into a renaissance age of prosperity and possibility. From what Canis had heard about last night, that prophecy may still be true. Canis interpreted his leader's stare not as hostile but as shocked. A month ago, no one would have dared question his motives. The man was untouchable. With their embarrassing defeat, however, all had been called into question and the Jark leadership subordinate to Brokk now insisted on involving themselves in more of the decision-making.

Canis viewed his role as the same. He was the caretaker of the remaining Marines; their guardian, confidant, and maybe even friend. They would continue to serve and fight for him, but they all demanded a reason, they all demanded to know the cost. While before Canis saw value in unfettering loyalty, he now viewed his role to be loyal to the men that served under him as well. The spoils had to be worth the blood.

"Explain," Brokk retorted. He kept his mouth parted as if he was a snake ready to strike; as if he was the grootslang incarnate, fully prepared to beat down any dissent amongst his most trusted commander.

"How can you trust her?" Canis asked. He considered his question to be an appropriate one. Canis, of all people, was wise to be wary when it came to things he didn't understand. After all, it was Canis who was nearly sacrificed by the sadistic Jark priests attempting to summon a creature from beyond the dead. A creature that should never exist and certainly not exist within the same realm of the living.

His shoulder and ribs still ached and at night he still woke with terror at the thought of the beast wrapping itself around his bed. He still saw the Tassian soldiers that stormed the basement, watched night after night the terror on their face as the grootslang devoured them.

After hearing about a woman boil the blood inside another man's body, Canis wasn't just afraid, he was terrified that everything was repeating itself.

"I trust her completely," replied Brokk, glancing at Canis and then looking away. Brokk clearly didn't want to have this conversation and seemed even more aggravated that he was being forced to negotiate with his subordinates.

"I didn't ask you if you trusted her, I asked you how you can trust her. We don't know her intentions and you saw what she did last night…"

"Only after I told her to," Brokk cut in. "She was powerless without my prompting."

"Just like you told the priests to summon the grootslang?" he asked. Canis too was becoming angry at Brokk's clear denial of the facts. "You play puppet master with the lives of my men. We are loyal to you, Brokk. This world, it is yours for the taking. I only ask that you place value on our lives."

Brokk let out a snarl and looked as if he was going to leap from his rock and attack Canis, but then quieted himself, instead choosing to extend his legs out straight and cross one over the other. "How does a warrior like you get trapped by a few blind priests?" Brokk asked, choosing instead to mock his past and take away any legitimacy from his caution. Brokk startled to chuckle and reiterated himself "I mean, you. A seasoned infantryman. A true warrior. How does a blind man get the upper hand?"

The pigment in Canis' face was red and he was happy for that. It hid the embarrassment he felt at being taken advantage of and the anger he felt for being accosted by Brokk. He would not take the bait. Instead, Canis chose to remain silent, locking his eyes on Brokk until the man conceded.

"Do you know she can hear us right now?" Brokk finally asked through the quiet morning breeze that ruffled leaves and swayed the treetops above.

Canis' hair prickled and his heart leapt in his chest at Brokk's suggestion and for a moment he realized he was yet again powerless. Not caught in the smoke, as before, but instead trapped in an invisible psychic energy that the new guest had brought with her.

"She's not a witch," Brokk added, seeing Canis' distress. "Have you never met a Lysop before?"

Canis hadn't and shook his head so that Brokk would continue.

"Then I understand your fear, but you have to trust me that she is harmless." Canis shot him a glaring look to convey shock at the omission of last night and Brokk corrected himself. "Mostly harmless," he conceded. "Have you heard my story about graduating the military academy?"

Canis had. At least, he thought he had. "I know you were a hero. You saved Lago's life on Coridon, but that is all. I know nothing else."

"We were both doomed," Brokk said. His eyes glazed a bit as he recalled the horror of Coridon. "Lago fell and I could see his leg was broken. The bone had ruptured his outerwear and he would have died for sure. I rappelled down the ravine to try and save him, so yes, perhaps I was a hero for trying, but we would never have made it."

Canis examined Brokk as he told the story and tried to determine his angle. The breeze picked up now as convection from the sun heated the cooler air and forced it upward, allowing for more cold air to rush in to take its place. Leaves and branches cracked and fell disturbing the peace and once again cried out to Canis to run deep into the mountains to take refuge in them.

"I could see fog rising from the valley," Brokk continued. "It was dense and icy. I could feel the cold coming off the fog like a thermocline in the water. Visible and frigid. All I could do was deploy an avalanche shelter and cover us. We were starving, freezing, and stranded. We should have died."

"What did you do?" asked Canis, leaning in to see how any of this tied back to the Lysop.

"I heard a voice call to me from the crest of the rock face, a woman's voice. She told me to open the tent and let her in. Lago was unconscious and I knew I was dead. The cold had surrounded us and my bones ached as the blood started to freeze inside my own body. The pain was excruciating. I thought I was hallucinating when I heard the voice but when I unzipped the tent, a woman with eyes as green as an emerald and wearing only a cotton blouse came inside." Brokk paused and Canis could tell he was still trying to make sense of it all. "She healed Lago's leg, stopped the bleeding, repaired his clothes and before I knew it the tent was warm as well. With her, she carried three white-headed rodents, already cooked and hanging on strings. I was sustained and by morning she was gone along with the storm."

Canis leaned back again and rubbed his hairy chin with his thick red hands. He wasn't convinced, but he couldn't write it off either. Brokk may have been cocky but he was no fool. Even in desperate situations, Brokk was not the kind of man that would hallucinate. He was resolute in battle and steady in uncertainty.

"She told me something," Brokk continued, shifting his weight against the tree that supported him. "I've never repeated her words, not to anyone." Brokk paused again and Canis could tell he was debating telling him the words she spoke to him. Instead, Brokk looked over his shoulder and into the densely wooded forest behind him. "You can come out, Tamara. I know you are there."

Canis, again shocked, watched as the slender woman crept from behind a tree and onto the dirty path that led to his meeting place.

"Come, Tamara," Brokk motioned. "Sit with me." Tamara sat and Canis felt terror grip him, but he refused to let it own him or control his life. Stoicism was the mark of a soldier and Canis would show it now if it were the last thing he did. He had to speak to her though, he had to understand who she was and what she could do.

Brokk remained quiet, allowing his ground commander to assess the threat. Canis stared deeply into her green eyes and she returned the same stare, but she was not hollow as the priests on Tassi had been. She had substance, meaning, and depth to her stare. "Can you feel my heart?" Canis finally asked.

"Yes," was her reply. "I sense it beating. It's a strong heartbeat, but I can tell you are aged and have demanded a lot from it."

"Do you want to destroy it?" he asked, trying to catch her expression before she had a chance to lie.

Tamara looked taken off guard for a moment and shot her eyes at the ground. Suddenly she blushed and looked ashamed. "It's okay," Brokk assured her. "You did what you had to do, last night. Tell him the truth, he is with us."

Canis nearly choked on Brokk's words. *He is with us. Was Canis now an outsider? Was this Brokk and Tamara now just like Brokk and Lago before?*

"I love hearing your heartbeat," she finally replied. "The beating is like music and it is combined with the beautiful lighter tones of your blood rushing through your veins as it supplies vital nutrients to your muscles. I can tell that your body has prioritized the nutrients to go to your ribs to repair the bones, muscles, and cartilage there." She paused as her dilated pupils became as small as pins and then returned to their normal size. "I can help you to feel better too if you'll let me."

Canis was furious at Brokk's blindness and no longer cared that he was going to hurt this girl's feelings. "Do you see, Brokk?" he shouted. "This girl just reached inside of me and told me everything about myself. How soon until she decides to turn the temperature up inside and boil my blood too? Or yours? That doesn't worry you?"

"Not in the slightest," Brokk retorted, climbing to his feet and choosing to sit on the large rock behind him rather than in the dirt below it anymore. "I could come over and kill you right now. I could have killed you and your marines on the ship by opening the pressurized hatches in your section. You place yourself into positions of vulnerability all the time. This is no different. We need to make allies and that requires trust Canis. Trust."

Brokk looked at Tamara and she returned his gaze before looking back to Canis. "I owe you my gratitude. Your people saved me, let me serve you in exchange," she said.

Canis had enough and labored against the ground and the pain in his ribs to climb to his feet and leave. "Stay out of me," he responded, furious at Brokk and desperate to get away. He had experienced enough magic on Tassi for the rest of his life. Canis stared at the mountains and thought about joining them, about living off the land and taming the wild beasts that lived there. A place where he was the master and far from the magic that seemed to follow Brokk's army where ever he went. He was tied to his men, however, and he would not leave them now.

* * *

Tamara watched Canis leave and then turned again to Brokk. "Do you want me to heal him?" she asked. "Would that win him over?"

He shrugged. "Why not have a bit of fun with him."

Tamara smiled and gleefully allowed her mind to rush towards Canis' body. She climbed over his hairy back and dug deep into his red skin. Soon, she was flowing with the nutrients in his blood towards his damaged ribs. She soared over his bones and sunk into the deep cracks and crevices of the damaged bone. Three were cracked. The muscle was stretched and mangled and cartilage and ligaments had pulled in the wrong direction, struggling to reunite.

As delicate as a spider spinning web, Tamara went to work, first filling the ribs with new bone and then untangling the mangled mess of sinew and muscle. She then rushed upwards towards his shoulder and massaged the knots, pulling them loose and flattening them out, creating marrow and filling bone where it had been lost.

Canis suddenly stopped and turned to face her but her work was done and she felt satisfied. She simply returned a sheepish smile to his scowl and turned her attention back to Brokk. He was gazing to the south.

"What do you know about the main city," Brokk asked her.

"I know a little, but I was a slave there for only a short time. After they captured my ship, they brought me there. A man came out and inspected all of us. His skin was dark green and he was cruel. I wanted to kill him but I knew I could not. There were too many enemies and I was wrought with sorrow for my crew.

"He examined me and then held me down and screwed the slave's band into my skull. After that, I could feel nothing. All my senses were dampened. They put me on display and finally the man you know as Orno bought me and put me to work."

"Who was the green-skinned man?" Brokk asked.

"They called him Kostia and he always barked orders. He had little patience for any of us. That is all I know."

"And the city, its defenses, who rules it?"

"I've heard some talk," she answered. "They call them the Iralene. They're pirates. The same that captured me. But they govern too. It is the Iralene that allowed Orno to sell his wine in the cities and I suspect the Iralene that control all the trade for the planet."

"And Kostia is the leader?"

"As far as I can tell," she guessed. "I never saw anyone that he had to answer to."

Brokk remained silent, deep in thought. As she waited she thought back to her time with Kostia. He scared her for more reasons than the power he wielded. Even with the slave collar, Tamara could usually judge a man through his eyes and the expression he wore on his face. Kostia was different and Tamara suspected that he considered eating his slaves as often as he considered selling them. His intentions were always mysterious and even now she shuddered.

"How far can you sense?" Brokk asked, breaking Kostia's memory from gripping her further.

"Up the last row of trees before the grassland," she responded. She guessed it was about thirty paces but couldn't be certain.

"And do you feel out that far all the time?"

"All the time," she hesitated wondering how much to expose. "I felt much farther when you touched me at Orno's. There is something inside you that helps me."

Brokk smiled, but even though she couldn't understand his thoughts she sensed his intentions to be mostly selfish—just like Red's. "We're going into the city today," Brokk told her. "You'll come with me and be my guide. I also want to see if we can't outfit you with some clothes to help you sense even farther. Get this slave garb off of you. Do you think you can do that?" he asked

"Yes," she smiled. "I think I can do that."

CHAPTER SIX

Thilgod Furstil grimaced and covered his face to protect it from the sharp breeze that pushed dust and the flaking remains of decomposing bodies into his nostrils. He had hoped the balcony attached to the villa would provide relief from the stench of the dead. It didn't. At the capitol's request, he had traveled north to investigate allegations of a ship. Reaching the northern garrison first, Thilgod thought it wise to bring a handful of men to canvas the northern farms beyond. This was wild territory and coming across this present situation left him glad that he did.

Technically, the Iralene didn't have jurisdiction here. This was a place where slaves, purchased from the city, were brought to the countryside to live and work. Their life expectancy wasn't long but they *should* have a life expectancy. The start of the day was slow and expected, each farm telling him they had heard and seen nothing and that all was quiet. *The slaves worked hard and the slavers feared nothing*, the owners told him, careful to thank him and the men of the garrison for his time. *Lies.*

Thilgod knew they weren't truly thankful. The garrison in the north represented everything that the farmers beyond the gates despised about the Iralene rule. They paid their taxes to avoid any backlash from the government, but if a wounded soldier walked up on their property asking for help, there was a greater chance no one would find the man's body as opposed to the poor sap getting aid. Best to just stay away was Thilgod's motto, which is of course exactly why the Iralene sent him instead of the northern garrison. In the wild, the people preferred their privacy over protection and had gotten used to living life on the fringe. A man asking questions would be seen as far less burdensome than government troops, far less risky if something bigger than just questions hung in the balance.

When he reached Orno's lot, however, what he discovered sickened him. He suspected it would sicken the other farmers too, maybe even change the relationship a bit between the farms and the garrison. The corpses of two dozen slaves lay strewn across the ground with many still rotting in their beds. Some clutched their hearts and others had faces frozen in the agony they felt at their point of death. Orno himself lay clutching his table cloth, food sprawled on the floor around him. Only the flies moved in the tan sandstone villa that rose up out of the ground, and only the flies knew in what peculiar fashion so many could have died.

From his vantage point on the balcony of the villa, Thilgod could tell this was no ordinary event. Folks didn't just die for no reason and from what he saw so far, there was no reason for this.

"Poison? Contamination maybe?" the man to his left asked, pulling him out of his thoughts and back into the gruesome room he so desperately preferred to avoid. The question was rhetorical, Thilgod knew that. Still, he turned around and faced the wiry, pale skin man that uttered it. Jilken, a doctor from the northern garrison returned the stare. Jilken's eyes were narrow and his head small. He spent far too much time in an office and with patients than he did on patrol and, clearly being bothered by the sun, he squinted as he stepped out onto the balcony to avoid its light. His leathered face, wrought with wrinkles and accompanied by long gray shoulder length hair showed Thilgod what he already knew, the man had no clue what they were up against.

"Maybe," was Thilgod's response. "Maybe. It doesn't answer our question about the ship though, does it?"

"The alleged ship," countered Jilken, turning his eyes from the dining table on the second floor of the villa and towards Thilgod who remained unmoving on the balcony, surveying the plantation below. "Are you here to investigate the ship or the murders or both?" The doctor was suspicious and hostile. He didn't like being roused on an early morning investigation for a man that had no allegiance to his garrison. Thilgod was an outsider; the doctor hadn't told him that verbally, but he knew well enough.

Bounty hunters were always kept at a distance from the Iralene regular forces. If he had to put himself in their shoes, it could have been for good reason. During the Iralene's war, bounty hunters and assassins were utilized on both sides and a bounty hunter's allegiance was rarely tied to much more than the size of an employer's purse. Thilgod liked to think he was different, but the stereotype was mostly true. He was a vagabond soldier for hire. He cared little for politics and even less for the lives of those he hunted. To be a bounty hunter, you didn't need friends; couldn't afford them, because they were always being bought by someone else for more cash than you had on hand.

"It would have come from the north, those mountains right over there," Thilgod said, pointing towards the horizon and deciding to ignore the doctor's frustration. Even Thilgod had to admit it seemed coincidental at best. All of these people dying at the same time, most of them clutching their hearts with faces frozen in agony. Contaminated food or bad water should have been the most likely source. The problem was he didn't see any vomiting. The stomach should have tried to reject an invader. It did not, leaving Thilgod to ponder other causes.

He needed this to be beyond natural for other reasons as well. The northern garrison agreed to help his investigation because they believed there could be a potential threat in the wild. If a ship did land, criminal activity would increase causing them more heartache than they wanted. If he wanted their help, which he desperately needed for the sake of their investigative resources, Thilgod would continually tie the possibility of the ship to the deaths they presently investigated. This might not be the garrison's territory, but it was certainly their problem if there was a connection, and that was sufficient for both Thilgod and the garrison's commander to come to an agreement.

"I know of nothing on a ship that causes the hearts of men to stop beating," Jilken responded with a combative doubt that made Thilgod angry. "I'll have to take samples back to our lab to test the blood for poisons, but all of the people living in the outskirts are low-tech. It's not likely we'll find any evidence beyond their own bodies."

Thilgod knew he was right. No cameras, no logs, and no witnesses. Then it struck him. *Logs.* "The Iralene keep medical records of all the slaves on this place, right?" Thilgod asked. The doctor nodded as a sharp breeze ripped up from the north and rattled the cups and silverware that had fallen off the table from Orno's desperate grasps before falling dead on his back. "What if some slaves escaped; got a hold of some poison and slipped it into the well without the slavers knowing? What if there are a few of them that planned it but they couldn't trust the others? What if they're walking north towards their friends on the ship that landed, or south for that matter towards your garrison?"

"Wouldn't survive long in weather like this," the doctor retorted, trying to make a case against the useless hike north that he must have suspected was coming. "There's been no water for days. It's hotter than it has been in weeks. A still wind to further dehydrate. Rain is coming; you can smell it in the gusts. Hypothermia will follow a rain like this on a desperate slave body that hasn't eaten enough food to keep warm. No, they wouldn't last long at all," Jilken said with certainty. "Unless..."

Thilgod cut him off. "Unless they had help. Unless that ship was looking for their friends. Unless for the first time since the Iralene seized power somebody tracked Iralene piracy to Orno's farm and mounted a rescue for people that he took."

Jilken eyed Thilgod but remained silent. He was an old man and had been around for a long time. The doctor's Hestonian roots further gave him insight into the motives of men and allowed him to apply sound logic to a situation. His face was expressionless, unreadable, and unchanging. Thilgod saw it as a good sign; the man was considering the ship as a viable theory.

"I need a roster of every slave," Thilgod told him. "I want DNA samples of the dead and need to bounce them off Orno's roster. If one is missing we'll know I'm right and we'll be able to validate the theory that a ship landed on the planet without the Iralene's consent, with hostile intentions, and a desire to free their comrades."

"How," the doctor abruptly asked, "do you jump from a missing slave to a ship?"

"You know the power of those collars," Thilgod responded, desperate to clinch the northern garrison's continued aid. "They scramble the mind, confuse the thoughts, and make it impossible to touch without unbearable pain. No one has ever taken off their collar and no slave has ever been able to help another remove theirs; without removing a collar they don't make it far from the farm. Since there are no bodies beyond the fence, we know someone else removed the collar. Since no one on any other farm would dare sabotage another slaveholder out here in the wild, it had to be an outside job—thus, my dear doctor, the ship."

The doctor grunted against an unrelenting wind that pushed Thilgod's long black rifle against his leg as it hung from his shoulder.

Already, Thilgod was thirsty from the heat. His eyes and mouth were dry from the constant wind that poured through the grassland planes from the mountains beyond. A miserable place this was. Guarding the north was no easy feat. Tracking a fugitive through it was even worse, but he was now convinced this was exactly what was going to happen. Bounty hunting came with its perks, however, and if Thilgod could solve this mystery for Kostia and link the events at this farm to a new enemy in the north, he was certain to get some relief. Maybe he would even get better work in the main city. Thilgod turned and looked back into the villa where he could see the doctor collecting samples.

Flies continued to buzz as they fought each other for the right to suck any remaining nutrients from the dead. These weren't the same flies from Hestos though and Thilgod knew to be cautious. The breeze might dehydrate, but it kept the flies away. With a two-inch wingspan, a stinger on the tail, and a three-needle sucker on the face, those were flies you didn't want to bother.

Returning his eyes to the ground below, he watched two soldiers drag a woman dressed in maids clothing out and lay her in the dust. Whatever happened, it was a strange day when even a helpless house servant met her end. A white apron covered a dirty tan canvass blouse and on her face she wore a combination of shock and terror. She knew something; of that, Thilgod was certain. It would just take a little detective work to figure out what that was.

CHAPTER SEVEN

Hunting in the void of space came with unique challenges that were rarely encountered when conducting missions like planetary interdiction or counter smuggling. Still, the similarities were also vast, and for advanced warships, those differences were easily mitigated. After completing over twenty hours of route assessment and pattern analysis, Terre developed target packets on nearly a dozen mid-tier pirate vessels. None came close to matching the Juggernaut in size or tenacity. To Terre, snatching ships and slaves would be like shooting fish in a barrel. A crew, however, that would be Brokk's problem.

The twelve vessels Terre selected were part of a comprehensive plan to rebuild the fleet. Terre believed the best method would be to rebuild in phases and Brokk had given him the green light. First, he wanted to capture enough ships to field a mercenary fleet that would later be used to seize the bigger ships. Pirates were loosely affiliated and this would be their downfall. Where a pirate cared only for his crew and his booty, a fleet could be tasked to work together to bring down bigger prey. Resources could be consolidated, crews could be trained together, and larger objectives could be met. Their selfishness would be their downfall.

Terre had no room for individuals. What he needed were privateers. The twelve ships he selected, of course, were crewed and manned by individuals. They would have to be executed after capture so that Brokk could fill them with disgruntled and marginalized pilots from the planet's surface. Once filled with people and outfitted with Jark munitions, Brokk would turn his rage against the Jark Space Fleet itself, selectively choosing destroyers that regularly patrolled shipping lanes his crew knew about. Terre smiled to himself as he thought about dispensing justice against the Jarks that so readily disowned their own people. He only wished they would be able to do it sooner.

From the cockpit of a prototype attack class warship called the Shadow Stroke, Terre waited for his prey. As he waited, he allowed himself to unfocus his eyes and drift through the vast cosmos. Space didn't bother him the way it did others in the fleet, and while many men couldn't bear to drift in a powerless ship light years away from any help, Terre reveled in it.

The Shadow Stroke reveled too. The most modern ship in the fleet, the Shadow Stroke was almost entirely computerized. Functions such as monitoring climate, preparing food, and routine engine maintenance were fully automated. The advanced functions too were automated and where an ordinance officer would be needed to select and load munitions or a targeting officer was required to identify enemy vessels for destruction, Terre needed neither. As a result, crew cabin space was minimized while the room available for armor was maximized. Speed and durability reigned supreme with the Shadow Stroke and in her class, she knew no equal.

There was one other function unique to the Shadow Stroke that only it possessed. The cockpit rotated independently of the ship and was in its center. Instead of a triangle, like Brokk's battleship, this one was spherical. Engines and weapons pointed outward where ever the ship was oriented and the only orientation that mattered was where the enemy was. The ability of the pilot to orient his cabin based on the enemy vessel separate from his direction of travel was paramount to his ability to react to and eliminate multiple threats in a nearly instantaneous fashion. Most importantly, it was the only assault sized vessel in the galaxy that had the ability to engage in wormhole travel during combat, something that increased his advantage ten-fold over an unsuspecting enemy.

While on the outside, the warship was a dark gray, to Terre, it was as if he floated in space without a ship at all thanks to a complex array of cameras that gave him a three-hundred and sixty degree view of the space around him. Lurking silently with the power off, Terre scanned the space beyond through an eyepiece that wrapped around his head. The device he wore was connected to his ship, making it an extension of his own body. Like a hunter in the woods, Terre was at peace—and then he saw it.

His headband vibrated once on the right. A small dot, then two. The computer in his ship worked feverishly to detect the type of vessel that was approaching, but Terre already knew what and who it was. It was an armed mining class vessel and a standard ship for a poor pirate just trying to make an honest living in the vast universe. Equipped with two front-facing cannons, a half dozen more cannons on each side, and a grappling hook and cutter underneath used to mine asteroids, it would be formidable against most transport vessels; but to Terre or a modern space fleet, the ship was a joke.

As soon as his computer detected the ship it began its scans and data suddenly poured in all around him. His computer told him his target would reach him in eight minutes, that the Shadow Stroke would be in range of their weapons in six minutes, and that they would be in range of his weapons in four minutes. If he wanted to, he could simply obliterate the ship now, but that wasn't the goal. He had to seize it. He knew the armor depth was three meters, that the atmosphere inside the vessel was mostly oxygen with some carbon dioxide and a small amount of nitrogen. Most impressively, he knew there were thirteen pirates on board and over one hundred slaves, as indicated by the size and positions of the living area on the ship. The slaves might survive, the pirates, however, would not.

If only we had this technology ready for the battle of Tassi, Terre thought, remembering how entirely outmatched they were against the surprise attack of the Mateen fleet. But there were limitations and against modern armies with sensor and wormhole dampening, advanced radar, and even more advanced thrust, it always became a dogfight and often times, the one with the element of surprise won the day. Terre was glad they were not in a fair fight this time.

Terre swiped his hand and illuminated the once dead vessel. Everything hummed to life and in a few seconds the enemy ship would detect the Shadow Stroke ahead. Terre didn't want to give them that chance but Brokk's plan insisted on fear. Opening up his communication array and broadcasting on all known short-range frequencies, Terre called to the bronze pirate vessel bearing towards him.

"Enemy vessel bearing 378.2 marks towards Charoth. This is the Shadow Stroke, I order you to halt and surrender your cargo." Terre waited and repeated the message. They would of course not halt, but they would hopefully transmit a distress call to Charoth. Thirty seconds elapsed. A minute. The ship remained on course. Terre waited. Intuition told him they were getting too close. His ship warned him he would be within range of their weapons in just one minute.

Terre repeated the message. The veteran pilot's intuition once again begged him. *Move.* He would not. Suddenly the ship changed course and swung to the side. He was within range. Smoke erupted from the barrels of six steel cannons, three stacked upon three. The display in his eye went red. They fired upon him. Terre pressed hard on his yolk, taking the Shadow Stroke into a steep dive as the six depleted uranium rounds rippled past his vessel.

The Shadow Stroke dove but his cockpit centered on his enemy. Again he could see smoke erupt from the cannons that tracked his movement, but Terre was getting the hang of piloting this new craft. He rocked his yolk to the right and pulled up hard as six more rounds snapped past his ship. It was his turn, but he had to take them alive. Terre allowed the targeting system to lock onto the top three cannons and depressed the fire control button on the yolk. Three green orbs full of liquid plasma sprung from directly underneath his seat towards the enemy. He banked left as another volley of rounds missed.

The ship turned to avoid the oncoming plasma bursts but they were too slow. Terre watched as the green blobs connected with the enemy's cannons and sunk into them like a drop of water into a pond. The barrels warmed and contorted in the space beyond the ship and began to melt, drops of liquid steel floating away from the vessel at all angles.

Diving, he passed underneath the ship, again learning the benefit of a free-floating pilot's cabin. Facing up, Terre fired another burst of plasma munitions and melted away the cannons on the far side. A few more passes and the ship would be finished but suddenly another flash of red from his heads-up display nearly blinded him. Two more vessels were approaching. Before he could react a second flash of red indicated rounds were being fired at him. The pirate's friends must have received a distress signal. *But so soon?*

Terre again pressed hard on the yolk. His ship dove downward and spiraled to his left. Algorithms on the craft's computers sensed he was trying to escape incoming rounds and throttled the engines faster than he believed he could go. His hands were damp and he struggled to keep his fingers tight against the controls as he spun and weaved. Proximity rounds erupted around him. The sound of metal vibrating off his armored hull told him some found a home in the Shadow Stroke's armor. *How did they get here so quickly?*

Irrelevant. Destroy them.

Centering his cockpit towards the threat, Terre saw them. Two Jark reconnaissance ships that had been patrolling several light years from him must have received the distress call. *But to answer pirates?*

Don't stew. Figure it out later.

Proximity rounds continued to explode but a new threat suddenly leapt into his mind. The Jarks had neutronium and he wasn't sure he could dodge those.

Keep moving. Keep spinning, find a chance to reorient and then let them have it. His ship selected his own neutronium rounds but the reconnaissance ships weren't forced to remain in one place like the mining craft had been. New technology allowed them to fire and move. This was a dogfight.

Terre pulled up on his yolk causing his spherical assault vessel to change directions and center on one of the ships. The second altered its course to drop behind him. Terre dove. His cockpit spun around backward and without warning, he was now charging the second ship. It pulled up just before Terre could fire his volley, but now the first ship had considerable distance on him, pulling away so it could target him from farther out; so it could avoid the dogfight. He couldn't let that happen. He had to bring them both in close and outmaneuver them. More rounds zipped past him from the second ship that had come about, but Terre was alerted and pulled hard to his right.

The ship charged, desperate to keep him in their sights. Terre was quicker and dipped down. The scouts rocketed past him and Terre pulled up, firing round after round of dense neutronium. One, then two found their mark and the back half of the triangular ship splintered. Fire erupted from hull and bodies were ripped into space. Terre didn't watch.

Pulling the Shadow Stroke about, he found the first ship just as it launched another volley of proximity rounds in his direction. Suddenly, the computer flashed yellow and he pressed a button accepting its recommendation. In an instant, the space between him and the enemy vessel became hazy like water. Proximity rounds erupted but they were nowhere near him. When the haze disappeared he realized he had just used a wormhole to jump behind the scout. They could never react in time. Terre lined up his target and fired three rounds directly into the side of their vessel.

It was over. Terre won his prize but knew more would come. He had to leave; and fast.

CHAPTER EIGHT

Getting into the capital city was easy enough, if not a bit unnerving for the once enslaved Lysop. Using Orno's borrowed and no longer needed terranean transport vehicle, Brokk and Tamara whipped along magnetic highways into the epicenter of the habitable part of the world. They made the three-hour journey in silence, but that didn't stop Tamara from hearing. Metal rippled and hummed as it bounced back and forth off of the magnetic field used to sustain and propel magnetic travel. When oncoming vehicles passed she could sense a screeching followed by a snap, caused by two vehicles rocketing past each other at several hundred kilometers per hour.

On occasion, Tamara found herself lost in the elements of the magnetic field, reaching into them with her mind but unable to truly grasp the powerful force. Where her previous journey left her entirely unable to sense anything beyond the metallic headband and black hood she wore over her face, this one captivated her. Brokk seemed to not be the talkative type and so she didn't try. It didn't bother her either. She was safe in his presence and he seemed to have no desire to use her as Orno had. That made her happy and she felt as free as she had when she served Red and his band of mercenaries.

Beyond the highway, skyscrapers shot upward where rolling hills and farms had been mere moments before. Stone streets and sidewalks blanketed the landscape and free Hestonians, Charlothians, and others bustled about, looking busy and concerned with only themselves. At each intersection, Tamara saw slaves standing on pedestals to be auctioned off by their captors. It was a heart-wrenching sight and remembering her own captivity, Tamara resolved in her mind to be an agent of freedom for these poor souls—if she could find a way that is. Perhaps Brokk would help her.

Deciding to give the magnetism a break, Tamara looked down at her hands as they pushed deeper into the city. Brokk had given her a new outfit, one he claimed would help enhance her ability to feel the elements. Instead of the blue dress that she wore at their first meeting, Brokk fabricated her a black and gold shirt that was armored at the chest and along her ribs. The armor wasn't heavy, it was light and moved as if it was an extension of her own skin. She wore jet black pants with hints of gray across the knees—another reinforced area that would make it easy for her to kneel, sprint, and slide. Instead of thonged sandals, she wore boots, with three straps to pull them tight across her ankle.

The season was unpredictable this time of year, and so he had also given her a black and gold trench coat with a golden hood, which he claimed was the color of his priests and would serve to give her the recognition she deserved in his army. The most significant gift her bestowed upon her though was on her hands. She flexed her fingers in and out examining the ornate jewelry. Gold rings that started as bracelets and extended as spikes beyond her fingernails were beautiful to look at but deadly to the touch. Tamara could feel her energy surging within her as she open and closed her palms. It was as if she was one with the car and with Brokk. She sensed more now than she ever had in the first few hours of meeting Brokk or any time before. Whereas before, Tamara believed she could only manipulate elements, with her new gloves she thought as if she might be able to forge elements out of nothing. It excited her. It seemed to excite Brokk as well.

Despite her enhancements, Brokk still was able to shut her out just as he had resisted her at Orno's villa. He shut her out now, a blackness of unmoving atomic particles as dark as space and just as immovable. It didn't bother her, not really, but she couldn't help her curiosity and was desperate for him to once again open himself up to her.

The magnetic transport pulled to a stop along the side of the street and was suddenly whisked up to a holding zone for vehicles to wait until their owners were complete with their business. Tamara watched as their ride climbed upward along the exterior of the building—lines of light flashing every four meters until they had been tucked into a space all their own. "Are we here?" she asked, suddenly realizing she had no idea where "here" was or where it was even supposed to be.

Brokk looked strangely at her. His golden skin was darkened by the shadow of the enclosed holding zone. His eyes, black as coal surrounded by white corneas flared. Something was going on other than the trip to the center. Suddenly she noticed a small implant just above his left ear. He was getting a transmission. A report. He didn't look happy. Finally, his gaze returned to the present and gave her a smile. "Yes, I believe we are here," he told her. Then quickly adding, "Do you think you can remember enough of this place to take me to the green-skinned man's business?"

Tamara was now the one caught off guard. Sure, he'd asked about Kostia. He asked a lot. For her to take him there though, that was entirely different. All she felt was pain from this city. Pain and remorse for Red and her friends. She never saw any of them again after the capture. Never knew if Red had survived or was killed in the raid. Now, this Brokk wanted her to bring him to meet the man that was responsible for all this pain. Would he recognize her? Would he associate her with Orno?

"What if he recognizes me?" she asked softly. Afraid to tell this man "no" but more terrified of letting him down; desperate for assurances that were likely just assurances without any real substance behind them.

"You are powerful, Tamara," was his response. In the dark, she couldn't quite make out his expression to be encouragement or a true belief in her, but luckily, he didn't stop with that one phrase. "I have business with this man. You've only seen a small portion of my force back at camp. This very morning, my ship captured one of his vessels. There were thirteen men on board and nearly one hundred slaves."

Tamara gasped and was suddenly hit with a flurry of doubt; that her meeting him was not just wild circumstance, that his intentions grew beyond a camp of outlaws in the mountains, and that Brokk was more dangerous than she wanted to believe. It was freeing still. Along with the doubt was hope—hope that perhaps her dreaming along the road to rescue slaves was not a dream. Hope that this man Brokk would help many people, not just those on Orno's farm. *Orno's farm.* The thought trampled hope into the dust along with reality. Brokk had only helped her at Orno's farm. She was the one that burned them.

"What do you intend to do with the slaves?" she asked expectantly.

"That depends on him," he replied, indicating to Tamara that this man was colder than she thought.

"And the slavers?"

"That, again, depends on him."

She said nothing for a long time in that dark hold. They descended stairwell after stairwell, the sounds of their feet echoing off the steel walls of forty or fifty stories. Ever downward they traveled. The light grew as they got closer to the surface and soon she realized they did not just spiral downwards but they were in an angled stairwell, moving closer to the outside of the building. Eventually, with one last step, she had reached the bottom. Tamara stuck out her hand to find the door but Brokk stopped her and forced his face level with hers.

"What would you prefer I do with the slaves?" Brokk asked.

She was taken aback, stunned. Her heart skipped a beat and in what should have been an eternity she said nothing, simply thinking about the possibilities. "Free them," was her response followed by a refusal to exhale.

He thought for a time longer than hers. Light from the window in the door danced fiercely off his drab gray overcoat. "Okay, Tamara," he finally said. "But I want to give them the option to work for me first, as freed men. I want to recruit them into service."

"Recruit them for what?" she splurged as she found herself guessing.

"I'm sure many of them have talents like yours. I intend to bring down the slavers and then I have my sights set on a greater prize." His eyes were cold and black. His seriousness was not to be underestimated. There was no convincing this man of anything else. She had seen the look before, the same on Red as he fired round after round at a dozen boarding pirates before she blacked out.

She wouldn't resist him. He offered to free the slaves and he offered her that same freedom. She would work for this man, might even recruit for him. "Okay," she said, pulling her hood up to cover her face as they prepared to exit onto the city street. "On one condition."

He eyed her but waited patiently, as if to tell her, *I'm listening.*

"I'll be loyal to you and your cause, but I want you to let me in on the whole plan."

Brokk let out a grunt and shoved through the door, exposing them to the bright light and wind of a city at twenty thousand feet above sea level. Tamara raced to catch up and slipped her hand onto his arm to match his pace. She would try again later.

* * *

The walk through the city reminded Brokk of everything he hated from Tassi. On Jark, the entire society strived together towards a common purpose; minds were set on warfare with the ultimate goal of pleasing their leader. Tassi, and now Charoth, had people that were aimless. They wandered, not out of necessity or drive but out of boredom and desire. Brokk passed countless residents meandering through shops. They rubbed their hands against silk and linen and mouthed words to their partners that held their change purse.

Vendors called out to him to show off goods as meat and fur hung on ropes in front of tented stores along the busy street. Slavers were more aggressive, seeing the ornate jewelry that hung off Tamara's wrists, they assumed wealth and continually confronted Brokk as if they had something he needed. All of it, every last thing being sold was either a good stolen from piracy or a person conquered during piracy.

"This one's got a strong back," one slaver hollered at him, reaching up to grab a large pale-skinned man's shoulder. The man grimaced and Brokk noticed his skin had been burned by the sun from countless hours of being marketed by his harsh new owner. Before Tassi, Brokk would not have cared. Slaves ran deep in Jark history and he was no fool to know that some captains in the Jark fleet even delved into the slave trade themselves. He cared now, though, for reasons he did not fully understand.

Call it compassion, although he did not. Things had changed. He'd missed a rebellion under his nose. He thought he could instill fear and discipline in the face of democracy but he only sowed discord. Chancellor Ebb had been right when Brokk threw him from the building as he seized control over Tassi. Those people would not yield under threats. Brokk began to believe that these people might not yield much longer either. He began to believe that perhaps enslaved societies were already on the downfall of their peak and that people demanded more from their leaders than simple direction.

Brokk wanted to keep going. His operatives had found someone he had to meet with, but instead, Brokk stopped and to the slaver's delight he sized up the slave. The man was big but it wasn't the muscles that caught his attention. It was the markings. Black ink swirled in spiral patterns across his chest and three red lines pulled across his stomach. These were the markings of a warrior. Despite the fact that he stood on a stone pedestal and kept his eyes cast down, Brokk knew this man was more than met the eye.

"What was your occupation, Slave?" Brokk asked the man. He felt Tamara nudge up closer to him and the slaver, delighted to find a customer, stepped towards them both.

"It matters not," the fat-bellied Hestonian said, inserting himself between Brokk and the slave. "This is a man built for work. Whatever you need a slave for, whether it be protection for your wife or work on the farms, he will do the job."

Brokk grimaced and felt his old self surge within him. This worthless slaver would not last a day against this man nor anyone in Brokk's fleet and yet he had the courage to try and make a sale.

"I was speaking to the slave," Brokk growled, allowing the half Jark part of him to be exposed, along with a row of carnivorous teeth. The slaver smiled sheepishly and backed away. "Slave," Brokk said again. "Don't fear my gaze. Look up at me and tell me your profession."

As Brokk said the words, he knew again exactly what this man was. He was a soldier, likely captured during some foreign war.

"I fought for the queen's army on Despona," he said. His deep voice was weary but confident, shaky in delivery and yet smooth and courageous.

"Despona," Brokk mused. "You were a member of the rebellion then?"

The man nodded and Brokk realized why he was hesitant. Despona was a planet that had long been conquered by the Jarks during the early conquest. The Jarks did not stay and this man would have been too young to have lived during that war. Despona though was weakened by the battle and left open to warlords and criminals. Many of the women were trafficked with the promise of work elsewhere in the galaxy, only to learn they were lied to by their potential hires and forced into a life of prostitution and labor.

"A freedom fighter," the man said, fixing his gaze on Brokk. Deep brown eyes looked steadily through a thick brow. The man's mouth was wide and his teeth, healthy. But he was fatigued, exhausted, overworked, under-fed, and a dozen of other issues that should ward off an astute buyer to damaged goods.

Brokk looked now at the slaver. "How many of his people are there?"

The slaver was perplexed. "You mean in this shipment?"

"Yes, how many do you hold?"

"Fifty-three," was his response.

Brokk felt Tamara's grip tighten again and wondered what she was sensing. Suddenly, just as she had done at Orno's, he felt hands grab his head. He fought them, but she was stronger now, free from the slave collar. Her metal fingers dug into the flesh beneath his coat and her hands, the ethereal ones that held his face pulled not his head, but his mind—forcing him to look at her. Her eyes were wide with expectation and the rich green of her iris expanded until Brokk believed for a moment he was on an ocean in the middle of the sea. His heart wanted to relax, to float with the waves but his mind told him this was wrong and abnormal and dangerous.

"Buy them," she hissed. "Buy them and they will surely help fulfill your purpose."

Brokk shut his eyes and forced her out. Hands disappeared from his skull and her grip loosened on his arm, but not without leaving their mark. He felt the damp trickle of blood run down the inside of his bicep to his elbow. It wasn't much, but it was enough to cause his shirt beneath his coat to grow damp.

Brokk looked at her and she returned his stare. "Those are daggers we put on your finger. Be careful with them, yeah?" He then looked back at the slaver whose face dripped with confusion. "Get him out of the sun. I want his whole group. Take the collars out of their skull and feed them a real meal. I need healthy workers, not dying ones. How do I arrange shipment?"

CHAPTER NINE

"A keen observation," the man mused. He was short with skin as black as the night itself. Long red hair flowed from his scalp and rested on his shoulders and scars speckled his arms and wrists. He wore the clothes of a slave, a brown canvass blouse with matching pants but three ornate gold necklaces, strands that intertwined with gold and silver and various colored gems, hung from his neck. As if the necklaces weren't enough to show stature, silver and gold bracelets adorned his wrists and clanked as he moved them freely about. "And your men? There are many of them watching me?"

Brokk nodded. His height was nearly twice that of the man that introduced himself as Atworth Kierce and his skin was as gold as ever when contrasted with the nearly black skin of Atworth, the self-declared ruler of Charoth. "We aren't watching you," Brokk said with a chuckle. "We simply took notice of you." He added, pausing to shoot Tamara a glance. "We're glad you took notice of us too. We're especially glad you agreed to meet with me on such short notice. I know it can be difficult to trust anyone these days."

Atworth Kierce picked up his glass containing a brownish liquid and took a sip. Tamara sensed his heart flutter as the sharp smelling sludge hit his tongue and slid down his throat. "It's bitter," he said, looking at her. "Would you like a taste?" She shook her head and the men behind him laughed. Bodyguards, she presumed, but remembered back to the utter inadequacy of Orno and his men and realized that it was Brokk who had the upper hand. "This is the good stuff, dear girl!" Atworth bellowed, returning his half-full glass to the dark wood table. The glass vibrated against the wood and sent shudders through her body. Moisture from the cooled liquid inside the glass created a ring of water that the table was quick to absorb. "This is the good stuff," he said again, quietly now.

Brokk picked up on the sudden change in tone. "It can be good again, Atworth." He said.

Atworth cut him off from adding anything else to the sentence by raising his hand and swirling it flippantly through the air. Despite the size difference, Atworth had an ability about him to command respect and wasn't afraid to demand it. Brokk wisely obliged, as did the men in the root cellar three levels below the busy capital streets. Tamara looked around and tried to count the people in the dimly lit bar off the main drag. Fifteen at midday. Not packed and likely capable of fitting four times as many patrons during the peak hours. Maybe more if they didn't mind standing.

A barmaid in a short canvass dress wiped spilled sludge off the counter and returned a rag to her shoulder. She busied herself in her work but was clearly as interested in the conversation as the other patrons of the bar. Her skin was dark, too, and matched Atworth's color. His daughter perhaps.

A single set of wooden steps, permanently fixed to the stone walls had carried them down. It would be difficult to escape, but Brokk didn't seem worried and neither was Tamara. For the first time since her arrival here, this was a meeting among allies, perhaps even friends.

Tamara returned her attention to the table where the two men sat opposite each other. Both stared into their drinks. Finally, Atworth was ready to continue his musings.

"Did you know it's been nearly twenty years, Brokk? Twenty years since my exile; since the Iralene purged our government. It wasn't perfect, but we were united. We were skilled and happily provided visitors with our goods."

"What happened?" asked Brokk. His heart was strong and steady. He seemed genuine but she wouldn't be able to tell. He had asked her to monitor Atworth, but she couldn't help herself but to sneak into Brokk's body as well. If she didn't focus, she could be lost in him, just as she had at Orno's, diving into his strength while trying to explore the parts that were entirely off-limits to her prodding mind.

"The Jark Empire found richer mining elsewhere," Atworth continued. "Decided we'd be better off as a marketplace for the illicit rather than a trading post for the rare minerals required to fuel spaceships. It didn't seem like anyone cared and despite our cries to the Galactic Order, we were ignored."

"I want to turn you back into that," Brokk said resolutely. "I want to give the people here work they can be proud to do."

"You'd bring more war to our people," Atworth retorted.

"I'll bring you freedom," Brokk hissed, before taming the wild Jark inside of him and bringing out the cool-headed Tassian once more. "Above your planet is the most advanced battleship the Jark Empire has ever built. On it is a battle-hardened force of pilots and marines. There will be no war that cannot be swayed from the bridge of that battleship."

"What is one battleship against the Jark Empire?" Atworth asked.

Tamara sensed Brokk's heartbeat rise and thud violently in his chest before settling back down. Atworth had angered him, but his face remained expressionless. "The Jark Empire will lose ship after ship if they come close to your planet."

"How?" Atworth questioned. He didn't challenge Brokk with his question. Instead, he seemed truly curious. "How does one ship stand up to an empire?"

"Your planet is special," Brokk told him, shifting in his chair and spinning his own drink around against the wooden table leaving rings of water where ever it touched. "The nebula protects you. It's almost impossible to go around. It's the same reason you didn't develop nearly as quickly; the same reason you were behind the curve when the galactic powers arrived at your door."

"And in return?" Atworth prodded, raising his glass and downing the second half of his drink, coughing once but still being careful to swirl his tongue in against the rim to lap up any last drops. "You wouldn't simply give me my planet back I presume?"

"Something like that," Brokk responded. "I'm not interested in governing, but I do want all the resources my fleet can handle. I want a safe haven to re-crew my ship and a place to make repairs to the fleet. My men are tired and war-weary. We want sanctuary. In exchange for a continued relationship, I will keep your government supplied with the latest weapons and ammunition."

"That's not all, is it?" He prodded again. "A man like you doesn't simply track down the exiled leader of a planet to find a place where his men can rest." He laughed. "The Iralene would have given you that, Brokk! They would have given you all the slave women you could handle too. You might have made a mistake coming to me," he grinned, winking at Tamara.

"No, that's not it," Brokk replied, shooting Tamara another look and letting his gaze linger on her for a moment longer. "I want revenge on the Jark Empire for betraying my crew."

"Ahh," Atworth said understandingly, as if a great philosophical truth had just been illuminated in his mind. "I've always believed that a man with a carnal motive could be trusted because one can project his direction." He looked at Tamara now. "This is a beautiful woman you have brought with you. Where, my dear, do you come from?"

Brokk nodded approval and suddenly Tamara felt flush with embarrassment. "I was a slave here until Brokk rescued me," she managed to say, diving her ethereal self into Brokk's chest and hiding from the gaze of Atworth and his men.

"You must be very important to him to have been brought to such an event so soon after your own recent meeting."

"She is," Brokk interjected as he took a sip from his drink. "Do you have the ability to organize a resistance if I provide you the weapons?" Brokk asked changing the subject to get back to business.

Atworth reluctantly returned his gaze back to the golden-skinned man that towered over him at the table. "This is easy, Brokk. We've had an organized resistance since the day we were ousted."

CHAPTER TEN

Corelves were ferocious creatures. They walked on four legs and at a meter and a half tall, could eat a man's face without having to jump. Their fur was thick and gray with speckles of brown and was desired by the rich for all types of clothing. Just one was formidable but these liked to hunt in packs and in the wild mountains to the north, a pack of corelves could kill a hunter with ease and even do damage to a twelve man scouting party if they let it.

Luckily for Thilgod, the two he used for tracking were bred in the capital rather than borne in the wild. Even luckier for Thilgod, these two were trained. Luo, the bigger of the two now took the lead down the narrow farm road and toward the wild. His shaggy tail weaved back and forth as he sniffed the ground, stopping to paw and whine as he found a trace of their outlaw and to look back for direction. Dacia followed close behind Luo, ensuring to catch and inspect the scent. If Luo was headstrong and arrogant, Dacia evened him out with sound logic and caution. As much logic that could be applied to an animal that was. After she confirmed he remained on the trail, she would trot back to Thilgod. Luo was the bait, but Dacia was the one that would make the kill.

Taking his eyes off the beasts, Thilgod looked towards the mountains. The path the animals had taken him on led him straight into the wild. At the last sniff, Luo had veered north, trotting over the road and towards his prize. Thilgod would have thought better, and probably still should, but he believed he had the upper hand. One slave had escaped, a female purchased nearly five years ago named Tamara. After the garrison pulled the slave records and identified the dead, they realized one was missing. After their doctor pulled her examination records, everything he found at Orno's farm made sense. *No, it didn't just make sense, it fit like a glove.*

Orno had unknowingly bought a Lysop—a race of vagabonds whose minds could be channeled to control the elements of nature. What Thilgod couldn't figure out is how she managed to channel the elements with the collar still wrapped around her head or how she had managed to get the collar off by herself in order to use them in the first place. He had captured Lysops before and knew to his bones that the collar wasn't defective. If the collar had lasted for five years on this slave woman without incident, it would have lasted for another five unless there was some type of intervention. Either way, the dead bodies from the farm had answered his first question—a Lysop had escaped and she no longer wore a collar; these two revelations made her extremely dangerous.

After reporting their findings to the Iralene council, Thilgod's contract was modified to find the Lysop. His orders were clear now, ignore the ship, find the woman, report what happened, and bring her head to Kostia so he could deter others from trying the same thing. Let the army take care of the rest.

Luo stopped and smelled the air and Dacia left Thilgod's side to join her partner. They circled, sniffing the ground and returned to their original spot in the grass before sitting. The trail had gone cold.

Thilgod now believed he had the answer to his second question. One did not simply disappear; not even a Lysop. She had help.

Thilgod reached the spot and stuck his hand into Luo's thick fur. The creature whined in a frustrated tone. *I feel the same way,* he thought to the beast but neglected to speak those words out loud. Despite the indicators, he knew where she went. The outlaw had gone to the same place that all fugitives go when they stage an escape. She was headed for the mountains to try her luck against Luo's cousins. One animal pack, a trained Lysop might be able to handle, but corelves weren't the only things out there and not even remotely the fiercest.

Beyond the foothills, hunters returned with terrifying tales of giant beasts, some with six legs and some with more. Fangs as long as a man's arm and claws just as fierce. Scouts would return from reconnaissance missions with stories of narrow escapes. They spoke of trees that came to life and slithering creatures that captured dozens of men in their party. It was wild country out here and whoever her accomplice was, they would not be able to protect her for long. In fact, it was likely him that needed protecting, thought Thilgod. She was the dangerous one.

He turned his eyes towards Orno's farm. The road had long since disappeared and he guessed they had walked about three or four hours since the scent of rotting bodies were no longer carried by the wind. The sky looked like rain. Clouds pooled and swarmed above him. Storms on the prairie were not gentle and the one brewing overhead looked especially vicious. Soon they would gather enough moisture and dump an ocean's worth of rain onto his head.

"Good for the soil, though," he said to Dacia. She whined. She was right, they needed to find some trees to set up camp out of the wind. "We'll find some lower ground," he said to her. The beast's eyes grew soft and his two companions rose to their feet, this time allowing Thilgod to lead the way.

He wasn't alone. He wished he was, but it was a rare day that the commander of the northern garrison allowed a bounty hunter to wander around by himself to track an outlaw. Hunting and tracking was what he loved and being alone with nature, his thoughts, and his pets was the most rewarding day he could think of. Luckily, the men in the garrison knew as much and in the absence of a real threat, they allowed him to do what he loved without much objection. He wasn't alone though.

As Thilgod moved toward lower ground, dozens of other figures rose from the grass behind him and pressed onward. They wore drab olive clothes with twigs and leaves sprouting from their shoulders and helmets. Most had faces coated in brown and black grease. Some had gone a step further and stuck dirt, grass, and leaves into the grease itself to further camouflage their faces. Thilgod refused such measures. He had decided long ago that if the white of his face was the difference between being detected and slaughtered or the difference between getting the upper hand or losing a battle, they may have lost the war before it began.

For a representative of the Iralene party to move beyond the safety of Iralene territory required a company of infantry to escort him. Though he wished otherwise, this was no different. Thilgod slowed and allowed the lead squad to overtake his position and lead them into the thick brush towards the bottom of the valley. Due to the climate and landscape of the prairie, harsh winds prevented trees from taking root in the highland region. Instead, the trees followed the contours of the ground, seeds finding places to sprout along dips and valleys where the wind wasn't as strong and where water was in greater abundance. The trick, Thilgod thought, was to find a spot where trees grew but water wouldn't pool in tonight's storm.

* * *

Wind howled and Luo whined. For being the bigger of the two, Luo was a real coward. Thilgod shifted on his foam mat and instantly felt cold liquid pressing up against his skin. *Soaked.* The company had failed to find suitable cover from the storm. A gust of wind ripped through the trees and knocked heavily against the flap of his canvas tent. *This will not do.*

"How long was I out?" he mumbled to Luo, as he squirmed his way out of the warm feathered sack and onto his knees. Dacia was outside pacing. The storm had her nervous, but maybe it was more than just the storm.

Outside, the wind was fierce. Leaves rocked back and forth on their branches and trees groaned under the weight of the relentless gusts. Despite their outcropping of trees, massive water pellets fell from the sky as if a god himself was thrusting them onto Thilgod's head. He shuddered and pulled a hood over himself. The hood barely helped. Red flashlights illuminated the forest as other soldiers roused.

Lightning cracked, revealing the cloud-ridden sky before thunder exploded directly above them. Curses from his men followed that threatened both the rain god and his mother. Thilgod didn't realize the rain god had been born like the rest of them and another flash of lightning indicated the god didn't either.

"This won't do," Thilgod shouted over the wind as he found the patrol leader packing up his own shelter.

"I know," he returned, lifting his head just long enough to acknowledge the bounty hunter that had caused them to endure the storm and catch a face full of cold wet daggers from above. Grease bled from the man's face and pooled down his neck as water droplets the size of hailstones rolled off his hat. "We're packing up," he shouted.

Dacia whimpered and shoved her black nose into Thilgod's hands. She must have appreciated the news. Thilgod did too. He made a point to never view circumstance as a setback. He was eager to find the outlaw and whoever had aided her escape and now the storm would help move the element towards their final goal. There was no way the witch was moving in this storm; likely huddled down somewhere at the base of the mountain. They'd gain good ground marching through the night and when the weather finally cleared, he was certain they'd be close to the base of the mountain.

Another crack of lightning and another ear-splitting rumble sent his corelves into a panic. "Half day's journey to the foothills," he shouted at the patrol leader. "They're eager to get back on the trail too," he added, standing to gather the rest of his belongings. The younger man nodded but didn't dare look back up from his work. He had learned his lesson the first time.

In a matter of minutes, the company was off and marching again. They stuck to the hillside, avoiding the open plain where the wind would be roughest. Rain pelted his face relentlessly, but it was better than laying in a puddle at the bottom of his tent. He had done that before too, and the experience of an old soldier told him marching was always better than shivering to death. Marching kept a man warm and allowed his mind to consider other things.

Thilgod focused on trying not to slip. The hillside was quickly washing away as not only rain but torrents of mud flowed under his black boots. He looked down at his companions and envied the four-legged beasts. They sniffed at the ground now, focused on their own task. Their fur was wet and they kept their ears back, but they kept moving. *Eyes on the prize,* he thought to himself and then *this too shall pass.*

CHAPTER ELEVEN

Bring him to me at once. Orders. Brokk once loved the prospect of watching men jump at his every command. He had earned it; graduated at the top of his class, was the youngest to command a space fleet in the history of the Jark Empire, and was even selected to rule a conquered planet. All of that had changed now and the only badge that mattered to him was the one of betrayal. He was thrown out, discarded, trashed. He was nothing in the eyes of the empire and everything he had learned was irrelevant.

For too long, Brokk attempted to rule the way Jark society demanded. Be a warrior. Accept nothing less than perfection. Demand men excel or die trying. This was the culture of those that betrayed him. He was no longer sure he wanted that to be the culture of those that still served him.

Over the last month and even more so in the last two days, Brokk had time to examine what he really wanted and how he was going to get it. Revenge, yes, that was always at the end. Those he led, however, they deserved better. Jarks like Canis were intelligent. Jarks like Terre were successful. Jarks like Lago were brilliant. Why did Brokk need to stifle their own leadership?

Because it is the Jark way. If you do not rule them heavy-handed, they will think you are weak and will destroy you.

Perhaps, but no more. Brokk leaned against a rock that had become his favorite resting place as a Jark guard brought Remmel into his presence. The old general's eyes were heavy and he looked even more exhausted than he had the day of his capture. Captivity was wearing on him. If he didn't act worried, Brokk now saw that he was wrought with it. His skin now stretched across his tall frame revealing high cheekbones and deep-set eyes. Shackles dangled from the man's wrist and clanged as he shuffled towards his captor.

Canis, the commander of his army, appeared behind him as well. He breathed heavily but looked better, lighter on his feet. *Healed.* The work of his sorceress had done exactly as it was supposed to. Scars from the battle with the grootslang still remained but his body was healed, and Brokk was happy to see him looking better. Canis did not smile, however. He was all business and after their last exchange, he had kept himself distant. It was the Jark way, never good at defeat but always capable of understanding their place in the pack.

At his side, the beautiful Lysop stood. Her green eyes flared with anticipation and excitement. He had not told her the purpose of this meeting, but as soon as she saw Remmel he knew she was marveling at the chance to explore this new person.

"Take his chains off," Brokk said to the guard as they came within earshot. He watched with amusement as Remmel's face sunk even deeper into despair than it had been mere moments before. The unshackling of a prisoner of war in the absence of negotiations typically meant execution. Remmel would have known that and even though he surely expected his time was nearing an end, the weight of a man's own death could never be fully prepared for. The guard, confused at first, obeyed and immediately unshackled his prisoner and left the group of four.

Merely a month ago, Brokk would have enjoyed toying with a man's emotions. He would get into a deep conversation about the meaning of life and what was going to happen next. Brokk had changed though and did not want to torment Remmel with anticipation.

Rising to his feet, Brokk smiled at the old general. "You will not die by my hand, Remmel," he said to him. Remmel lifted his eyes but did not speak. He was weary and expected games, so Brokk continued. "Please sit," he said, motioning to a stool that had been set out. "You as well Canis. I have something I must say."

Canis grunted but obliged. *Jark for "get it over with."*

Brokk would not let it phase him. His trip with Tamara, the city, the slaves, all of it had changed his perspective. His destiny was clear to him now; his path obvious.

He looked at Remmel first. "You are a free man, Remmel." These words captured the general's attention. "I cannot return you to Tassi, as they would surely hang me for my crimes, but I will not sell you nor kill you here." Remmel's mouth hung wide and his eyes opened wider. "I hope, that between two military men we can come to peace about the events over the last month. We were both acting on orders from our governments and we have both done things we regretted."

Remmel finally caught his breath and opened his mouth to speak, wearily and shakily as if he had not used his voice for a long time. "I don't understand," he finally managed to utter.

"Nor do I," Canis growled. The Jark had shifted to the edge of his seat and if his skin had not been born red, Brokk was certain it would be as red as the lava on their home planet.

He didn't let that deter him and addressed Canis now. "We're outlaws, friend. Betrayed and now hunted by our own people. We were set up and thrown out. How many did you lose? Thousands? Millions? We'll never know how many were captured or if the King is even negotiating for their release."

Canis knew the truth when he heard it and settled back into his chair. "Truth," he said, grunting.

Remmel was now perplexed. Brokk expected as much and had hoped his curiosity would spur this meeting forward. He had never apologized to anyone before and certainly never asked a man for his help. As Remmel's eyes narrowed, Brokk became acutely aware of the rain that began to fall on them. Small drops at first but they grew in size. Wind howled and pushed at the trees above them, the storm trying to exert its will against the ancient plants.

"Tamara?" Brokk asked, looking at her. "Can you do something about this storm?"

She smiled, eager to please Brokk and show off for his guests. Suddenly the branches on the trees above them stretched and grew. A thick canopy of wood and leaves intertwined, wrapping themselves over and over again and blocking out the sky until the four were nearly encapsulated in a cave of branches. If Remmel was surprised by the Lysop, he didn't let it show and Brokk suspected he had come across her kind before.

"So what is your angle, Brokk?" He said at last, wiping the remnants of the storm from his face with his sleeve.

The tree cave that Tamara had given them for shelter was dark inside and Brokk could hardly see Remmel's face. Removing a red flare from a pouch on his chest, Brokk lit it and dug it into the center of the circle. Red light flickered back and forth across Remmel's aged features, playing with his mind and revealing a far more sinister general than had appeared at the beginning of the meeting.

"I intend to free the slaves and lead a rebellion on this planet. The Jarks are profiting from the slave trade, my pilot encountered two Jark escorts during a raid against a slaver's ship." Remmel leaned forward at this but Brokk continued. "The slaves here outnumber the free ten to one. I want to arm the farms in the north, give them a reason to rebel and create a distraction for the northern garrison that is barely able to flex enough strength to tax the farms, let alone put down a rebellion. I want to hit the Jarks in their pocketbook, take away a source of their income and establish a slave free economy on Charoth. Then, once we've gained enough strength, I want you and I to take our full revenge."

Remmel sat motionless considering the proposal. "What do you mean, take our revenge?" he finally asked.

"I don't know yet," he admitted. "Maybe they will come here and try to stop the rebellion, maybe they will begin guarding the slave ships. However this happens, I want to be a thorn in their side until the Jark ruler cannot hold a meeting without my name seeping from his magistrate's mouths."

"And you've found a Lysop," he said, motioning towards Tamara.

Brokk grinned. "Yes, the first of many slaves that we have set free."

"She serves you now?" he asked, raising his eyebrows at Tamara in a way that sent a flash of anger across Brokk's vision.

"I owe him my life," responded Tamara elegantly. "I am grateful to stand by his side."

Remmel said nothing and Brokk looked at Canis. "I owe you an apology as well, Canis." Canis grunted and looked away. Jarks did not apologize but Brokk continued anyways. "Things are different now. If we are to be successful, I cannot run this army like a dictator. I need you at my side to provide counsel rather than blind obedience."

"Always," growled Canis, eager to end the apology. "I will echo the General," he said, motioning at Remmel. "What is our next move?"

"I've purchased a shipment of slaves. They'll arrive at Orno's farm tomorrow at midday. I don't have the money, of course, so I want you to ambush the shipment and give the men an ultimatum. They were captured freedom fighters from Despona, so I believe they will fight by our side. Simultaneously, I want to arm the farms. Dispatch a patrol tonight to the northernmost farms and supply them weapons." Brokk paused to look at both Remmel and Canis but saw only nods. "Terre is intercepting his second shipment of slaves in a few hours. We will continue to enlist those that are sympathetic to our cause."

The dome of trees was silent except for the beating of rain against the branches. Torchlight flickered as the four sat quietly. All that had to be said was said and neither Canis nor Remmel had objected to his plan. Brokk took that as a good sign and rose to his feet. Tamara, sensing the meeting was over loosened her grip on the branches and water began pouring in. Canis rose as well but Remmel remained seated.

"You have changed, Brokk," he said at last, water flowing steadily over his features. Then he rose and stood face to face with the golden-skinned man that had caused so much pain to so many people. "Do not think that my cooperation with you equates with my forgiveness. You freed me willingly and I am grateful for that. We are now entering into a relationship of convenience and mutual needs. If I get the chance, I plan to leave."

Brokk gritted his teeth but nodded and Remmel walked out of the circle a free man. It was going to be a difficult change of pace for the man that believed he was the chosen one.

Canis, reading his mind put an arm on Brokk's shoulder. "You are walking a very narrow path," he growled before walking away.

CHAPTER TWELVE

Explosions tore Thilgod from his sleep. *Thunder? No, more distant.* This was duller, broader. Thunder had a way of cracking. This was almost hollow.

Thilgod rubbed his eyes and pushed Luo's head off his thigh. His back ached and his clothes were soaked. They hadn't made it as far as they wished last night. A soldier from the patrol slipped in the rain and broke his leg bringing the whole company to a halt. This was the way things worked beyond the northern gates. The land was just too wild to tame; but the Iralene, through the bodies of the northern garrison, certainly tried.

The skies were clear now, if not for a few thin finger-like clouds above and some fog blanketing the lowlands below. Thilgod cast his heavy, sleep-laden eyes across the predawn grasslands. The prairie was a deep gray in the early morning light. Silhouettes of soldiers lay scattered across the landscape and the smell of wet soil, drawn out from the downpour, was pulled into Thilgod's nostrils with each breath. Most of the soldiers had fallen asleep sitting against their packs or leaning against one another as they waited for their wounded comrade to be treated. Eventually, the patrol simply set up camp and slept.

In the low dawn light, a few men roused just long enough to see if their commander was alarmed from the noises. Others ignored them completely. Thilgod finally brought his gaze back his pack. Luo had curled himself into a ball and Dacia readjusted her head on Luo's back.

Another dull explosion to the east. Something was happening. Someone was under attack.

"We're headed towards the explosions," said a man behind him. Thilgod looked up the hill to see the patrol leader standing above him. While he typically wore a wide-brimmed hat and forewent face paint, the man had chosen his green helmet and had coated his face with green and brown grease. In his hands, he carried a standard issue rifle for the Iralene forces—black with a leather sling that was about as long as a man's arm. The rifle still used a propellant to launch dense copper balls into its desired target and increased the weight and size of the load each soldier had to carry. Thilgod believed they were probably fifty years behind a modern military in armament, but these rifles were top of the line for Charoth and had served the Iralene well enough to unite the planet.

"You think you'll see some action?" Thilgod asked, pointing at the man's helmet.

He grunted. "You never know. Better wear it and not have to worry about a stray round turning my brain into soup, you know?"

Thilgod smiled. "Do you know who's killing who over there?" It was a valid question. In the wild, farms were often pitted against each other for resources or because of family dynamics. Gangs that managed to evade Iralene taxes operated on the fringe, as well. Thilgod suspected they'd get there too late to find out.

The patrol leader grinned white teeth through the dark grease that covered his features. "I suppose if we show up too late to find out you can track them down too for some extra beat," he said; insinuating that Thilgod would revel at the chance for more money and another contract.

He wouldn't let it bother him. Soldiers always viewed all bounty hunters the same. He suspected they also envied him. "I can't go with you," he finally responded. "I've got orders to find the woman now and I know she's gone north."

The man's eyes narrowed as he assessed Thilgod's news. Already his soldiers were headed uphill towards the east, towards the battle. The column of weary warriors, carrying more weight on their back than a normal man should, walked silently past the two men speaking. Water dripped from the sleeves of a soldier's blouse, his weapon dirty from the flooding. "I'm not supposed to let you go off by yourself," the commander finally said.

"It wouldn't be the first time I've been out here, you know?" He tried to look convincing to the younger soldier. "I've got my corelves here for company," he added, grabbing a handful of Luo's scruff. Luo growled but settled almost instantly. "Plus, I've got my rifle. I'll be fine up here."

The patrol leader looked his rifle up and down. It was an older model, wood stock, long barrel, and single shot with a twenty round capacity before having to switch magazines. He had a scope on it, too, which could magnify a target at nearly two thousand meters. Anything more, Thilgod would be guessing; but he had hit further targets.

The last of the column trudged past their leader and he had not yet made his decision. Finally, with a sigh, he conceded. "You're heading north, huh? Can't convince you to take a detour for the day?"

"You and I both know it could be more than a day. We lost time in the storm too; Luo's eager to pick up the scent again."

"Fine," the man responded, turning with his heavy pack and walking quickly to catch up to the others. "If you die, I'll be lying about the circumstances. I'll tell them you snuck off."

"Fair's fair," Thilgod grinned. "Let's go, Luo," he said, waving his hand north.

* * *

Being out on the hunt again was a good feeling. Thilgod was headed north and he was alone. The blue sky and a gentle breeze had all but erased the memory of the torrents of rain that fell last night. Rolling hills covered in knee-high prairie made for soft, easy walking. He preferred it this way—being alone with his animal pack. Luo had trotted ahead to sniff the air and Dacia was off on his right flank. They both looked as if they had picked up her scent wafting along the breeze. To Thilgod, this was good news. It meant she was close by.

After another hour, he was starting doubt that closeness, but then he heard it. Talking. *No.* Someone was barking orders. Luo and Dacia heard it too.

Thilgod whistled twice, shrill and short to mimic a klack bird and the two corelves lay down in the grass to conceal their figures. The hunt was on again and they were close. Crouching himself, Thilgod unslung his rifle and scurried to the top of the nearest hill overlooking the east. Luo and Dacia both whined, quietly at first but then impatiently. Thilgod foolishly mistook their cries as selfish, wanting to get ahead of him for the hunt.

Fool. Upon cresting the hill, he realized his error. He should have known. He should have been quiet. He should have heard their voices. He had been too hasty, too eager to appreciate the solitude of the hunt rather than to focus on the hunt itself. The east. Somehow, his pack had wrapped him around to the east.

Louder than before and not nearly as dull, an explosion ripped grass and dirt a mere fifty meters to his front. The heat of the blast scalded his face, knocking him off balance and sending him rolling backward. Had they known? *No, a misplaced shot.* Gunfire erupted from both sides as he scrambled to get off his back and find the rifle he wasn't supposed to drop during combat. Low crawling, Thilgod crested the hill once more and looked down.

A few thousand meters beyond in the valley below he could see a farmhouse burning and an outcropping of four brown buildings. No more than a three dozen slaves were scattered across the lowlands, taking cover behind gray wood fences and watering troughs. But they were armed and their focus was not on Thilgod. Not yet anyway and he intended to keep it that way. These weren't the source of the explosion, however, but the whistling of more rounds told him to cover his head.

Four more explosions ripped through the otherwise peaceful day, they were closer and better aimed, peppering the ground around the farms and startling the slaves. Still, the men did not move from their positions. *Slaves marked for hard labor until death, it is no wonder they would rather die here on the open plains than surrender to the army.* The northern garrison had arrived to put down the rebellion. To his left, he could see the company of men that he had walked with through the night. Their scouts crawled on their bellies over a hill. The glint and reflections of sun against glass indicated to Thilgod they were using binoculars and calling in the mortars that reigned down from above.

Intuition told him to leave. It told him this battle was not relevant to finding his slave. That even if he wanted to help the garrison from his position any shot from this distance would be impossible. The valley was simply too far. Intuition told him he risked being a casualty of war, a misplaced mortar that would land just a few too many meters to the west of the farms and turn him from living and breathing to a puddle of mush for his corelves to enjoy.

His corelves told him to stay. They had smelled the fugitive, no doubt about it. Whatever this uprising was or had been was instigated by the Lysop. The woman that had miraculously escaped her collar and caused unimaginable pain to nearly forty others.

Thilgod pulled his brown rifle through the grass by his sling and brought the stock to his shoulder. Uncapping the lens he looked through it, first at the rebels. They were well armed with black weapons that Thilgod had never seen before. These were smuggled in, not from the capitol but from another planet. Even on Hestos, Thilgod hadn't seen weapons like this. Their thick black stocks and heavy barrels were not just modern but appeared state of the art. He could see no ammo wrapped around the slave's bodies which indicated these were propellant-less, capable of storing several hundred rounds in the weapon itself.

Suddenly, Thilgod realized these men had a chance. Not just a chance, but a good chance. This wasn't an opportunity rebellion, it was planned, plotted, scripted. *But what are they waiting for?* The thought tormented him. They could range the northern garrison, yet they waited.

Swinging his rifle to the south, Thilgod watched the garrison creep forward through the grass. If not for his optics, he would not have seen them writhing like snakes towards their prize. A pit grew in his stomach. They were being lured in. *Tricked.* Smoke puffed upwards from behind the garrison's front and another half-dozen mortars landed, peppering the farm. None hit their mark. *Was the garrison that bad or was something else at work?* And then he saw her and knew he might not get another shot.

* * *

Lure them in. Make it a public showing. Pride and confidence are the only way for a sustainable rebellion. You will be their symbol, their priestess, their sorceress, their goddess. Brokk's words. Not hers. She liked the way they sounded, though. She liked what they were doing even more.

She could feel them all; six high explosive munitions fired from six mortar tubes entered her consciousness as they soared through the air.

These were launched by savage men trying to keep the collar on free people. Her people. One of the tail fins on a round was loose. This one would miss anyways. A second was a dud. She supposed the poor construction had to do with purchasing the weapons second-hand rather than making it themselves. Of course, with slaves as laborers, it was likely that constructing your own weapons was out of the question as well. Regardless, first or second-hand munitions would not have helped.

As Tamara sensed the incoming rounds, she played with the air around them and pushed the mortars outward towards the boundaries of the farm. She hadn't planned on letting the main home burn, but that was a mistake she didn't intend to let happen again.

The slaves, Brokk had told her, weren't supposed to fight. That would come later. This was a demonstration of their power and once the northern garrison saw what was happening, fear would spread throughout the division.

After deflecting the last volley, Tamara looked at Brokk and smiled. Standing by her side, he returned a warm look but did not smile. No, not this man. It was all business. She didn't mind and refocused on the men in the grass, inching ever forward.

"Can you feel them now," Brokk asked. His voice was calm and steady. A gentle breeze pushed through his black hair as his golden skin sparkled in the sunlight. He wore his camouflage today, deep brown and green patterns that seemed to shift and change depending on where he stood to match their background perfectly.

"I can feel them. Should I wait longer?" she asked. She wanted to explore them now. Expose their insides to the outside, merge body and nature and everything in between. Send a signal to the rest to run from her, that this was her farm now and that these were her people.

"Patience, Tamara," was Brokk's response. "There are a hundred more beyond that hill. In a moment they'll realize their mortars aren't working and then they'll charge."

Tamara only heard the first part of Brokk's response. She suddenly sensed many more breaths in the field pushing away the warm air from the cold, exhaling carbon dioxide where oxygen had once been. "I think they're coming," she told Brokk with excitement, and then, without waiting for his approval, Tamara allowed her mind to race from her body through the tall grass. She bumped over little knolls and inconsistencies in the prairie until she was swarming around the soldiers. First the scouts and then the main assault. They were crouched, just at the crest of the hill. She could smell their sweat, sense their anticipation. The hands trembled on some as they gripped their rifles. Knuckles were white where blood could no longer circulate from the tightness of their hold. She felt them all and then she sucked the breath from their lungs and collapsed their insides. She pulled the oxygen and swirled it upward so that their gags were silent and their death was immediate.

She was having so much fun she almost missed the lone man to her east. In the back of her mind, she had always sensed him, smelled the salted scum that stuck to his hair from days of walking and the musk that came from sleeping with two large animals. Hoofed, no, clawed. It was the metallic ping that brought this man into the forefront of her mind. She suddenly sensed anticipation mixed with fear as he depressed a trigger that caused a hammer to fall against a single steel round, propelling it from a twenty-four-inch barrel.

Tamara froze, curiosity gripped her initially but as she realized what was occurring it was fear that kept her from reacting; the sudden realization that luck was nearly as good as skill and that she had just run out of both.

Her savior was a man of action, however, and where she missed the signs he moved swiftly. She couldn't tell if it was the flash from the muzzle or her grip on his arm that alerted him to the threat but as the single round left the barrel she felt a stiff shove and heard a snap past her head, followed by the sickening sound of steel smashing through flesh. A wheeze and a grunt of air being pushed from a damaged chest behind her.

Brokk staggered and fell to a knee, breaking the spell of her concentration to feel as far out as she had; but she knew where her target had been even if she could not feel him.

Tamara grabbed flame from the farmhouse with her outstretched hand and hurled it towards the grassy hill to the east. Fury gripped her and she seized another handful of the fire, spun it into a ball with her silver and gold fingers and thrust it again, watching the flame explode against the prairie. Her concentration was fully out of focus now and she charged the hill, but again Brokk grabbed her and threw her backward just in time to avoid colliding with a massive animal that leapt from the flame.

It skidded past her and into a fence before regaining its balance. This time, Brokk was in the creatures sights but it no longer had the element of surprise. The beast circled, snarling and dripping spit from finger long fangs. It leapt, but Brokk was faster raising his weapon and firing three rounds before diving out of the way to the right. The bullets exploded inside the creature's chest and it landed lazily, wheezing for oxygen. Brokk stood and circled closer to Tamara as the beast's legs failed it, causing it to drop to its side. Its breathing slowed and Tamara suddenly couldn't help but to reach out and wrap herself around the creature using her mind to comfort it in its final moments.

Brokk gripped his shoulder and watched the interaction until its last breath. "What were you able to learn about it?" Brokk finally asked.

"Not much," she said, coming to him to examine his shoulder. "It had been hunting me since Orno's, but that's all I know."

Brokk grunted, pushed her hands away, and walked towards a radio he had set up in one of the farmhouses. He carried his injured shoulder low and gripped it with his other hand. Tamara could see blood pooling around his fingers but try as she might, she could not use her mind to reach him. This was all business, and Brokk wouldn't let anything slow him down from monitoring the start of the rebellion. "The ambush on the slaves we bought from the city should be getting ready to start," he said over his good shoulder, "I want to warn them about the garrison's troops."

CHAPTER THIRTEEN

His lungs burned from smoke exposure as he descended the final hill into the gully. Each inhale brought searing pain from his throat to his lungs and back out again. It felt as if his chest itself had caught fire in the inferno he had just narrowly escaped. Thilgod couldn't say the same for Luo and the thought of his lost companion caused his chest to ache even more. Looking over his shoulder, Thilgod could see smoke still rising from the village but the sound of explosions and gunfire had completely ceased. For the poor souls of the northern garrison, the battle was over before it began.

He should have been smarter; could have been smarter. Everything had changed, the contract didn't cover him hunting a rebel army. His job was simple, investigate the foreign vessel beyond the walls. But he knew Kostia. Kostia would expect Thilgod to finish this or would insist that he die trying. That much was obvious—you didn't just give up on Kostia, no matter how complex the situation had become. A warning first then. He would tell Kostia that the slave was not alone; that she had been rescued as part of some greater plan. A warning that there was a man out here arming slaves, killing slavers, and instigating a rebellion. A warning that he had just witnessed an entire company from the northern garrison suffocate to death while completely surrounded by oxygen.

He tried his best to move quickly over the rugged terrain but his strength failed him over and over again. His left leg burned, as did his hip, ribs, and shoulder. Doing his best to hustle down the steep slope that separated the prairie from the river country, Thilgod failed to see a root and tripped, slamming his bad leg hard into the muddy hillside. Pain shot up his knee and throbbed in the front of his skull. Before he could roll over, Dacia was there with her big black nose and long red tongue covering his face in kisses. He imagined she too felt more pain than she could possibly let on for losing Luo.

"We'll be alright girl," he whispered, grabbing her ears to push her face from his so he could sit up. Obedient as always, Dacia sat next to Thilgod as he checked himself. "Good girl," he comforted, knowing that he was really comforting himself.

Delicately, he rolled his shirt up at the waist to reveal blisters where the witch had burned him. She'd gotten him, he had to give her that, but the man with her was even more intriguing. Thilgod gingerly took his pack off his shoulders and found a black pouch containing medical supplies. Inside, he removed a white canister and unscrewed the lid. Medical cream. He'd be good as new in a few hours. Thirty years ago, when he started this job a blistering burn like this would take days if not a whole week. Lost out in the prairie like this and the wounded were lucky to make it back alive before infection got to them. Not so anymore. With new technology from Hestos and other advanced societies, a person could break a bone and have it good as new in a day. Despite the misfortune, he decided this was another thing to be thankful for.

Thilgod dipped his fingers and began to lather the thick white cream around his ribs. *The man with the golden skin.* Each rub of the cream sent stabbing pain through his body. It was almost unbearable. Almost. Dacia sensed his pain and decided to leave him for another resting spot. A good pet that one was. She was the smart one; kept a good head on her shoulders unlike that dull littermate of hers that rushed off to be slaughtered. *Probably owe that thing your life. If he hadn't have acted, you never would have escaped.*

True, he considered, wondering why he was arguing with himself. *But what now?* Tell Kostia the whole thing is going downhill fast; that his slave has linked up with an eight-foot tall man whose skin literally sparkles in the sunlight. Tell Kostia that this man can take a half inch wide steel round to the shoulder and stand up moments later to slaughter a four hundred pound corelve. That this man put weapons in the hands of slaves that were more advanced than his entire northern garrison. There were dozens if not hundreds of things to explain, but that stubborn man inside him continued to play the devil's advocate.

Do you even tell him at all? There was a thought. Never give bad news to your boss unless you want him to pull you off the project. *Project, look at you, it's as if you were working in an office somewhere and not headed out to butcher a woman.* Project was easier to stomach though. Kostia thought himself a generally good person, and even though he knew the tricks to coping with who he had to be, he preferred the word project as opposed to murder. Regardless, Kostia wasn't the kind of man that would just pull him off the project, this was the kind of man who decided a requirement to send a replacement meant you were no longer useful at all. Being useful to Kostia was what kept him alive during the purge; he wasn't about to give that up.

It was settled. He wouldn't waste his time reporting to the Iralene. He had been tasked to hunt the slave and leave the vessel to the northern garrison. While it looked like the two were interrelated, no one could expect Thilgod to take down a small army. The rebellion was in the garrison's hands. Thilgod would continue to hunt this witch and only after he brought her head to his employer on a silver platter would he risk returning to the city.

Complete with his treatment, Thilgod looked at the valley before him as he zipped up his pack. Through a dense layer of trees, Thilgod could see a swollen river flowing forcefully below him. The water looked clear and was likely good for drinking. The noise from the storm swell would mask his movement well and he would be able to catch some fish for him and Dacia, as well as, resupply his canteens.

The man with the golden skin. A thought tormented him as he tossed the assault back and forth in his mind. As soon as he fired his round, the two had separated. The man pushed her away and took the bullet to his shoulder. He stumbled but she, despite not being injured, looked worse. She had been confused; almost a different person from the woman that pushed mortars away with her mind mere moments before. He had crawled far closer than the men from the northern garrison that she had killed moments earlier, yet she couldn't find him. Then the answer struck Thilgod so hard he felt dizzy. There must be a link between them. The key to getting her was to remove the golden-skinned man.

But how?

"Patience, Thilgod," he whispered to himself. *That is a man who is brimming with ambition. He will separate himself from her and then you will strike.* Thilgod pushed himself back to his feet and grimaced. The pain was still there but he could feel the salve beginning its work. He turned back towards the smoke that continued to billow dark black puffs into the sky and whistled. "Let's go, Dacia. Let's pay them back for Luo."

* * *

"You're hurt," Remmel said at once, observing Brokk enter the wooden slave quarters with his good arm still holding his wounded shoulder.

"It's nothing," Brokk hissed behind clenched teeth, hoping his voice didn't waver despite the pain that he felt. He wasn't about to show Remmel any weakness. It had only been sixteen hours since Brokk had released the old man and showing vulnerability would surely inspire opportunity inside the old general's mind.

"It doesn't look like nothing," Remmel responded from the end of a wooden bed where he had set up a makeshift operations center. A table from the corner had been pulled over and placed upon it was a disk with four claws holding it upright. From that disk flowed all the information the Jark operatives would need to communicate with each other, mark locations of enemy forces, and distribute that intelligence to the rest of his force.

From Brokk's now wounded position, he felt foolish for letting Remmel in on the operations center so quickly. Remmel wasn't alone, of course, but despite the ten other Jark staff officers that occupied the operations center, Remmel seemed to be the one in control. Brokk reminded himself that this man, despite his gray hair and wrinkles, had outwitted him on Tassi. This was the man that led the rebellion to dethrone him; the man that had coordinated an uprising mere days after the Tassian army had been pushed from the city.

No, he would show no weakness. "Perhaps to a Tassian it looks painful, but these are Jark bones," Brokk mocked, pushing past Remmel to look at a monitor that showed him his forces at Orno's farm. "They'll heal quickly."

Remmel wouldn't let it go. "That's the same Jark arrogance that left you beaten on Tassi," he said, drawing looks from the rest of Brokk's staff.

"Careful, Remmel." Brokk said now fully acknowledging the tall thin man that dared challenge his authority in his own command post. "These men never got their fill of Tassian blood. Besides, if it wasn't for your government's corruption, you would likely have been rotting in a jail cell somewhere rather than commanding an army when I arrived."

Remmel looked shocked but this time kept his mouth shut. Brokk saw the weakness and capitalized on it. "You must need a reminder about how you slaughtered your own comrades as a prisoner of war just to survive," he hissed walking towards Remmel to threaten him.

Remmel didn't back up, it wasn't in his nature and instead stood face to face with the man that held his very life in his hands. "How did you learn about that," he said quietly.

"Your government is just as corrupt as mine," Brokk responded. "They kept records of you. I assume in the event they needed to blackmail you later," he added.

Remmel turned his head and sat quietly on one of the wooden slave bunks that they had pushed to a corner to clear the way for an operations center. "It was a long time ago," he said at last. "I was desperate to survive. It might have been better to die."

"Maybe better for both of us," Brokk grunted. As he turned to walk away he saw Tamara standing in the doorway. Rays of light pushed past her body, gleaning off her dark hair and reflecting brightly from the clawed jewelry on her fingers. The rest of her was merely a shadow with features that were indiscernible as she faced into the darkened room. She still wore the long trench coat and it flowed freely from a gentle breeze that pushed in from the open door.

"I'm sorry," she said, staring at Brokk, afraid to move closer to him from the doorway. "I should have seen him coming."

"You need to practice," he responded. "We have to make these people believe that you possess all power. They are superstitious and will be inspired by you." Remmel raised an eyebrow at Brokk but Brokk ignored him. "You have to be able to act through the chaos, to be able to continually feel the elements around you no matter what you are doing in the present. That man shouldn't have gotten the jump on us. I've told them you are a sorceress. Act like one."

"I know," she said, looking down now at her hands. "But I..."

Canis' voice on the radio cut her off. "Trucks inbound," he reported.

Brokk spun around to watch a hologram in the center of the room populate three cargo vehicles gliding across a magnetic highway towards Orno's farm.

* * *

Canis swirled his thumb around a small button attached to a remote the size of his palm. His fingers were steady but the day was hot. He had done this dozens if not hundreds of times before. Still, his palms were wet with anticipation. A bead of sweat rolled through the thick hair on his forehead and down across the skin on his dark red nose until it finally fell, landing in a patch of dirt that was his shelter.

Canis looked to his left and then his right. Ten other men lay in the tall prairie on the other side of the hill from the magnetic highway. The road curved slightly allowing him to form an "L" with his formation. He didn't need to look any further down the road; he knew what would be there. More of his soldiers, waiting and watching for the first explosion, a signal to seal the trap and initiate the ambush.

Three blue and silver vehicles, each with high backs capable of transporting twenty or thirty men, shone brightly in the sunlight as they raced down the magnetic trail. Another team, five miles closer to the city had scanned the trucks and reported that men with guns were in the first and last vehicles and that slaves were in the center. At the high speed of travel, his team wasn't able to get any more specific and Canis suspected that the first vehicle might also be carrying slaves. His goal was to minimize slave casualties to be able to continue to replenish his force.

As they rounded the bend, Canis made one final circle of his thumb around the button on the detonator. He was targeting the last vehicle in the convoy to seal off any escape. Beyond the bend, his engineers had severed the magnetic track that hovered above a dusty brown road. By the time the slavers saw the damage, it was too late. The first vehicle swerved violently trying to halt their forward motion before they hit the break in the track.

It didn't work and the truck was suddenly airborne, free from the magnetic barriers that had held it so perfectly above the dust below. All five tons plus passengers fell the four-meter height and shattered on the earth. Force from the impact caused the glass on the windshield to explode outward and with it, the driver, whom Canis suspected had failed to properly secure himself. The middle truck, realizing what had just happened slowed hard and stopped just in time to avoid meeting the same fate. The last would not be so lucky.

As soon as the driver of the first vehicle flew from his seat, Canis depressed the button on his detonator, sending a signal to an explosive charge nestled in the ground underneath the magnetic track. An electrical burst in the device detonated the bomb causing an explosion to rip upward, pushing hundreds of steel ball bearings through the body of the vehicle and turning anyone inside into mush. Instantly, his team on the hillside charged the center truck, pulled the driver from the cab and executed him.

As Canis approached, his armor-clad soldiers were already pulling men in cotton rags from the back of the vehicle and looking for survivors in the first and last truck. Two gunshots rang out from the front truck but as he looked over, he realized it had come from his own soldiers putting the wounded out of their misery.

"Did anyone in the back survive?" he shouted.

The Jark soldier shook his head. "Nothing but mush back here."

He wished that wasn't the case. Canis had wanted to get all fifty. Kneeling on the dusty road in front of him were thirty-five men. They had placed their hands on the backs of their heads and Canis was certain they expected to be executed. Most were olive skinned as were the majority of people from Despona—the planet that they had been captured on. One man was larger than the rest and Canis instantly recognized him as the one Brokk described. He decided to address the group instead.

"You're free men now," he shouted at them. "You do not have to kneel any longer."

The slaves exchanged glances before one finally had the courage to stand up, followed by others and eventually the rest.

"You won't survive out here for long though," Canis continued. "I ask you to join our cause, help us free other slaves and liberate this planet. Once we've completed our task, you are welcome to remain and help us forge a new society or to return to Despona. The choice is yours."

The larger man stepped past the rest. "There's nothing for us on Despona anymore," he said through yellow teeth. "We'll join you, and when we are strong enough, perhaps we can return to Despona better prepared."

Canis nodded. "Arm them!" he shouted to his soldiers. "Let's go."

CHAPTER FOURTEEN

Gunfire and explosions were constant now. From a distance, Thilgod could hear the snaps and cracks of shots being taken at random. Likely slaves and slave owners trading shots from homes and barnyards. Other times he heard what sounded like a firing squad and assumed that the slavers were executing their workers for fear of rebellion. News had spread and surely there would be fear spreading throughout the north. Explosions accompanied by gunfire were likely instigated by the slaves and rebel forces. Thilgod assumed these noises were ambushes set by the rebel militias attacking government convoys, slave transportation trucks, or merchant goods. In less than a day, the whole countryside had transformed from a peaceful outcropping of farms to all-out war.

Chaos was how Thilgod would describe it. Uncontrolled chaos. Sure, the rebel commander, whoever he was, thought he could control the various groups, but Thilgod knew otherwise. Just look at the history of Charoth, for example. Dictators armed a few tribes and before you knew it, the tribes had their own ideas for getting even and their own ideas for controlling justice. They didn't want governance, they wanted revenge. It was impossible to bring order to these people on the fringe and before Kostia, all attempts by a central government to do so only brought back messengers missing their heads, or worse, messengers sliding through ten-foot spears that started in their legs and came out at their throats. Kostia brought an iron fist, and with it, much needed control that only a firm leader could bring.

Chaos. Thilgod wanted none of it and he stayed as far away from this type of chaos as possible. Thilgod looked down at Dacia and suspected that she agreed. Instead of taking the lead as she typically would do in Luo's absence, she hung by his side, patiently pacing her master's steps and allowing him to set the speed and direction of their hunt.

Her tongue hung from her mouth and draped lazily over sharp teeth. She was nervous. She had a right to be. Her ears were perked and her wet black nose constantly sniffed at the air. He suspected she knew more about what was occurring than she could let on. If someone had told him twenty years ago that he would see a four hundred pound corelve get nervous, he would have called them crazy. These were different times.

Hugging the stream, Thilgod had decided to continue north rather than to retreat to the south. He remained convinced that the originator of this whole situation had been the unknown ship that landed at the northern foothills a few days ago. Having never seen or heard of the golden-skinned man that accompanied the witch, he suspected this was a man from another world, maybe Hestos or maybe even farther. The suspected landing site of the alien vessel would undoubtedly be close to the rebel base camp and most certainly be the group fueling this overnight rebellion. With sturdy conviction, Thilgod knew he would find the woman at that main camp; he could only hope it would be when her guard was down.

He couldn't be certain how long he had walked, but the sun had once again returned to the south and was being blocked by the plateau that the capital city rested on. Darkness had engulfed the northern half of the planet and only small hints of light now illuminated the underbellies of thin stratus clouds high in the atmosphere. Beyond the clouds, Thilgod marveled at the stars that speckled the sky. In the sky to his west, rich orange and teal hues hung still as if a painter with a brush had swirled the Rainbow Nebula into existence and onto a window pane above his head. What was beauty down here, however, was a nightmare in the nebula.

Hot gasses long ago emitted from its dying star were thousands upon thousands of degrees. If your ship was strong enough to withstand the heat, the journey still was not without worry. That was where Kostia's pirates hunted, and because of the time and distance it took for merchant vessels to bypass the object, the pirates often had an easy time finding their prey. *Beauty from my point of view though,* Thilgod thought to himself.

"This is what living is all about," he told Dacia, not expecting any type of response as he tied her to the nearest tree and walked towards his pack. She didn't disappoint, but her attention was suddenly elsewhere. Fur on her neck bristled and she pulled her tongue into her mouth and crouched her body low to the ground. Thilgod crouched too and listened in the silence.

A snap caught his attention. Leaves rustled and Thilgod and Dacia swung their heads to the right. It was impossible to see anything in the dark. Another snap, this time a twig cracking under the weight of something larger. *An animal?* No. Dacia didn't respond this way to animals. This was something else. Something bigger. It moved intentionally, with purpose, but he could not say for certain it was sentient. Stories of beasts on the fringe were enough to sway any traveler that considered a vacation to the north.

Thilgod moved only his hand to grip the trigger of his rifle. It was cold and moist from dew that had gathered on the ground. He slowly wrapped his hand around the stock and squeezed it tightly. If he had to move fast, he wanted to be able to move fast with a weapon. Another snap and more leaves rustled to his right. Dacia licked her teeth and crawled to the end of her rope. He suddenly wished he hadn't tied her to the tree. He wondered if he could sneak over without making any noises to untie her or how long it would take cut the rope if he was being pulled off by something bigger than he.

Suddenly another noise ripped through the cold dark air sending whatever was moving into the darkness and scrambling away. Engines hummed and then roared to life from beyond the hill. A bright light illuminated the skyline and the very ground he stood on began to rumble as a small shuttle lifted vertically into the air and then launched itself into space. His suspicions had been confirmed, he had reached the camp.

* * *

Dacia cried and paced the tree nervously. Between short breaths, bursts of steam rose from her mouth in the cool clear night. She wanted to come with him, but it was too risky. Thilgod didn't want to lose her if things went south and she decided to rush the camp. He needed to be quiet for this one, he needed to be smart. After grabbing her mane and ruffling her fur coat, he pulled his canvas backpack from his shoulders and started digging.

"Ah," he exclaimed to Dacia, feeling the soft fabric of a prototype Mateen combat uniform. He pulled it out to examine its features. The light gray material began to darken and reflect the shapes and colors of its environment. The shape of a branch appeared with dark brown leaves and grass suddenly sprouted from the legs as if an invisible artist was painting in his midst. The Mateens had called this a Chameleon Suit, capable of blending into its environment for scouts and soldiers to be able to sneak upon an unsuspecting enemy. This was old technology now, but it still worked wonderfully.

He paused to examine the one flaw, a one-inch hole through the chest of the man that wore it before him. Thilgod quickly shed his brown overcoat, undershirt, and pants and climbed into the one-piece outfit, being careful to pull the material over his boots so that only their black soles could be seen. He stretched it carefully over his shoulders and pulled it neatly over his arms and legs to make sure the fabric had no wrinkles.

As he moved around, the material continued to adapt to its environment, shedding the branches that had once formed and taking on entire tree trunks with blackness beyond. As he fiddled to make sure the suit was perfect, fog began to roll down the hill and collect along his makeshift campsite. His suit reacted by matching the misty white that pooled around his feet. He looked nearly invisible.

Next, Thilgod removed a metal mask from his bag and stared at it. Its eyes were wide and covered in a red-tinted glass that would enhance his vision and monitor his surroundings. In addition, the computer monitored his rifle and was able to project his rifle's point of aim and how much ammo he had left. Instead of a mouth and nose, a metallic grate acted as a filter to ensure he could breathe clean oxygen in the event the sorceress found him before he found her. While the suit was Mateen, this piece of technology was made for the Hestonian military, and Thilgod had used it more times than he could count. He wished he had used it earlier.

Placing it to his face, he heard the system hiss as it sealed around his head and hummed to life. Suddenly the darkness of night disappeared and his surroundings were illuminated by an advanced light filter in the eyes of the mask. Data streamed across his face giving him temperature, wind speed and direction, atmospheric pressure, and a dozen other things that might influence his ability to kill his target. He looked at Dacia and she was silent now, simply watching the stranger that was once her master complete his transformation.

Thilgod grabbed his trench coat and shoved his arms back through the brown canvass sleeves. It was a cold night and he still had some walking to do. While the Mateen combat garb would be effective if he had to sneak into camp, his trench coat and assault mask would protect him from the witch if she tried to throw more fire at him.

"Stay here, girl," he whispered through the mask, grabbing his rifle and heading into the night.

* * *

Dark fingers lingered just beyond reach of the small lantern that provided a minuscule amount of light for Remmel to do his work. As the candle flickered, the darkness grew brave and surged toward him only to be beaten back by an orange flame that danced like the tail of a Hestonian salamander as it lured its prey. Remmel watched the battle for supremacy and appreciated the application. Darkness surrounded the lantern, moving quietly beyond its reach. It squirmed and slunk with an unrelenting desire to squash the flame. The flame, desperate to maintain its grip fought against one side and then the other; forgetting that its time was limited not by the darkness but by the wick on which it set its trust.

Brokk is that flame and I am the wick. His desperate attempts to salvage his brutal campaign on Tassi were pathetic. Brokk was a desperate man, fighting against the Iralene on Charoth below and the entire Galactic Order above. His own people, the Jark Empire, was just as desperate to turn Brokk into a distant memory. There would be no forgiveness. There could be no peace. Brokk's desperation was highlighted by his pathetic attempts at making peace with his own prisoner. Remmel was not so stupid as to ally himself with the slaughterer of the Tassians. The enemy of his people.

Feet scuffed the dirt outside his tent and Remmel pulled his green wool blanket over his work to hide it from the guard. The Jark remained outside, however, and after a few minutes, Remmel was again comfortable enough to resume his work. Peeling the blanket back, he revealed the black matte sheen of a Jarkian long range sniper rifle. It was a weapon intended for the rebellion, but Remmel's new found freedom had allowed him the opportunity to hide it.

He had found a scope as well, although not native to the weapon, his work until now had been successful in securing it to the rifle. The most important aspect still remained, sight the scope to the barrel. On Tassi, this would have been an easy task. Simply head to the firing range and figure out where the bullets were striking compared to where you looked. In a guarded tent with a stolen rifle, however, this was a much more difficult task.

Remmel removed a small laser pen from his pocket and shoved it inside the barrel of the rifle. Another stolen item taken from the desk of a Jark staff officer. Brokk was not only desperate to make amends with Remmel, he was foolish too. That was certainly not someone he wanted to ally himself with.

Turning it on and climbing onto his bed, he shot the laser across the twenty-foot tent and looked through his sights. Through his scope, he could see the laser was to the lower left. Remmel lowered the rifle, adjusted the windage and elevation on his sights and aimed again. Closer, but not perfect. Another adjustment. Check the door, make sure there isn't any movement. Aim again. Adjust the sights. Rotate the pen in the barrel, and take up aim yet again.

It was a slow process hampered by the guard that continually wandered near the door but never entered. Finally, the laser matched his scope, but only at twenty meters. If his aim was off by even a centimeter, he could risk missing his target by nearly a foot. *Aim at the torso then and wait for the furry beast to face you.*

First get Canis. Then Brokk when he comes back to mourn his loss. Maybe toss a grenade into the command center and head for the Iralene. Buy a ship and head back to Tassi. Simple enough, he supposed. Time to get to it.

CHAPTER FIFTEEN

A destroyer waited for him at the edge of the nebula. Terre felt trapped. He was trapped. But there was always a way - he just had to find it. Hunting pirate ships had led him to a gold mine inside this nebula. The dense soupy structure made it almost impossible for a vessel's sensors to detect other craft until they were on top of you. With a ship as advanced as the Shadow Stroke, hunting in the nebula made it almost impossible for him to lose.

He'd learned another thing too. This nebula was the main source of the piracy back to Charoth. Merchant vessels from Hestos traveled the nebula almost constantly and the pirates had their pick of goods, people, ships, or all of the above. Terre decided, and Brokk agreed, that if they were going to attract the Jark Empire, disrupting piracy from this nebula would likely do the trick.

Unfortunately for Terre, it worked before he was ready. Jarks had increased their patrols with the recent raids and Terre had unknowingly attacked his prey while a Jark corsair was patrolling nearby. The corsair, he could handle, but the pilot, certain he had found the ship that was causing their fleet so much trouble, had called for backup. Now, Terre was trapped inside the Nebula. If he restarted his engines, powerful sensors on the Jark destroyer would be able to locate him. If he called for help, any signal he sent to Brokk's crew on the Juggernaut would be intercepted by the Jark Empire.

He wasn't about to give up Brokk, instead hoping that the destroyer would grow impatient and decide to join him in the nebula. At least inside it might be a fair fight. Might.

"This is the destroyer Kemnaut of the Jark Empire," a voice broadcasted over a generic frequency that all ships were capable of monitoring. "You are wanted for piracy in accordance with intergalactic law. Submit to boarding or you will be destroyed."

Piracy. In the eye of the beholder, he supposed. Ironically, Terre was actually aiding a merchant vessel that had been ambushed mere moments before. That too occurred on the corsair's watch but because the real piracy was being sanctioned through bribes, the Jarks were prepared to turn a blind eye. Now that Terre was interfering with business, they sought to halt his legal activity. How the tides had turned.

Colors from the nebula swirled around his ship and radiated through the unique optics that allowed every spectrum to penetrate his cockpit from all sides. Orange gas buffered by bright teal danced and swayed, parting as his ship floated powerlessly. Beyond the superficiality of the beauty, heat and radiation threatened to melt his body in seconds should his ship's thick armored hull be breached.

"This is the destroyer Kemnaut of the Jark Empire, I say again, submit to boarding or be destroyed." His second and last warning. Terre knew the rules and just as he suspected the Shadow Stroke's computers flashed a red warning to indicate shots fired as two bright explosions erupted inside the nebula. They were shooting proximity rounds to flush him out.

Another flash of light and another warning from his ship indicated more rounds bursting through the thick gas of the nebula. They had gotten closer and this time, the Shadow Stroke indicated something new. Two Jark Corsairs had entered the nebula to hunt for him. They wouldn't see him, not yet. His engines were still out and the density and heat of the nebula would hide his vessel for some time longer. If they got close enough, however, he would be forced to turn his engines on to fight the corsairs, simultaneously alerting the Kemnaut to his position.

His radar continued to track the vessels that he could not see. They swept in from his flanks with more flashes of light below him as the destroyer hammered the nebula with proximity rounds. The corsairs were getting closer, using their own radar to cover large swaths of the nebula. Hide and seek was over. He would soon be detected and had to be the one to make the first move. It would be his only chance and if he could find a way to get close enough to the corsair, perhaps the Kemnaut would be unable to engage him simultaneously.

Terre pulled his harness over his chest and grabbed his controls, wishing there was some way he could alert the Juggernaut without the Kemnaut hearing his transmission. Wishing he didn't have to weigh his own death against selling out his beloved commander. To die then, and hopefully inflict enough damage on the destroyer to make the Jark Empire pay for their betrayal.

The corsairs inched closer on his screen, one to his left, one to his right. The destroyer had shifted slightly beneath him and was more aligned with the ship on his left. He would go right. Put the other corsair between him and the real enemy. Destroy the first, then consider the second. If he could outrace it to the far end of the nebula, perhaps he would have a chance at wormhole travel and an escape.

Terre squeezed the controls and swiped his hand across the clear screen to his front. Instantly the sound of engines hummed and he jerked the controls to the right. Detecting his engines, the corsairs changed direction, the leftmost in pursuit while the one to his right charged. Explosions ripped upward through the hot gas from the destroyer below sending shudders through his ship's hull, each one closer than the last.

He could see it now, the shadow of a red and gray vessel with two large wings and a tall tail fin to allow maximum maneuverability in a dense atmosphere. *Or a nebula.* A flurry of orange cannon fire erupted outward from the vessel, Terre dodged left letting loose his own volley, forcing his attacker to pull his ship up. Another round exploded beneath him sending a flash of white across his eyes. A blue flame flared from the nebula as it regurgitated the explosives that caught the heated gas on fire. The second corsair had closed on him now and fired its own volley of neutronium rounds that ripped passed his vessel as he dove downward.

Get behind one of them. Avoid the bursts. The first ship leveled out and then dove down as well, swimming through the dense nebula that had been his refuge mere moments earlier. Terre pulled his controls to the right and thrusters burned as he dodged more cannon fire from above. In open space, he would be able to outmaneuver the two smaller ships, but the nebula was their world. The Shadow Stroke struggled to maintain its speed in the dense cloud.

Corsair wings suddenly appeared from his left. Another volley of cannons peppered the thick gas in front of him. They were forcing him down towards the destroyer and he had no choice but to dip again, launching round after round to cover his retreat. The screen on his ship flashed accompanied by warning sounds. Dense neutronium rounds had been launched from the destroyer. He pulled to his left and tried to climb as more flashes erupted around him. Corsairs battered down against him, both ships attacking in unison.

He released mines as he sped, hoping to slow their descent but could see them easily avoid the traps. More warnings, more flashes, a thud that stopped his heart as he realized one of the rounds impacted and penetrated his hull. Hissing of oxygen through his cockpit told him they'd punctured his armor and embedded the round into vital life support systems.

The ships automated functions worked to seal the breach, firing fast-acting foam to seal the hull and protect him from deadly radiation. *I have to dive. Escape the nebula. Charge the Kemnaut destroyer.* It was his only chance. He could avoid the proximity rounds, maybe even the neutronium. Force a two-dimensional fight out of the corsairs as they pursued.

He dipped downward, palms sweaty with anticipation and fear and he gripped his controls, squeezing the trigger to give everything he had at the destroyer beyond. The ship thrust and outmaneuvered his rounds that traveled slower in the nebula than they would have in open space. Still he fired, spun, swerved, and avoided. Everything depended on it. Colors from the gas zipped past his face and beamed into his eyes. He squinted through the optics trying to block out the light and maintain his awareness. More cannons descended on him from above, rattling his vessel, and sending more flashes across his interface. Red and white warnings flared across his vision with blue and orange just beyond.

The gas began to thin, blackness could be seen beyond. Open space was almost upon him and whatever may come after that. Then he heard it. A warning. Hope. An explosion.

"This is Commander Brokk of the Juggernaut. Cease your hostile action against my vessel and surrender your ship."

Cannon fire ceased as the destroyer to his front shifted its focus. Brokk had come. Terre struggled to hide his elation. One last push and he was through the nebula, beyond the reach of the dense clouds. His thrusters picked up speed. Terre tapped the joystick and the Shadow Stroke responded brilliantly. In open space, survivability was determined by thrust and velocity. He now had both against the corsairs.

Terre spun his ship back towards the nebula. Gas swirled as the shadows of two vessels circled violently inside the dense cloud. Both launched projectiles but Terre swooped beneath them peppering the ships with his own munitions. White flashes lit up the space in front of him, blinding the corsairs and giving Terre a chance to maneuver to their flanks. The two ships were slower out here, far less maneuverable hampered by the size and position of their engines. Terre fired two neutronium rounds which found their target in the side of the nearest corsair. It splintered in half sending dust and debris outward to float aimlessly in the void.

The second ducked downward to avoid his wrath but his Shadow Stroke was able to calculate the enemy's trajectory. Like shooting animals in a cage, Terre launched two more rounds. They both found their mark and he watched as the second ship's hull erupted from the sudden loss of pressure.

The fight was not over yet. Breathing hard, Terre throttled his ship towards the destroyer. In the battle, he had sunken under the nebula and couldn't see either vessel. Terre raced around the nebula, staying near to the walls while avoiding getting pulled back into the soup that had slowed his momentum down so significantly. The two ships remained on his radar but he could not see or hear what had happened. Even with the size difference, a lucky shot from the destroyer could disable the Juggernaut and even kill its crew.

"Juggernaut, this is Shadow Stroke," he called. There was no answer. "Juggernaut, Juggernaut, this is Shadow Stroke." He said again. Zipping in and out along the nebula's border, fear gripped Terre for his companions. They should have responded. There was no reason they wouldn't. Something was wrong. *Had the ship been lost?"*

Then he rounded the last bend and he saw it. Relief flooded over him and his could no longer hold his shaking hands to control the ship.

The disabled Kemnaut sat motionless. Above it, the Juggernaut hovered like a king over its kingdom. Its two golden spears, two massive prongs at the front of Brokk's triangular ship, were lodged into the hull of the dead destroyer. Brokk had speared a Jark destroyer, a feat no space commander had ever achieved and was now boarding the vessel to seize the crew. Suddenly it dawned on Terre just what had been achieved.

Brokk had just commandeered a Jark Empire destroyer and would add it to his fleet. He would likely kill or ransom the crew while simultaneously declaring war on the Jark Empire.

CHAPTER SIXTEEN

It called to him. The dark winding trail that led to who-knows-where. The trail that wrapped through trees and pushed him ever towards the mountains. Towards the wild. Towards whatever made its home between an inhabitable, life-filled land and the frozen tundra of the dark side of the planet. Canis probably should have turned back, but he couldn't. His feet continued to push him. The smell of reptile and mammal was rich is his nostrils. He was wild. All Jarks were. The call to adventure was too much for him to bear and the insurgency that Brokk was instigating was merely a small adventure compared to what he desired.

Canis hadn't tested his hands or his ability against anyone in a long time. Too long. He desired more. His muscles ached from stagnancy. With Brokk gone to put pressure on the Jark Empire above, Canis had the freedom to explore on his own. "Take care of her," were Brokk's only instructions. He did.

"You need practice," he told her, leading her out into the wild with him; leaving her at the head of a river that roared south and split in two separate directions. "Do you see the waterfall," he asked her, pointing below them to a crystal pool of water that was as frigid as it was beautiful, filled from the glacial runoff of the mountains above. "There's no heat in that water. Can you feel it?"

She nodded that she could. Her eyes had been distant, in a different place as she swarmed her senses around the elements of the wild. "If you can heat that water and continue to track my movements away from you, you'll know you have the focus that you need."

She had stared at him for a while, wondering what he thought he knew about sorcery. Or was it conjuring? "There's no heat in the water," she finally told him. "I can only manipulate things that are already there, not create new ones."

Canis was too old for a young girl to protest his training methods. He still didn't like her and she knew it. He trained infantrymen for war, not witches to learn magic. He knew where she faltered though, it was in her attention. Her ability to capture two pieces of information at the same time. This was neither sorcery nor conjuring. Neither magic nor trickery. This was something he could teach.

"The elements are already there," he told her. "If there was no heat this water wouldn't be flowing. It's simply cold. Bring it to a boil and pay attention to my heart beat, my footsteps, my breathing and my pace. Then," he said giving her a grunt and showing his distaste for her worth, "you will be ready."

She had nothing to say and Canis was glad for once. Turning he started to run; *make it hard for her.*

* * *

Close your eyes, Girl she could feel Red saying. *Keep them closed and just focus. Feel what's around you.* His fire-red hair and large frame was intimidating but calming. He was on her side and wouldn't hurt her. She closed them now and slowed her heart. *You care too much about everything else,* he continued to chide. *Stop caring. Just like me.*

She cared then and she cared now. Even alone, it was hard to block everything else out. Tamara opened her eyes again and faced the river that flowed fiercely over the cliff and into the pool below. Mist sprayed upward against the green leaves of trees that dipped their branches towards the river for a drink. The nebula above her shone down in reds, yellows, and blues. Brokk was up there. She imagined red was up there too, somewhere, still sailing his ghost ship and ordering his ghost crew around the cabin. *Work to be done,* he shouted while giving her a wink.

Focus. Tamara grabbed the hood on her coat and pulled it over her head so that her eyes were barely showing. She couldn't close them, not here, not alone in the wild. But maybe she could block some stuff out. The nebula above sent colors to dance off her silver jewelry that formed jagged claws on her hands. They empowered her, but she felt empty without Brokk by her side. *Focus.*

First, the river then Canis. Feel the water, search for the heat. Spin the particles. She found a warm spot floating to the top of the water and tried to grab hold of it but a torrent of cold poured in from above and hammered the warmth down and away. Try again, grab some more. The rushing of water pounded in her eardrums. A breeze rushed through her hood and pushed at her long black hair. Another warm spot, spin it faster, gone.

Work with what you've got, Girl. Red's voice echoed in the back of her mind. She wasn't strong enough to help Red that day and she regretted her weakness ever since. She told herself it wasn't her fault, that there were five other mercenaries, good men, that weren't strong enough either, but it didn't help. She had been Red's secret weapon. His confidant. He never faltered, never disappointed her, and never tried to live up to anything. *Work with what you've got.*

Then it hit her. Why boil water when you could freeze it? Why animate particles when you could stop them. She boiled blood because she was already working with something warm. Now, she had something cold she could work with and that would be easier.

Tamara switched gears and looked back at the nebula. Its brilliant colors danced in the sky and she shifted her mind back to Canis. Search for him first. It was easy. His footsteps still carried the common thud she had come to expect from a heavy Jark body attacking the ground. She traced his footsteps through the air to its source and suddenly she could feel all of him again as if he were right next to her. His heart pounded in his chest and adrenaline raced through his veins as he explored the wild. His breath was steady and constant, his ribs no longer ached.

Now track him, and think of something else too, Red told her. But it wasn't Red talking this time, it was Canis and he had been right. A soldier had to be able to multitask to take on multiple threats at once. She had to be able to sense her surroundings while protecting the people she cared about. She had to be distant yet intimately close with the things she controlled.

Tamara pushed the stomping of his feet into the back of her mind, focus on his feet, you can follow him again later, but keep the noise there. Keep the rhythm. Thud tap thud, thud tap thud, thud tap thud. *Now the river. Stop it.* Raising her jewelry clawed hand, Tamara dove back into the water. Cold rushed around her mind and numbed her thoughts. The pounding of the waterfall made it difficult to hear Canis but she relaxed her mind just enough to anchor to his hands and feet pounding against the dusty trail that wound towards the wild. Thud tap thud. Thud tap thud.

Slow them down now, she told herself. *Not Canis, just the water.* Her raised hand shook against the pounding of water falling into the pool. *Slow it down, slow it down, push against what heat remains. Disperse it and stop the elements from spinning.*

Silence. The pounding stopped and all she could hear now was Canis thudding against dirt. She opened her eyes and looked at the river. It was frozen. Jagged ice crystals now sat where water once flowed. She had done it, but a new noise entered her mind. A single thud, soft and tender compared to the pounding of Canis' feet. Thud. Thud. It was distant but rode the same waves as the wild Jark's footsteps. It was near him. She had to follow it. She had to know who was out there. Who was stalking him?

Suddenly, aware of danger, Tamara crouched and ran from the open to find the cover of a tree. Follow the steps, climb over the sound waves, reach the source. She slithered over the ground, following thud after thud, step after step, until she found the boots that made them. Black with a rubber sole. Not as large as the Jark's, not as heavy either. Metal hung by the walker's feet, a rifle, one she had seen before. She crawled up his shirt, followed the noise his body made as it cut through the air, and she saw him. The prisoner. Remmel. He was following Canis, but for what reason, she could not tell.

Thud, tap, thud. Thud, tap, Thud. Canis halted. Remmel halted too. Tamara started to run. She saw it all now. Canis was being followed. Remmel had betrayed them. He betrayed Brokk, but she had to get closer. He was out of reach.

Tamara pushed herself faster, ducking under tree limbs and hurtling logs. Focus on the Tassian. Stop his madness. His knee hit the dirt, his boot scuffed past a fallen branch and crinkled leaves in its way. Remmel raised the rifle to his shoulder, lifted his head to feel the direction of the breeze. Three clicks clockwise on the scope and raised it to his eye. His eyebrow brushed against the metal and his eyelashes blinked against the glass that now had Canis in his sights.

Remmel's finger swirled around the trigger of the Jark rifle that he had stolen from the armory. He had planned this whole thing, this very night. Execute Canis and then come for her. His finger swirled again before resting on the trigger, rubbing the flesh against the cold steel as he made sure he found his target.

Tamara could see his target too, only a few hundred yards from this would be assassin. Canis had kneeled to inspect footprints in the dirt. A man, she gathered, as Canis ran his fingers against the cold wet mud that had shaped around a fourth person's boot.

Cold and wet mud. Cold metallic trigger. She could feel that too. *Work with what you've got. You can feel it,* shouted Red into the back of her mind. Suddenly she realized she too was in range.

The thin white finger of a desperate man pulled against the trigger slowly. He had killed before. His breathing was steady. Tamara pushed her hand forward, extending her range as the firing pin engaged a single round, igniting a spark and then fire within the barrel of the rifle, sending the projectile at nearly a mile per second towards its target. She had it now and felt the heat as well as the cold. Grabbed the barrel of the rifle with her mind and jerked it upward just as the round was nearing the end.

* * *

Patience was the key; leave a track and then circle back. Quietly. Slowly. Deliberately. Stay downwind from your target.

Thilgod recited the fundamentals over and over again in his head. *Keep your eyes towards the threat.* His helmet illuminated the big, red-skinned Jark that was kneeling to examine his tracks. He could hear the man's breathing—heavy but steady. The optics highlighted two weapons on him. A long black combat rifle was slung over his back and a hatchet hung on a belt at his waist.

Toe first, then the heel. Feel for something solid before you shift your weight. He had to be careful now, he was too close. Bugs buzzed loudly past his head and other insects in the bush chirped and called to one another. Leaves bristled as a slight breeze rushed up from the east and died down again at random.

He had decided he had to use a knife on this one. A rifle would be too loud, might alert the witch before he could dispatch her bodyguard and finish her off with a long shot. When he left her, she was by the waterfall gazing at the nebula. He had to keep his distance, maintain his silence.

At three feet, Thilgod could smell the hairy Jark. He fought back the urge to lunge at him. The red-skinned man's size alone made it a formidable fight. No need to rush it. Find the throat and cut through the head. It was how all creatures died, this one would be no different.

Suddenly a round fired from a rifle snapped past his head smashed into a tree. Bark flew outward from the impact. Someone else was there. Someone had been watching them.

Thilgod jumped backward to conceal himself but it was too late. The Jark rolled forward and out of the way, spinning around while reaching for his rifle. Before the Jark could aim at Thilgod, another round smashed into the ground to his front. Dirt sprayed upward and stunned the Jark for a second as he tried to find his threat. This was his chance. Thilgod rushed the behemoth and the Jark too, seeing Thilgod in the bush charged, swinging the butt of his rifle like a baseball bat.

Thilgod ducked and swung his own rifle but it was parried by the larger man. He was quick. A flash of light from his left, another crack. The shooter was firing at them both now, but his rounds weren't accurate and Thilgod paid them no attention. Focus on the Jark. Eliminate the bodyguard.

Another swing by the Jark, but Thilgod saw it coming and stepped into the swing, bringing his own rifle down on the Jark's wrist. The man grunted and let go of his rifle but Thilgod's second swing towards his head struck only air as the Jark rolled to his side and reached for his hatchet.

The man was too fast. Thilgod had hoped for an easy fight using the element of surprise. He had hoped to catch him off guard. Now he had his full attention and it was almost too much. Thilgod tried to recover from his last swing. He tried to pull his rifle back into his body but the Jark had rolled to his side and brought his hatchet down towards Thilgod's arm. Thilgod jerked and the hatchet narrowly missed his coat but connected with the rifle, smashing through the barrel and nearly spitting it in two. His hands vibrated as steel met steel. A metallic shriek rung in his ears as the hatchet rendered the rifle useless.

Thilgod ditched the gun and rolled backward, grabbing for and drawing his machete from inside his trench coat.

* * *

Remmel steadied his left arm on his left knee and held the Jark rifle firm along the stock. It was bulkier than he was used to, but the weight felt even throughout the length of the rifle and would make his aim even steadier. Sensing the wind had just picked up, Remmel twisted his windage knob one more click clockwise and brought the sight to his face. Four hundred meters away, Canis kneeled inspecting something on the trail. Through the scope, Remmel could see the scars on his face from his battle with the grootslang and a scowl across his mouth.

The beast should have died on Tassi, but his luck would now run out. Remmel would make certain Canis paid for his crimes. And after Canis, Brokk would pay as well. There was no forgiveness left in Remmel's heart. No forgiveness for the crimes Brokk and his Jarks had committed against the Tassian people. It had to end tonight, this new campaign of terror that Brokk and his goons wreaked everywhere he went. Remmel would get the revenge so desperately needed by his people, and if he survived, he would bring closure to himself too.

Looking at a man through the sights of a rifle was liberating. He could feel his powerful heartbeat thudding steadily in his chest. His arms and legs felt powerful as he became acutely aware of the strength he held within him.

Canis turned his eyes and looked directly at Remmel. *Did he know or did another noise in the wild surprise him?* It didn't matter. Remmel held the rifle firm and felt the cold steel trigger with his finger. It wasn't that much different than firing a Tassian weapon. *Steady your breathing, pull the trigger back slow, watch the rise and fall of the barrel and then finish the motion.* He had done it a hundred times. Just once more now, and maybe once again after this to cut off the head of this fleet. Remmel squeezed the trigger, but as the stock rocked against his shoulder he felt it pull up.

A miss! Impossible! Re-aim. He's moved. Fire again.

It was ruined, he felt blood rush to his face. This had to work. He had no other chances. Find him again through the sights. The Jark had rolled, was hiding behind a tree. Suddenly, a second figure appeared and Remmel fired a third round, again narrowly missing his target. It was then that he realized what was happening. He should have heard her footsteps; her heavy panting. Somehow she had known and she had pulled his rifle upward.

Brush was moving to his right. Brokk's sorceress was near. He swung his rifle to meet her as she leapt from the trees. He squeezed off a round but it went wide right. *Ten feet now, she's closing fast, ditch the gun, grab your knife. Finish her off that way.*

He flung the weapon at her to slow her down, but she ducked it and as he reached for his knife she was on top of him. Pain surged from his stomach as her metallic fingers dug deep into his abdomen, opening a hole in his flesh deeper than he cared to consider. Remmel stumbled backward as Tamara regained her balance and stood above him. Blood dripped from her hands. His blood. Her eyes flared an emerald green from behind her hood. Her face darkened by the night. Impossible to see anything but those green eyes, those bright green eyes.

Wonderful. Beautiful. Terrifying. Captivating. Words bounced back and forth between his brain and his tongue as he processed the speed at which all of it occurred. He wanted to ask her so many things. He wanted to warn her about the brutality of the Jarks, about how terrible

Brokk had been. He wanted to tell her she was in danger, not from him but in danger from Brokk. He couldn't though. Tamara was Brokk's now. The sorceress had fallen under an even more powerful spell. Brokk's spell.

Remmel fell to a knee and finally found the knife on his belt he had been looking for. He gripped it with his hand, refusing to take his gaze off the woman with emerald eyes that flared like the toxic fire of a nebula. He tried to pull the handle of the knife but couldn't. It was heavy. It was cold. So was his hand. His body was paralyzed. Whether she had learned this new trick or whether it was fear that captured him, he did not know, but as she came closer to him he realized his complete inadequacy to defend himself.

She knelt close to him for a moment, grabbing the back of his head with her hand to keep him from falling over. He wanted to thank her for that. He felt the need to show her appreciation for keeping his head off the ground. The words escaped him and his mind was suddenly consumed by the rapid beating of his own heart. Then he felt hot and then nothing.

CHAPTER SEVENTEEN

There was no time to revel in her victory. Before Remmel's eyes had a chance to fade and before his blood could stop pouring from his wounds, Tamara took off in a full sprint towards Canis's last location. She couldn't feel him anymore, sensed no heartbeat, felt no footsteps. Ducking under branches and diving through thick thorny brush, she pushed herself ever faster despite the pain of jagged tree limbs attacking her arms and thorny briars slicing at her legs.

A bright flash ripped through the trees ahead and a concussive boom followed, rocking nearby leaves back and forth against their limbs. The flash blinded her; the noise was disorienting. The elements vibrated and hummed, further confounding Tamara's ability to sense the world around her. Smoke suddenly filled her nostrils and she no longer knew which direction she was running. Her ears rung and her head screamed. A fire was burning ahead and the swirling of elements made it impossible to pick out Canis from the burning forest. Like a needle in a haystack, his heartbeat would be impossible to find.

Luckily, she wouldn't have to.

"Tamara," growled a weary voice behind her.

She froze, spinning around in the darkness until she found him leaning against a tree. He held his side with his hand and propped his other arm on his rifle. One leg was stretched stiff while the other held his massive frame. Even in the darkness, she could see dark spots on his clothes where fresh blood was pooling.

"What happened?" she asked, rushing to his side, touching his arms delicately and feeling around his ribs. Easing him to the ground where he could sit and avoid the billowing smoke that smothered the air. His pants were torn and his left knee damp from the steady trickle of blood that flowed from a fresh and open wound. His heart was steady, though and his eyes were sharp. *He'll survive.*

"Ambush," he groaned trying to mask the pain behind gritted teeth; voice shaky from the drop of adrenaline after a fight. "Two of them."

"I got one," she said gently. "It was Remmel. He was shooting at you from the trees over there," she said, pointing to the spot she thought she had come from. "I surprised him; he wasn't expecting me."

He nodded. "Good. He shouldn't have gotten the jump on me." Canis groaned as he inhaled a breath into his lungs, stretching his ribs and forcing more blood from the open wound. "A second. Not with Remmel." His breathing was labored as he tried to fight the sheering pain. "He had a rifle but got me with a knife. Long, like a sword or a machete. Sharp. Too sharp with serrated edges like teeth."

Tamara listened and gently pulled his hand from his ribs to examine the wound. Blood gushed from a three-inch long gash as he shifted his weight. His red skin parted and cured upwards away from the injury. The damage the teeth on the knife had done was now visible. A rib was missing half the bone and muscle and marrow that connected the ribs to one another had been torn and pulled apart. His breathing quickened as she touched the skin near it, trying to avoid the wound itself but desperate to clear the area so she could begin treating him.

"It's deep," she said at last. "But you'll heal. Just one slash?" she asked, shocked at the damage that a well-built knife could do.

He shook his head. "Got my knee too," he managed to say, gritting his teeth once more and pointing with his free hand towards his extended leg.

"Not as bad though," she said. *No need to scare the old warrior.* "You'll be up and fighting in no time."

His eyes widened as if he'd forgotten all about the concept of fighting. "He's still out there. Somewhere," the hairy Jark stuttered.

Suddenly his weight shifted and she could feel him trying to get up. Fear coated his scarred face. Desperation filled his eyes and drove him to try to find a position where he could defend them both, as if he had not considered until now that he was vulnerable.

Tamara pushed him back against the tree and more blood surged to the surface of his open wound, pouring over his clothes and coating her hands. "Whoa, you're not fighting anyone like this. You've got your bag?"

"The enemy," he snarled preparing to double his effort to get up.

Tamara wasn't about to let him dictate anything. She had learned a lot in the few hours she was alone and she could feel the power within her. She had just killed Remmel and frozen the river solid. She deflected bullets and saved his life. Tamara pushed him back harder and let her eyes flare a sickly green. The glow stunned Canis and he fell back against the tree once more but she wasn't done. Extending her hand, Tamara grabbed the fire that now simmered behind her and flung it in a ring around them. She pulled it upward sending the simmering flame into a roaring inferno. Sparks flew and the heat growled against them, devouring the brush in its wake yet being contained by her subconscious.

"I don't sense him," she said definitively, "but if it makes you feel better, I doubt he will come through the fire to find us."

The old Jark's face relaxed a little and he fixed his eyes once more on hers. "The first aid pouch is on my belt," he said at last. "There is a white spray in there. It should do the trick."

Tamara reached in and grabbed a cylindrical bottle. Pointing the nozzle at his wound she sprayed until a white film had coated his ribs and solidified against his skin. She then moved down to his knee, repeating the process. In the spray was enough anti-septic to kill whatever was on that knife. It would also bond to his skin, act as a clotting agent, and eventually repair the damage.

It was the same stuff Orno used to heal her after a night of torture to ensure she was fit to labor the next morning on the farm. She hated the spray then, wishing instead for death. Now that she saw its real application she was grateful for it, but the smell still made her sick. Made her angry. *No time for it Tamara. Not yet. Focus on Canis. He needs you now.*

"You'll be better in no time," she said, pushing the spray from her mind and patting him on his good knee. "We'll wait until you feel strong enough to move on your own, it should only take a few minutes to take effect."

He gave her an uncertain look as if to say *you can start an inferno but you can't limp me back to camp?* but instead asked, "What happened to Remmel?"

"I killed him. Stabbed him," she said, looking down at her hands to make sure he knew what she meant. Even now, the nebula above reflected its colors off the jeweled daggers that Brokk had gifted to her. Flakes of Remmel's blood, freshly dried, fell to the ground below as she flexed and contracted her fingers, staring at the objects that took the life of a man she wanted to call her friend mere hours earlier. The tips of her fingers were as sharp as ever, deadly spears that would serve her over and over again. She should be thankful to Brokk, but she felt burdened by them. She wanted to feel empowered, but only dread gripped her as she examined the weapons more closely. "Stopped his heart too," she added, pointing at her mind.

Canis looked at the ground, refusing to give her any acknowledgement for a job well done. Instead, sorrow seemed to coat his face as if he had felt the same burden she was now experiencing. *Introspective perhaps.*

"I don't blame him," he finally said. "If it was me, I wouldn't have taken Brokk's offer either." He was quiet for a moment but she knew he wasn't finished talking. He fixed his eyes on a night beetle that struggled to climb onto a fallen stick. Its black shell weighed heavily on thin legs and frustrated its efforts. "The man's changed. Brokk has. I guess all of us have." He stopped again, playing with the dirt on the ground. Fire blazing behind him, illuminating his back and showing off the animal side of the Jark race. Such a contrast Tamara could see now, such a war-weary creature that didn't know where he fit in anymore.

Introspection perhaps isn't always good for a soldier.

Changed. The words resonated with her; almost made her feel guilty for taking so much pride in the death of their mutual enemy. But she had changed too. She had to be stronger. She had to be less reliant on men like Red; men like Brokk. The world would not allow her to trust those she wanted to call friend; and if it did, the world would rip them from her as soon as she let her guard down.

"Things are different for all of us now," she said, examining the artificial skin that had sealed around his wound. "I spent five years as a victim because I was unable to protect the people I cared about. It won't happen again." He stared into her green eyes and she gave him the chance to know that she was serious. He didn't break his stare. Always a warrior. "Your bleeding has stopped," she told him, smiling and rising to her feet. "We should get back to the camp to alert them that Kostia's men have found us."

Canis rolled over and tenderly pushed himself up, using a tree for support with one hand and the barrel of his rifle as crutch in the other hand. His breathing quickened but he didn't make any audible sounds to indicate he was in pain.

Tough, she thought to herself, offering a hand only to have it slapped away. *Tough.*

Steadying himself, Canis faced her. "Brokk's not going to put up with this slow stuff for long. He might be half Tassian, but the Jark half of him will be itching for more. Brokk is a warrior. He always has been. He has his eyes set on Kostia's chair, and if that means obliterating the entire northern garrison to do it, he'll do exactly that. We sit in our base arming slaves and looking for the ones that have talent. Ones that can pilot or repair ships we've taken. The rest are fodder, Tamara. Fodder."

"Do you know how long I stared at these mountains," she retorted. "I took beatings because of my daydreaming for rest in these hills that didn't include a slave's color and the whip. They might be fodder, but they're free," she insisted. "Free to be fodder or free to walk out into the wild and disappear. Kostia won't be able to contend with this rebellion. Already weapons are flowing past the northern garrison and into the villages beyond. Brokk's name is being passed with each bullet that is distributed to their cause. They'll fight with him because he is the only chance they have at freedom. He is the unifying presence that all of us have been waiting for. Brokk is our conqueror, now. What comes afterward, I do not know."

Canis grunted again and turned from her. She thought she saw a smile or a grin through the fur and beyond his scarred face and sharp off-set teeth that protruded outward and upward to allow him to tear through flesh just as easily as the claws on her own fingers. She didn't know if she was looking at the animal half of Canis or the logical part, but it didn't matter. She could feel his heart rate was still steady, and she took that as a good sign. As a sign of trust that she had been so eager to earn.

The ring of fire around them slowed to simmer at Tamara's command and other than the scurrying of rodents and steady breathing of birds hunting in the trees above, she sensed they were alone.

"Back to camp," he ordered, limping through the ash.

CHAPTER EIGHTEEN

"How could you?!" screamed an irate Kostia. "You were there, in the enemy camp and you did nothing?" Spit flew from his mouth as he yelled, coating Thilgod's forehead and cheeks with a sticky green slime.

After a two-day journey back to the city, he had tried to lay low, avoid the bars and clubs that Kostia or his cronies would visit. Nurse his wounds from the battle with the Jark. His shoulder still throbbed, and his hip, which was lucky enough to catch the handle of the ax instead of the blade ached as well. The bone was shattered and there wasn't enough medicine to heal bone. Only time could do the trick, time he had hoped to get before Kostia realized he had failed.

He had to go out though, had to leave his hiding place to find food for Dacia and that's when they found him. Horick and his men grabbed him and brought him to Kostia in shackles. Threatened him with crimes of desertion and abandonment, threatened him with execution. Thilgod wanted none of it.

"Well?!" Kostia boomed again, waiting for the answer of his once respected bounty hunter.

The man's green scales glistened in the light from his top-floor window. His big eyes bulged forward, waiting for Thilgod's response.

"There's a real army out there, Kostia," Thilgod implored. "A real army with real soldiers. They've armed the slaves. It's a rebellion. You can't win this by threatening me."

Big mistake. Shouldn't have gone that far. The warlord's face turned pale, then from green to red where blood rushed upwards. "Threatening you?" he asked with a hiss. "Threatening you? Is that what you think I'm doing? I'm not threatening you Thilgod..."

"That's not what I meant..." he tried to cut in, but Kostia rose his voice even louder.

"I'm not threatening you, you fool! I'm going to make an example of you. I'm going to show the citizens and the army of Charoth that you don't back away from a fight. Especially not a fight that threatens to change our way of life! Do you think the Iralene ruling party wants to see slaves set free? Do you think they want to work the fields themselves?" He paced towards the window angrily, shoving his way past Horick who yielded like a puppy eager to please his master.

"We don't just supply ourselves," he said, now looking out of his window at the streets below. "What will the Jark Empire think when the supply of slaves stops coming? Or the Hestonians with their indentured servants and underground brothels. This is an intergalactic business and the Iralene are rich. Now, news of this Lysop, this sorceress, has reached our city. They believe they can't be touched with her behind them. My men are busy executing slaves in the streets but somehow more slaves manage to get weapons and pick up the fighting."

Kostia turned back to Thilgod whose chains hung painfully from his raw wrists. His knees ached and his hip hurt even more from being forced to stand and put weight on the bone-deep wound that he feared would soon become infected if he could not treat it. Kostia came close to him and the stale reptilian odor of dry skin, harboring standing water, penetrated his nostrils.

"You should not have come back here," he said, turning from him again and heading back to the window. From the corner of Thilgod's eye, he could tell something had caught his attention. "I wouldn't have come looking for you, I would have assumed you had died trying to carry out my will and the desires of the Iralene. The same Iralene that made you rich and comfortable!"

The echo of gunfire reached Thilgod's ears and he suddenly realized what Kostia had been watching. They were executing slaves in the square below. He heard no screams but knew that Kostia and his men did things to make a point. The public executions were no different and Thilgod could be certain others were down there watching the horror. The men were likely only shot after torture; after being paraded about the city without any dignity to prevent others from following in their footsteps. *An Example.* Then it dawned on him and the pain on his hip came second to the dread in his chest being validated by the shackles on his wrists.

"So what will you do to me?" he asked, unafraid to be curious in his final hours.

Kostia looked at Horick and then back to Thilgod. "Lead him to the jail. Lock him away until this rebellion has been quelled," he ordered. Horick nodded and brought two guards to escort Thilgod from the room. "Once the fighting ends," Kostia continued, addressing Thilgod now, "we'll bring you to the square and let you rot on a pike. That is the punishment for failing the Iralene," he hissed.

* * *

Without anesthesia, a handheld drill drove four screws into Thilgod's skull. The pain was unbearable. His vision flashed from white to red and then all of the colors in between. Through gritted teeth he groaned and cried, doing his best to hold back tears that were a natural yet shameful response to the first of many tortures.

He had watched the act performed dozens of times to slaves; saw them scream and writhe in agony as bigger men held them down and screwed a collar into their heads. Thilgod could never have imagined the pain it caused. Luckily for him, he no longer had to. When the final screw had been inserted into his temple, he passed out.

The painful vibrations of a prison transport rocketing along a magnetic track woke him. He was inside a windowless box, a compartmentalized prison unit that would be attached to the ever-growing maximum-security prison that the Iralene managed in the south of the city. This was his new home and had been kindly equipped with a brown toilet and a blue and white striped mattress.

Through blurry eyes and dimmed vision, Thilgod could tell he was alone in the container. Guards no longer needed to escort a prisoner from a transport truck and into a cell; this was their cell. Instead, they simply shelved his container and shoved food through slots in the ceiling when it was time to eat. A horrible existence and a disorienting experience, no way to tell which way was up or down. No way of knowing if his box was on the outside of a wall or on the inside. No way to plan an escape or monitor guard movement.

The transport jostled violently, slamming his head back and forth. It throbbed in between moments of sheering pain and each time he squeezed his jaw to brace for the next jolt of the container, fresh blood would trickle down his forehead and onto his nose where it pooled; dripping steadily onto his mattress below. This was the cost of crossing Kostia. The punishment for failing the Iralene. It didn't matter how many times you helped them, once you failed them it was over for you.

Between the pain, when his brain gave him a chance to think on other things, Thilgod considered Dacia. He had no way of knowing how much time had passed, but she'd be starving, pacing back and forth in the one bedroom rental he had gotten two days before being captured. Maybe the owners of the rental would hear her crying and feed her. Maybe she'd attack them out of desperation and they'd kill her. It didn't matter now. Not immediately anyway. He had to focus on the present. Think beyond the pain that shattered his thoughts as the screws jiggled in his skull.

The prison transport bumped again sending him up towards the ceiling and knocking him hard against his cot. His shoulder burned where it hit the cold steel wall; his eyes flashed white from the pain in his skull. The transport suddenly jerked again and swerved within its magnetic tunnel, throwing him forward as the nearly two hundred mile-per-hour steel box slammed against the wall before finally grinding to a halt. *Ambush.* A hammering nose of gunfire slamming into the wall of the box and sent Thilgod diving to the floor; fully expecting rounds to penetrate the steel box. They did not.

Suddenly, an explosion that sounded like a well-timed grenade sent shudders through the box and rattled his teeth against his skull. More gunfire now, closer and deeper as if the guards were returning fire against the hammering of the enemy weapons. Then silence. Thilgod waited expectantly, lying prone against the cold ground. His hip throbbed and his shoulder ached. More blood pooled from the screws attached to his skull and dripped from the bridge of his nose and onto the cold steel floor.

Thilgod waited in the silence, expecting to hear more gunfire, voices, a door opening, or the motor of their magnetic transport warming up to continue the trek. None of that happened and suddenly he realized he had either been abandoned or his guards were dead. Great news for a condemned man, but the realization was also accompanied with the sobering fact that he was now stuck inside a prison cell and a steel box in the middle of the road at the heat of the day. How long could he last, a day? A week? Certainly not much longer. *Escape then. But how.*

Thilgod stood to examine his cell. Thin rays of light penetrated into the far corner of his rectangular box from where the slot for food had opened during the battle. It was the width of his hand and only about twice as long. *Not nearly big enough to slip through.*

The toilet though… He locked his eyes on a metallic stool, wide enough to sit uncomfortably and do one's business. It was anchored to the floor and contained no moving parts. Just a metal rim, not even a tank. No seat to lift, no screws to remove. There must have been pipes underneath; pipes that would connect his toilet to a water source outside. *Same problem, Thilgod,* his rational side told him. *The hole's too small. You're too fat.*

Rip it up, his non-rational side began to muse. *Rip it up and see. What's the worst that can happen, huh?*

Nowhere to do your business, that's what. You not only die in here, but it stinks as you find a corner to do your business in instead of going out the civilized way.

When did Thilgod get weak? He didn't know and instead of arguing with himself like a lunatic whose only friend was a wild animal, he leaned back on his bad hip and thrust his good leg forward, rattling the steel toilet hard but causing no damage. *When did Thilgod get weak?* His alter-ego asked again, chiding him to kick it again, which he did at least three more times before the pain in his hip was so intense he couldn't bear to stand any longer.

He had been right. Not an option. Not now at least. These transport vessels would have monitors on them. Maybe someone would be coming. Maybe plan to take whoever did come off-guard. Make weapons and wait.

Except you don't have to. His alter-ego told him, as he heard the sliding of a metallic bolt outside his door.

"Stand back prisoner!" a voice ordered from outside.

Thilgod quickly backed up again and sat on the ground, trying to look harmless but ready to take his chances against unprepared prison guards. The door creaked and popped. Suddenly daylight exploded through the open door accompanied by a gust of fresh air.

"You're free now!" Shouted the voice. "Don't follow us, you hear?"

Thilgod couldn't see the blackened figure from the brightness against his eyes but he knew who it was. Rebels. Freed slaves that took their time clamoring down from their ambush position to open the container. They had no idea who he was. He was lucky and had no intention of following them. It was time to find work elsewhere; work away from the Iralene.

Thilgod nodded and the figure disappeared. He was free.

CHAPTER NINETEEN

"She's ready," said Canis through the holographic display on the Juggernaut.

"And you?" asked Brokk from the large red captain's chair, at the head of the table in his executive conference room.

"Of course," he responded flippantly.

Canis's face told Brokk a different story. He was badly hurt and taking time to heal. Even though the hologram was a poor rendition of an actual person, Brokk knew the real Canis would look even worse if he was given a chance to see the old warrior face to face. Upon hearing about the attack sent Brokk into a rage, but Tamara had settled him down. "Without traitors," she told him, "how would I have gotten the practice I needed?"

Brokk was learning daily what it really meant to lead in such complex environments. A leader couldn't be everywhere at once and even worse, he couldn't even gauge the intentions of his own men. Leaders needed to empower and trust their subordinates. Countless mistakes were bound to be made, but how else does a fleet learn?

Brokk and Canis were joined in the briefing room by twelve newly appointed ship commanders, all sitting around the massive metallic table that had the ability to project holographic displays of the battle plans as they were developed. While some of the men had been promoted from within his own crew, others were merchant pilots that had been rescued during the anti-piracy campaign that Terre had led. All had agreed to join Brokk's quest. In exchange, Brokk gave them a captured ship outfitted with the latest Jark weaponry fabricated by the Juggernaut and an offer to become permanent, and paid, members of his armada.

In addition to the twelve, by his side was Terre, clothed in a gold and red flight suit of a newly promoted fleet admiral. Terre would command the destroyer and a fleet of three other ships. As their armada grew, Terre's fleet would grow too.

"How are the repairs to the destroyer coming, Terre?" Brokk asked.

"We're almost complete," he responded. "The maintenance bots are finishing up the last of the hull today, then we'll move to the inside and make sure the life support and defense systems are running the way they should. I'll finish in one orbit."

Brokk nodded approval. "Your destroyer is the last ship we can afford to repair. I don't think I need to remind you how scarce our resources have become. There won't be any more fabrication until we can come up with more material, and that won't happen until you take that spaceport."

"I am aware," Terre agreed. "Still, the material has lasted longer than any of us thought it would. We're in good shape from a fleet perspective and I'm certain we'll be able to seize those resources on the spaceport."

"Good." Brokk responded. "And your new crew?"

Terre grinned. "They're eager." He paused to see if Brokk knew what he meant, so Brokk nodded. "It is interesting having a mixed crew instead of pure Jarks. We're getting past the oddities of culture and moving into our roles."

"I know what you mean. If anyone can do it, Terre, it's you." Brokk said reassuringly. "Okay, let's get into the plan," he said addressing the group of pilots and ground commanders seated around the table." Since this is a new team, make sure we take it slow and ask lots of questions. I'm going to hand it over to my chief of operations, Kal."

A thin and hairy Jark lurched forward from the far wall and walked on his hands and feet until he was within reach of the hologram floor that spun at the center of the table. He was shorter than average, standing at a mere six feet tall, and had gray tips along his hairy back giving him a silver shine that signified age and wisdom in a culture comprised of young warriors. For Brokk, Kal was a creative mind and a savage tactician. He knew whatever Kal had been planning for the last few weeks would be sufficient, timely, and effective.

"This is a four phase war," Kal began. His voice was raspy and his movement stressed as he pivoted on damaged knees and elbows, gesturing with his fingers to bring up a map of the solar system for all to see.

Phase one has been occurring since we arrived. It consists of arming the rebels and sowing distrust for the current governing body. The special units we've sent into the city have done an excellent job with this facilitation and as of our last intelligence report, we've fabricated and provided over twenty million weapons, explosives, and ammunition.

Brokk leaned over to Terre and chuckled. "That's where all those rare metals went."

"Those that have not yet been armed," Kal continued "are waiting patiently for the rebellion, at which point there are plans to overthrow local government offices and seize the weapons from peacekeepers throughout the smaller towns and villages."

Kal paused to make sure that everyone was on the same page. Brokk nodded to indicate they were and he continued.

"So, here we are on the eve of phase two. Reports from our agents on the ground indicate that guerrilla forces are now waiting to move from unrest and civil discord to armed resistance. Those embedded with the ousted president tell us that he and his government have given a thumbs up to our moving forward as well. All they need is a sign. Much like a conventional fight, I propose that sign be something big enough to catch the attention of the entire planet." Kal paused and gave Brokk a wink. "To initiate phase two, I suggest an aerial bombardment of the northern garrison, providing Canis and his marines freedom of maneuver through the safe area and towards the capital city."

Kal spun the planet until the bright side was illuminated. Three red dots shone outward on the hologram and caught the attention of the group. "There are really three garrisons that the Iralene hold. The gates to the north, here. The Southern garrison below the capital city, here. And finally, the capital garrison, which primarily acts as a police force and guard for the Iralene ruling party. The other two garrisons primarily exist to maintain peace within the towns and cities beyond the capital."

"Because of its location," Kal said, zooming the three-dimensional map in on the northern garrison, "this would be the one to hit while minimizing collateral damage. This strike, launched by the Juggernaut will initiate movement for Canis and the marines to push south, past the city of Galamora, while proclaiming a message of liberation from the brutal and oppressive Iralene rule. Our intelligence believes that none of the cities in the north will fight against our men because Iralene supporters are only truly localized in the capital itself. The benefits of Iralene rule neither extend to the north nor can they without meeting significant resistance from those loyal to the previous government."

He paused giving Brokk or Canis a chance to ask questions. Neither had any. So far, Kal had put together exactly what the two had drawn up separately in his office.

Sensing approval, Kal continued. "Phase three is two-part and requires the simultaneous action of our armada above and the rebellion below. First, we must destroy the local defenses around the only spaceport and seize it. Terre," he said, looking at the veteran pilot and newly crowned captain of the Kemnaut, "You'll take the Kemnaut and three of the mining vessels we've seized and lead an assault on the spaceport. No damage can be done to this port; as you know, we desperately need it to be able to transfer essential items to our ships to replenish our stocks, as they are almost entirely depleted of organic material because of the fabrication of weapons and repair of vessels. If we lose this spaceport, it will take years after establishing the new government to rebuild it. We simply cannot take that chance."

Terre nodded and Kal looked to the hologram of Canis who was picking at a scab on his face. "Canis, you've got to establish a defensive position at the outskirts of the capital. We believe your very presence will be sufficient to start the rebellion required inside the city."

Canis, who didn't miss a beat between peeling the scab from his face and shamelessly rolling it around in his fingers, nodded. "We will do it," he said plainly.

"Excellent," responded Kal. "Phase four is largely ceremonial. Wait for Kostia and the Iralene ruling party to attempt to flee, capture him, execute him, and exploit the emotions of the people to establish a government free from slavery that answers to us. During phase four, Canis, you remain outside the city. The goal is to not project any concept of foreign rule. Let Atworth Kierce establish his government and provide a quick reaction force as required in conjunction with his own men."

With the framework established, Kal looked to Brokk for guidance. "Do you have anything before we break into groups to discuss the finer points of each phase?"

Brokk shook his head. "It looks good, Kal, thanks."

Rising, he examined the group. He never thought he would be standing amongst a mixed race armada striving for the eventual defeat of the Jark Empire—an empire he once thought he would help climb to the top of the universe. Some were young, but many of the men he looked at around the room were weathered and experienced. They might not have commanded a Jark destroyer, but they were talented and eager. That would hopefully give him just enough to gain the upper hand, not only against the Iralene but against the Jarks and other enemies he faced down the road.

"Remember," he told the collective, "there is a popular government ready to immediately provide services to the people once the Iralene dissolve. This place used to be more than just a slavers corner. There are rare minerals under the surface and the expertise and equipment to mine them. This is a place that can fund our operations indefinitely; we simply have to break it free from the influence of the Iralene and the Jark Empire.

"This should be an easy battle. Don't lose focus. Commanders," he said, now looking at his pilots, "I'll be back in one orbit to receive a back brief from each of you. Be prepared to walk me through your portion of this operation in detail."

Kal nodded and Brokk decided it was time to leave the room to let the team finalize their plan. There was nothing worse than a commander that meddled in the business of the staff.

CHAPTER TWENTY

"What will it look like?" Tamara was leaning against the side of a tan and green striped armored vehicle. Next to her was Canis, wearing a green camouflage outfit and body armor. He propped a rifle on his knee and was twisting a blade of prairie grass in his fingers. His eyes squinted in the sun as he looked out over the open fields.

"White light," he said at last. "Loud, like thunder except you know something terrifying is coming with it. You'll probably feel it too, the ground will shake and tremble as the rounds detonate." He turned the grass to mush and wiped the orange juice that oozed from its stem onto his pants.

"How many rounds will it take?" she asked, tapping her jeweled claws against the side of the armored vehicle behind her. The vehicle responded with deep metallic groans that signified the density of the armor behind the paint. Its black track, long rubber and metal pads that connected the rear wheels to the front had already proved powerful adaptations as they crossed streams and gullies as if the natural barriers did not exist at all.

"He'll probably give it two," Canis grunted. "One would likely do it though."

Tamara grabbed a pair of optical enhancers that rested on the hood of the vehicle and looked through them. The fortress, a few miles beyond their resting point, looked massive through the magnifying lenses. The huge stone structure jutted out of the ground at least thirty feet high. Embedded in the walls were guns and cannons that could surely launch a dizzying and deadly array of munitions. As she scanned the fortress, her optics illuminated other defensive objects such as wire and mines that speckled hills leading up to the impenetrable beast. Beyond the walled defenses was an entire garrison of soldiers, ready to attack an enemy at a moment's notice. In total, the sprawling fortress in the north covered nearly two whole miles of land and had a population of tens of thousands of people.

"One round," Tamara asked in shock, "would destroy that thing?"

"If you remember one thing, Tamara," Canis told her with a growl, "remember that you never want to be downrange of an aerial bombardment from a battleship."

Wind on the prairie picked up and now blew steadily, forcing dust and seeds from the grass to lift and sail where the weather beckoned. Her black braided hair blew violently as she looked behind her, grateful for the black trench coat that Brokk had given her. A row of hundreds of vehicles, just like the one she leaned against was formed behind them, waiting for the show, and afterward, the charge through the gates.

"In position down there?" a voice hummed on the radio.

Canis touched his throat. "We're ready for the show," he responded, giving Tamara a grin.

The show. Tamara had to remind herself that the people they were preparing to destroy were supporters of the Iralene; supporters of Orno. It was these people that killed Red and abused her over and over again to make sure she understood her inferior status while in captivity.

It was the corrupt and evil Iralene government that whipped her, beat her, and covered her senses so that the world was not only dark but miserable. Still, the thought of wiping tens of thousands of lives off the face of Charoth made her stomach churn.

"Will they feel pain do you think?" she asked Canis.

He looked at her with wide and confused eyes, as brown as the dust rising off the prairie. She felt silly for asking but suddenly he smiled. "I haven't wondered that in a long time," he said at last. "But rest assured, if anything in war is painless, this will be it for most of them. The concussion of the blast alone will create enough pressure inside their brains to cause them to implode before they even know what happened. Add to that the immense heat and flash radiation, and a person would likely vaporize nearly instantaneously."

Tamara nodded in agreement but a flash of light and a thick black cloud suddenly swirled in the skies above. "They've fired," Canis said, pointing at the darkened sky.

Through the black cluster of clouds, a white streak flew through the sky, arching across the horizon. The sun glistened off the silver object as it fell downward until she lost sight of it. Canis grabbed the optical enhancers from the hood of the truck and focused on the garrison. Tamara didn't need anything to see what was going to happen. Suddenly, the ground beneath her feet began to tremble and shake. The truck behind her vibrated and loose gear and weapons rattled as they fell lose from their resting places.

Fireballs erupted upward from the fortress, scorching the sky with red smoke and dust. The wind, which was once blowing against her back changed directions and pushed a hot dry blast against her face, causing her eyes to burn and her mind to go wild from the sudden battering of elements that it carried with it.

Canis touched his throat again and signaled the battleship above. "Up three, right one, part of a wall and who knows what else beyond it."

A second flash erupted from above and a second object, a harbinger of the death to come fell rapidly from the fire-branded sky. As it disappeared, Tamara squared her feet to balance herself against the violent shaking of the ground. More fireballs flew upward into the sky and the wind that came with the second blast was hotter and richer than the first, carrying with it the scent of charred stones and harvested souls from the single most devastating strike she had ever seen.

"Target," Canis said calmly into his radio. "Scanning, negative, negative, hit." She didn't know the code words but she didn't have to. It was clear the northern Garrison was nothing more than rubble and ash. Their way to the capital would be clear and Kostia's heart would surely be frozen with fear as he received the news.

* * *

In the dead of space, the two flashes of light to the starboard side of Terre's destroyer would have meant nothing if he didn't know the carnage those munitions were wreaking on the planet below. Seeing them sent adrenaline through his veins. He felt alive again. For Terre, the high-energy explosive shell was a signal to attack. The coordination required for his very own battle group to charge from his resting position on the dark side of Charoth and into the light to attack and seize the spaceport.

"Maximum thrust," he ordered from the command center of the Kemnaut destroyer. His pilot, a pale-skinned Hestonian freighter pilot before being captured by pirates on Charoth acknowledged his order and slid a magnetic lever forward. Trapped in the gravity of the planet, Terre suddenly felt his chest sink and his muscles strain under the immense force of the engines that pressed against his body as they accelerated.

Like a bird diving for prey, the Kemnaut launched from the safety of its perch and hurtled towards the southern pole of the planet. In space, where the only orientation that mattered was the target as it related to your weapon systems, Terre believed an attack from the south against the minor defenses of the spaceport would be perfect to both maintain the element of surprise and to minimize damage to the spaceport itself. Meanwhile, the smaller vessels could confuse the enemy from the flanks.

"Sensor report," Terre shouted as he strained to move his head to see his targeting officer.

"Holding steady," the hairy Jark responded from his seat. "Three ships orbiting clockwise across the face of the port; two others coming south from the northern pole."

The Kemnaut's advanced targeting systems could likely handle them all, but he had to make sure they made a clean sweep before boarding the station and seizing it. "Wings One and Two, initiate the sweep, break now," Terre ordered into his headset, watching as the two seized Marauder Class pirate vessels broke formation and began to circumvent the planet from opposite directions.

The plan was simple. Use the destroyer to attack from the South Pole while the Marauders came in from the east and the west. The patrols heading south would be destroyed by the Marauders while he was left to deal precision blows to those defenses immediately surrounding the station. His third wing was a boarding ship, also seized nearly a week ago and packed with Jark interplanetary marines. They had the hard job of blowing a hole through the spaceport and taking control without damaging the magnetic elevator that connected it to the planet's surface.

Light from the yellow sun shone brightly through their command center's windows as the Kemnaut made its final crest along the southern pole of Charoth. Thrust and velocity were the two biggest factors to fighting a war in space and at over ten thousand kilometers per minute, Terre had the advantage on both fronts. Within seconds his targeting systems had picked up the three patrolling vessels near the spaceport and calculated the munition and trajectory required to destroy them.

"Three locks," shouted his targeting officer.

"Execute," responded Terre.

The ship vibrated as three depleted neutronium rounds launched from their cannon bays at the targets beyond. From his computer terminal, Terre could see the three ships lazily coming about as they attempted to identify this new ship and potential threat to their existence. They were too late. Mere seconds after the launch the rounds tore through the pirate ships sending fire, shrapnel, and the bodies of their crews into the icy abyss. Seconds later the two northern ships thrusting south to confront Terre met their own doom against his marauders at their flanks.

"Wing three," Terre blurted into his radio, not waiting for his targeting officer to give the all clear. "Initiate docking and seizure. Wings One and Two, begin east-west patrols. Pilot," Terre finally said out of his radio and to his own crew, "Fast halt and come about. I want to watch that nebula in the event Jark vessels respond to any distress calls."

* * *

Hatches hissed white plumes of oxygen and carbon dioxide as metal screeched against metal. Sizzling could be heard beyond the copper and lead shield that protected Masai and his company of Raiders from the immense heat of lasers cutting through the steel exterior of the spaceport. A heads-up display in his pressurized combat helmet indicated the breach would be ready to rush through in twenty seconds. A lot could happen in twenty seconds.

Masai felt a nudge against the back of his space suit and twisted his body awkwardly to look back. A fat red face, coated in sweat, stared back at him through an amber tinted visor. "We've still got fifteen seconds before we do anything and you're already sweating?" Masai joked through his helmet's radio system.

"Give me a break," panted Mayo, the number two man in the stack. "I don't think my climate control is working well in here."

"You better have my back," Masai growled. He knew Mayo did. Masai was hot too and each of them were about fifty pounds heavier than the next biggest guy in the company. They didn't get their position because of speed. The first two guys through a door or the hull of a ship were bullet magnets. The thicker the man going through, the fewer bullets traveled through him and into the next man on the team. *Seize the foothold*, their commander would growl. *I don't care how you die after the foothold, but you had better get us through that door and into the next room!*

And they did, time and time again Masai and Mayo got their company into the next room, established a foothold to build up fighting power with the rest of the company, and always won the ship.

His heads-up display blinked quickly. Five seconds. Go time. Masai gripped his rifle and took the weapon off its safety, selecting the fully automatic feature that allowed him to send six hundred and forty-three rounds into the enemies fighting position before he had to throw in a new drum.

His shoulders ached, body rigid, slight rock back, work up the momentum. One second. The steel hull of the space station slammed down and his own lead and copper shield suddenly vanished. Push forward. He felt light as a feather running as fast as he could through the smoke that concealed the gap in the breached hull. Hot orange steel, melted at the frame, still glowed around the edges as he pushed forward. Flashes of light and bullets from enemy defenders snapped past him, slamming into the metal walls of their boarding bay behind them.

Through the door, turn right. Follow the wall. His heads-up display illuminated three combatants which he held down his trigger against until they fell to the ground. More shooting now behind and in front of him. A grenade rolled to his feet, which he kicked away just in time to watch explode in a flash of light. His helmet tinted black to protect his vision and his suit blocked the concussive boom that would have left him stunned and disoriented. Another target, another ten round burst, enough to penetrate the armor of the enemy suit and tear through flesh.

Hit the corner, swivel left, stay along the wall. The room was longer than he thought it would be and opened up into a wide bay that held boxes of supplies and wheeled vehicles to carry the equipment throughout the station. Smoke cleared and his helmet couldn't find any more targets in his sector. "Clear," Masai shouted, which was soon echoed by Mayo and about twelve other voices.

"Push to the next chamber," his commander calmly said through his radio.

No time to rest, and suddenly Masai was aware of his heavy breathing and profuse sweating. His head felt clammy and his fingers were cold. He noticed a red warning light flashing at the upper left of his display. Suddenly the arm of his suit tightened and compressed against his flesh. A needle stabbed him in the leg. Adrenaline; he'd been shot. Losing blood. Keep going, take the next room, but he couldn't, and before his left foot struck the ground he was falling backward into his own medicine induced abyss.

CHAPTER TWENTY-ONE

"They're surrendering?"

"In droves, sir," Horick responded with an insolence and incompetence that dripped laziness and self-pity.

Kostia turned from his chief of security before the urge to slap him was too great. Moving towards the window, he looked at the streets below from the high-rise conference room in the Iralene government building. Nothing moved except the guards mounted in armored vehicles that had sealed off the block. They wore the royal green color of the Iralene to show their devotion. A color that once represented victory and celebration. Kostia doubted it meant anything to the soldiers beyond the money in their pockets and the surface of their skin.

He turned again to confront Horick. The man's face was weathered and his eyes were droopy. Wrinkles formed on a furrowed brow as he feigned concern. *Perhaps not concerned enough.*

"Well, what are you doing about it, Horick?" Kostia asked at last, wondering why the solution would have to be pulled from his once trusted right hand rather than a solution being offered with zeal. There was a time when Horick would have jumped at providing a solution. Perhaps Kostia had kept him around too long and that the wealth of Iralene food and the warmth of Iralene women had hardened the connections in his brain. Perhaps he had always been this way but Kostia was the one too foolish not to see it.

"We can't get anyone on the radio," Horick responded, shifting his weight and shoving his hands into the pockets of his black cotton pants. "After the northern garrison…"

"Don't use that nonsense as an excuse!" Kostia shouted. "And stop fidgeting in your pockets as if you couldn't care less what your performance has to do with your lifespan!"

Horick pulled his hands from his pockets slowly and crossed them at his chest. "What I'm saying, Kostia, is that after the northern garrison disappeared, no one else has dared to lift a finger against this rebellion. Slaves are claiming that a sorceress did it, that she actually vaporized all those people. The fear of you is being surpassed by a fear of her."

Kostia couldn't believe what he was hearing. "It was a bombardment from above, Horick. You don't actually believe that Lysop girl wiped out the garrison too, do you?"

He shrugged a mindless and gutless shrug. *Useless.* "It doesn't matter what I believe. She's become a legend and the peace keepers in the towns won't lift a finger against her. More and more slaves have taken up weapons in the north to join the cause and now, the enemy has encamped outside the city. We've already lost two of the lower quarters and you know the rebellion will continue to climb. We have only the true loyalists now, only the ones that actually believe in what the Iralene are doing as opposed to those that were simply too scared to cross us."

"Too scared to cross us?!" Kostia was now not only mad but he was stunned. "And is that why you have worked for me too? So that you could enjoy our benefits until you no longer feared us? Are you that much of a coward, Horick?"

"That's not what I…," Horick began to say but was silenced by Kostia's hand.

"Watch yourself, Horick," he snapped. "What about the south? What does that garrison have to say?" Kostia asked, stunned at how quickly the old man would assess them as being on the losing side.

"They want to wait. I've asked them to reinforce the city, but they claim they are busy in the south."

"Gutless cowards," Kostia hissed. "They want to remain on the sideline until this is over and then pick the government that wins." Kostia turned and circled back towards the window. Reaching for a lever, he twisted it and felt the cool breeze force its way into his office. Pops and cracks could be heard below as freed slaves and rebels took shots at Iralene government buildings, signs, and anything else they decided they didn't like. "I sent a message to the Jark security station in this sector," Kostia continued. "That battleship and whatever else is up there are going to be destroyed. The Jarks are dispatching a fleet. Then what will you do, Horick? Do you expect me to reward the men that only fight with me for the money and disappear when a true conflict comes knocking?"

"Will they send marines too so we can quell the rebellion?" he asked dumbly. "We don't have enough fighters to put this back in line anymore."

That was the last straw. Kostia could not tolerate a member of his government that so lazily doubted his ability to squash the rebellion. "Horick," Kostia hissed walking towards him. "This is where you and I end our relationship."

Horick's eyes grew wide and his jaw sputtered as he tried to think of something to say. Kostia was closer now. Close enough to smell his fear and feel the adrenaline that had surged in Horick's veins as he realized his life was over. "Don't," he finally shouted, bringing his arms up to protect his face.

He was fat and slow and his arms couldn't possibly move as fast as Kostia's sharp dual-pronged tongue, which he shot out from his mouth and into Horick's left eye, tearing it from its socket and swallowing it whole. Horick screamed and tried to move backward, grabbing at his empty eye socket. Blood poured over his fingers and streamed onto the tile below. Kostia grabbed him, stepping past his legs with his own and swinging them back, tripping Horick and sending him to the floor. As he fell, Kostia jumped on top of him, pushing the fat man's arms up above his head and exposing his other eye. His pupil was wide with fear and it danced back and forth between Kostia's eyes and mouth.

"This is what happens when you fail the Iralene!" Kostia roared, plunging his snake-like tongue into Horick's good eye and tearing it from its socket. He crunched down with his teeth tasting a burst of salty water as the eye exploded beneath Kostia's jaws. Horick screamed and squirmed, finally settling on a whimper. "You'll see Horick," he told him. "The Iralene won't fall to this. My race may be few in numbers, but we will control far more than you could ever dream. This barrier is merely a hurtle, nothing more. Don't worry, I'm going to give you a front-row view."

Kostia climbed to his feet and grabbed Horick by the leg, dragging him to the clear glass door, while shouting for his secretary. "Put him on a stake in the garden!" he shouted. "Let everyone see that this is what happens when you fail the Iralene!"

* * *

Sliding the window up slowly, Thilgod paused and sniffed the air. Just Dacia, no cologne masking the scent of a stinking Iralene loyalist waiting to finish the job. Pushing the rest of the window up, Thilgod swung his legs around, careful to favor the gash on his hip and dropped himself gently onto the floor of his dark apartment. He made no noise, but Dacia didn't noise to know her master was home. Rushing from the entryway, she slathered him with kisses until he revealed the wrapped up leg of a stag he caught last night on his trek home.

Dacia tore into the meat and in minutes she was whining for more. "I know girl," he whispered, kneeling to pet her head. "We'll get more food once we're out of the city. We can't stay here any longer."

Dacia whined again and followed Thilgod to the next room where he flung open a dark wooden dresser drawer and pulled out an olive-green backpack. Inside he found his combat helmet, trench coat, knives, and pistol all untouched. *Just how I left them*, he thought to Dacia who didn't seem to care. Unzipping a side pouch, Thilgod removed the medical cream from its carrier and applied a generous amount to his hip and shoulder.

At this, Dacia growled, spun around three times, and flopped her body on the ground facing the other direction. She must still be able to smell the Jark that had inflicted his wound and she wasn't happy. Dacia hated being left behind on a hunt and almost a week later, she still hadn't forgiven him. "Oh, give me a break," he hissed at her. "You wanted to end up like Luo?"

She ignored him and Thilgod continued getting dressed. His ritual was always the same whether he prepared to hunt a target or flee the city, the green cargo pants followed by the trench coat always went on first. Attach the belt with two machetes, a pistol, and enough ammo to kill a small squad and finish it off with the combat helmet that tucked into the hood of this trench so he could pull it on quickly in the event of a surprise attack.

"Let's go, Dacia," he said, whistling and moving towards the front door. "Time to say goodbye to this forsaken place."

Outside of the one story, single room apartment in the lower quarter, the streets were nearly silent. Despite being gone, Thilgod could tell that the rebellion was in full swing. He had no interest in being identified as an Iralene sympathizer. *You're just a random traveler,*

Thilgod told himself. *You've got nothing to do with the rebellion.*

Curiosity, however, drove him up the darkened ally streets towards the upper quarter, where the government resided. With each step he took, his hip felt better from the medicine. After eating a solid meal, his muscles felt rejuvenated. He wanted to disappear, but he couldn't. There was unfinished business he had with Kostia. Perhaps he'd get a lucky shot off, perhaps not, but he was certain Kostia's grip would slip, and what new government wouldn't welcome the man that brought Kostia to his knees?

As he neared the upper quarters, the streets got wider and more people wandered. Quiet whispers filled the vacant air. "A sorceress is coming," a woman gossiped. "I hear they want to free all the servants," responded the other. "Her power can't be matched by the Iralene. They're worried, executing their own people because they think traitors sold them out."

Thilgod gripped the fur on Dacia's neck and walked faster. *So the news had spread and now the whole city waited expectantly for their savior.*

The next crowd he passed was even larger than the first. Dozens of men had gathered and were talking.

"You came from the north?" one asked above the rest. "What did you see?"

Thilgod stopped to listen, pulling his hood up over his eyes to cover his face in case there were any sympathizers in crowd.

"I was on patrol," said another man. His face was covered in grime and his hair buzzed short along the top of his head. His pale skin indicated he wasn't local to Charoth; a conscript then from another world, offered military service as opposed to slavery. "We had just crested a hill to the south, coming out of one of the towns when a light flashed over the garrison. They were wiped off the planet in a single flash." He covered his eyes and started to weep.

A man put his hand on his shoulder. "You can't blame the rebels, son," he told him. "It's the Iralene's fault."

The man nodded but Thilgod saw through the propaganda. *Blame violence on the other side even though yours is just as guilty.* Waging a war for the hearts of the planet was no easy matter, however. It was all about controlling the message.

Thilgod decided to move on, pushing up the stone covered street until he reached a barrier and stopped. A few hundred meters ahead of him, fire blazed in the streets in front of the government building. Men in green carrying riot shields and sitting atop vehicles still surrounded the building, protecting their totalitarian ruler inside. Gunshots rang out in the distance; soon the rebels would be upon them.

In the center of courtyard in front of the building, Thilgod saw a man hanging limply off an executioner's stake. The ten-foot spear, started at his thigh and came out of his mouth. A gruesome way to die. The rumors were right, the Iralene were executing their own and making a show for the others that thought to abandon them. Desperate efforts to save a failing government. It didn't matter, and in the face of riots and an armed guard, Thilgod decided it would be better to leave town rather than wait for Kostia.

CHAPTER TWENTY-TWO

Like a mighty conqueror, Tamara rode through the city in a steel white carriage. Atworth stood on the seat to her left. He waved but the people paid no attention to him. No, it was her they had heard about and on her they focused their attention. Tamara didn't disappoint. Canis had been certain of that. The hood on her long black coat covered her face so that an observer could only see the green flames that burned in her eyes. Her metal fingers, decorated with emerald and ruby reflected brightly against the sun. Rings of fire burned around all four of their wheels and left simmering tracks on the cobblestone street in their wake.

Onlookers gasped and cleared the road as the white, open-topped vehicle drove towards the upper quarter where the government center sat. Tamara reached out with her mind and felt the crowd. She could sense them all and their hearts beat hard with excitement. Tamara's beat hard too. She was eager to find Kostia and pay him back for the evil that he had brought against her; against Red.

Up, up, up the carriage drove through the lower and into the upper quarter. Gunfire was nearly constant and roared over the cheers of the citizens they passed in the street. *Liberator.* She allowed herself to think. *Murderer.* Crept into her mind later.

Perhaps she was, perhaps she would be again. None of that mattered to Tamara now. All she could think of was Kostia.

The carriage stopped and Atworth looked at her with a smile. "I'm so glad you joined me for our triumphant entry. Your presence here makes this day even more special than it already was." He climbed from the seat and onto the stone walkway and then offered Tamara a hand.

"Just don't forget why I came along, Atworth." She responded, refusing his hand and pulling herself over the steel frame and landing softly on the ground.

Atworth grimaced but recovered gracefully. "Of course Tamara, I won't keep you from the records. I will happily assist you in finding this man Red."

Tamara smiled but he couldn't see it. Her hood completely blackened her face so that only the flame of her eyes could be discerned. *Keep it covered,* Canis had told her. *You are a powerful icon, but the enemy does not fear what they understand. You must be a mystery to them; always.*

She followed his advice to the letter, and even now as she walked towards the government building, citizens and soldiers alike gave her plenty of space. At the next clearing, she saw it. The crown of the Iralene rule, a steel and glass structure that erupted from the ground forty stories into the air. Its windows were all decorated with Iralene pictures and a statue of Kostia rested over the long rectangular garden to the side. His fingers pointed to the sky and his sharp dual-pronged tongue hung from his mouth. *The statue of a fool,* Tamara thought.

As she walked closer into the courtyard she realized she was alone. Atworth and his soldiers remained at the barrier. Iralene guards, mounted on vehicles, guarded the main door. A fountain separated the two sides, shooting cool water into the air and letting mist fall back down.

All eyes were on Tamara. This was her show.

"Lay down your weapons," she shouted above the splatter of the fountain. "The battle is over. Do not die for such a worthless man as Kostia!"

If the guards flinched, she did not see it. Full face helmets, solid and white, covered their faces. Green capes draped delicately over their backs. In their arms were weapons she could only guess about. A machine gun or a rifle perhaps. One held something thicker, like maybe a grenade launcher. Tamara would not take a step closer to find out.

"Long live the Iralene," a guard shouted, raising his weapon to his shoulder.

Tamara was ready. In an instant, she pulled the heat from the fountain with her hands, freezing it solid. The first round from the shouldered rifle fired, but slammed into a block of ice between them, splintering it and giving her more than enough daggers to finish the job. Bullets zipped past her head but she could feel them all as they exited their weapons and adjusted their trajectory. Spinning the icy splinters around in the palm of her hand she let them go with a thrust, launching them into the chests of the guards.

The crowd gasped as she walked past the fountain unharmed. When she reached the door and shattered the glass inward, however, the show ended. *Find Kostia. Don't let him get away. Up the stairs.* Tamara sprinted and lunged through empty halls and over empty desks. Sweating she tore her hood off, finding the stairs and climbing them, jumping over every third and fourth step until her legs burned and her lungs ached.

"Kostia!" she shouted, hurling herself through a double glass door at the top of her steps and falling to her knees when she saw it. *Empty. Cleared out. Destroyed.* Small fires simmered as papers smoldered. He had left. Nothing remained "Red…" she wept. "How can I find you?"

* * *

By midday, Thilgod had made it to the southern outskirts of the city. The gunshots were nearly constant now and joining the fray was the distinct sound of automatic weapon fire as rebels traded jabs with the Iralene. It wouldn't be long. Kostia was outgunned and had few resources. He wouldn't be able to stand against the rebellion.

Feet propped on a rock, Thilgod lay his head on Dacia's back. Her stomach grumbled in discomfort and her panting was short and fast. She was hungry and dehydrated and Thilgod felt terrible for her. The leg of a stag was nothing to fuel a four hundred pound corelve that hadn't eaten in nearly a week. They needed food; fast.

The path wound through the towns in the south and eventually opened into low-lying fields and orchards where he could quickly make his way to the ocean. The trip wouldn't be easy but, unlike the north, it had been tamed. *The worst is behind us, Dacia.* Without predators to deal with, animals were in abundance and could easily be spotted and hunted. Fruit hung low on rich green trees and the dew that dripped from brown water vines called to Thilgod with each drop that fell from their engorged stems. A few more steps into the wilderness and he would be free, regardless the outcome of the rebellion.

Dacia lifted her head and sniffed the air. Her breathing shallowed and stilled. She'd seen something. "What is it, girl?" he asked, rolling to his side to see what she was looking at.

A shadowy figure crept along a far hill on all fours. Long neck, narrow head, slouching as it sniffed the air. A breeze blew against Thilgod's back. Would carry his scent right towards the cautious creature before they'd be able to get the jump on it. Dacia knew it too, but she couldn't help herself. Climbing to her feet, she started off slow, one foot after the other.

Thilgod thought about shooting it to put Dacia out of her misery.

No, too close to the city still. Best save ammo. He fixed his eyes on the stag as Dacia took another step forward.

The creature froze, head snapping towards the two of them. Dacia stiffened her body in response as the creature stared. Stalking prey was like bounty hunting. *A delicate dance.* Slowly, she moved a paw forward but the stag didn't seem to notice. Taking that as a good sign, she picked up the pace, moving from a standstill to a trot to an all-out dash. *Won't work,* Thilgod thought after her but saved his breath. *Too obvious, but fun to watch regardless. Better take notes, Thilgod, she might be more successful at catching her prey than you are at catching yours.*

The stag took one more glance in his direction just in time to see a four hundred pound corelve racing towards her. That was the last look she needed before taking off in an all-out sprint, bounding over the next hill before Dacia had a chance to reach the top of her own knoll. She stopped and turned back towards her master. "Shouldn't have bothered. I'm gonna find you something, Dacia. Just lay down," he said, patting his leg and imploring her to come back over and continue serving as a pillow for his head.

Suddenly, she stopped again, eyes fixed on the road. Teeth shone and lip curled. A low grumble surged up past her teeth before quieting again. *Threat,* she told her master, sinking low to the ground ready to pounce.

Thilgod spun around, rolling to his belly and grabbing his bag. Only a hundred meters past his position, a man walked. He was average height and wore a brown coat that fell down to his knees. He wore a hat and covered his face with a scarf. *Rebel?* Thilgod thought, discounting it as soon as the thought entered his mind. Something in his stride was familiar, the way he tilted his head and shifted his weight. The man's eyes weren't working right, or he was blind. His feet didn't walk, they shuffled, slithered almost by rocking from the outside heal to the inside toe before lifting again. *Or you've seen this before,* his mind screamed.

Dacia screamed too, not audibly but in her posture. She knew something, but what was it. How was the lone wanderer a threat? Then the answer hit him harder than the Jark swinging his hatchet in the forest.

"Kostia!" he screamed, pushing himself from the grassy knoll and sprinting towards the serpent man that had ventured from his government quarters all alone. As he ran, Kostia's head tilted, trying to see and understand what was transpiring.

Too late. Thilgod covered the open field in mere seconds, completely forgetting that he had a bone-deep wound on his hip and an injured shoulder still needing time to heal.

Kostia was alone but he wasn't defenseless. Just as Thilgod leapt onto the road, the green man opened his coat, pulling down two silver plated handguns and firing them wildly at Thilgod. But he was nervous, shaken, disturbed. Bullets zinged past his head as Thilgod dove and rolled to the side, feeling pain surge up in his shoulder as he climbed back to his feet. *Close the distance, Thilgod. Get inside his grip.* In mere seconds, the reptile had expended his ammo and was reloading when Thilgod smashed into him, driving his legs hard and pushing Kostia to the ground.

Kostia grunted and let out a gasp of air, but was stronger than Thilgod remembered and rolled, throwing Thilgod to his side and scrambling to climb on top. Pain shot from Thilgod's leg and his shoulder ached too, screaming into his mind that something was wrong. Thilgod ignored it and fought to his feet, but Kostia was quicker and swept his legs. Pain surged once again from his hip as he hit the dusty brown road. It hadn't healed yet and suddenly he realized he had made a big mistake.

"You should be dead!" Kostia hissed, rising to his knees and grabbing a steel knife from his belt.

Thilgod fought, but Kostia was too strong. He smiled and parted his scarf, revealing a slimy snake-like tongue, dual-pronged and as sharp as a razor ready to strike. Thilgod had seen this before and didn't want it to happen to him. *Squirm, get your belt, grab your knife. Defend yourself, shift your weight. Can't. Shouldn't have rushed in, should have just shot the man from a distance. Too foolish to survive your third mistake. Too foolish.*

Kostia brought the knife down but suddenly stopped and looked to his right. His eyes bulged and his mouth dropped at the sight of Dacia in midair. He exhaled hard as the four hundred pound creature sank finger long teeth into his shoulder and twisted its head, shaking him from side to side. Still hungry, still starving, and desperate to take out a week's worth of pent-up aggression on her master's enemy.

Thilgod climbed to his feet gingerly, grabbing his hip and feeling fresh moist blood where the injury had split open. Kostia screamed and clawed as Dacia tore through coat and scale and into flesh. Blood sprayed upward and outward in the mayhem, covering her black and silver hide in a reddish-green ooze.

Thilgod circled around to look at Kostia's face, who still screamed as the wild beast tore into his abdomen, grabbing at its ears and clawing at its fur. It was no use to struggle and soon Kostia realized that too. His cries quieted and became more accepting. They turned from pleas for help to whimpers, to shallow breathing. He blinked once, twice, then fixed his thick round eyes onto Thilgod's face. He wanted to speak but couldn't and was instead rocked back and forth by the feasting giant as it tore into and devoured his insides.

Thilgod sat down next to his head and looked off at the horizon; no desire to see the man's final moments no matter how bad he was. Dacia looked up at him satisfied. Dark red blood dripped from her snout and jowls. Thilgod suspected she saw this as payback for Luo. He nodded. "It is payback," he said. "I hope he tastes better than he acts."

She looked at him once more and then dove back into her feast, muzzling her head deep into his flesh. *Must have tasted a lot better,* he thought. Smoke billowed against the blue sky from the city center. It was over, the rebels had won, but that meant nothing for Thilgod. It was time for him to find a way out, there could be no reintegration. He was on the losing side. *Best to leave now before you wind up like him,* Thilgod thought, looking at the pale green head that returned a lifeless stare.

He whistled and Dacia leapt from her meal and to his side. "Let's get our things, girl," he muttered. "It's best we get out of here while we still can."

CHAPTER TWENTY-THREE

"Station seized," reported Terre over his intercom to Brokk. "Five fighters have barricaded themselves in their barracks room, the company is preparing a breach now. We're evacuating three wounded, one critical."

"Keep me updated," Brokk responded from the bridge of his battleship. "I want to be able to thank those men in person. Don't let them die."

"Of course, Commander," responded Terre. "They'll go straight to the chambers for revitalization."

"We aren't out of the woods yet. Don't let your focus be on the victory we just achieved, think about the threats that still linger beyond the nebula."

Brokk terminated his connection to Terre and stared at the monitors in his operations center. *Lago.* His face felt hot as he looked from the monitors to his large viewing screen that faced the Rainbow Nebula. Bright blue and orange clouds swirled around the dense gas that would vaporize a man in seconds. Fear and panic seized him. *Lago.*

The image of Lago being crushed and sucked from his battleship sprung into his mind. His bones ached as he remembered the pain; his skin burned. Suddenly his body felt contorted and squeezed while Lago's fear leapt into his mind. His eyes, Lago's eyes dimmed as space itself ravaged his body and snatched his soul from his chest flinging it into the underworld.

Brokk shut his eyes. *Get out!* He couldn't take the feeling that the psycho-transmission and done to him. He was permanently scarred, desperate to avoid another battle. Desperate to avoid the fate that he had already experienced once through the eyes of his closest friend. His companion. His brother.

But he would. The monitors told him that. Beacons, deployed beyond the nebula were vibrating. Ships were disrupting the subspace. Not just ships, but an armada. Brokk knew who they were. He knew they would come the day he seized the destroyer. The Jarks, desperate for revenge were knocking at his door.

"They're coming for us, Terre. Get ready," Brokk said over his intercom. "Remember the plan, lure them in with the destroyer near the planet. I'll head into the nebula and hit them from the side."

Brokk watched the holographic representation of Terre's ships in the center of the room begin to pilot away from the spaceport. They couldn't risk collateral damage against the port, it was their one means to rearm and refuel their ships.

"Maximum thrusters," Brokk ordered his pilot while taking a seat in his chair. The Juggernaut vibrated violently as massive engines roared to life and propelled it forward towards the Rainbow Nebula and his enemy. Nine other vessels, small marauders captured from Iralene piracy operations, flanked Brokk on his sides. They were small but equipped with Jark weaponry and could release a blistering array of dense neutronium rounds.

The nebula swirled around Brokk and soon the deadly hot gas had engulfed his ship. Engines churned and strained to push the massive

Juggernaut through the dense clouds that acted as the perfect concealed position for his attack.

Brokk looked at his sensors. Six ships exited the subspace and had risen onto the spatial plane. They were now formed into an arrow.

"Kill the engines," Brokk said to his fleet. "I don't want them detecting us. They need to focus on Terre and his fleet around the planet until it's too late for them to respond to us."

The longer the ships existed on top of the spatial plane, the more Brokk's sensors were able to detect the type of ship that was approaching Charoth. Of the six vessels, his ship's computer now showed two Jark battleships and four destroyers.

A deep Jarkian accent suddenly came through his intercom system. "This is the third fleet, hailing Commander Brokk."

His heart stuttered. The prospect of fighting against other races in the galaxy always excited Brokk because he believed the Jarks were the best trained warriors in the galaxy. Being confronted by the third fleet, a storied and feared fleet throughout Jark history, sent shudders down his spine.

"Commander Brokk," the thick voice said again over their intercom. "This is Commander Tajdar Szega of the Third Fleet. I demand your unconditional surrender. Respond immediately or be destroyed."

Tough words. Maybe tough in action too. Brokk didn't doubt the man's intentions but there was no way he would surrender. *Just stay quiet. Make him wonder.* His beacons had done their job; they'd diverted enough negative energy in the subspace to completely shut down wormhole travel beyond the nebula and into the planet.

More data was coming into his ship now. They were flying in an arrow formation at nearly 20,000 knots. On two dimensions, this would have been an easy ambush. The third dimension, however, added a height element, making it impossible to simply fire at will along the same spatial plane. While the targeting system on the Juggernaut was sophisticated enough to attack multiple targets, the enemy defense systems would be advanced enough to destroy many of his incoming rounds. Brokk would have to concentrate an entire volley of fire on one battleship while focusing his small armada on just two destroyers.

"Come on line with me," Brokk said into his radio to his fleet, watching his ship's display to see the smaller vessels maneuver until they were all aligned with each other. "The Jark Armada is closing in," he told them. "Remember, we stay in the cloud. Force them to come to us and target enemy ships simultaneously. Their countermeasures are too advanced for us to shoot one or two rounds, we need a volley of twenty or thirty rounds simultaneously fired to defeat each vessel."

On the hologram, he could see the enemy formation closing in on Charoth. Closing in on Terre. They would have certainly known that the destroyer Terre flew was the captured Kemnaut. It was Brokk's hope that they would think he had hidden his battleship behind the planet rather than in the clouds.

A battleship formed the tip of their spear, two destroyers flanked it at each side and two more at the rear. The sixth vessel, Commander Szega's battleship, was nested safely in the middle.

"Target the lead battleship and come about," he ordered his crew. Thrusters fired, positioning his ship sideways where he could use all forty of his cannons. "The rest of you," he ordered over the intercom, "target the nearest destroyer."

His fleet acknowledged and Brokk broke the transmission to speak with Terre. "Terre," he called. "Don't play with these ships. Get behind the planet once the shooting starts. I want to degrade the fleet and force them into the nebula before you come in from behind."

"I hadn't planned on playing with anything," Terre responded. "We'll run as soon as I hear your fire command."

Brokk slouched deep into his chair and closed his eyes. His ritual before most battles was to remind the dead that he had given them what they desired. The dead had failed him at Tassi, however, and with no one else to pray to, he simply took three deep breaths. *Nothing worth doing is easy, Brokk,* he said to himself. But it wasn't his voice that said it. It was Lago's; the part of Lago that didn't die in the explosion orbiting Tassi; it was the part of Lago that lived in his dreams and nightmares every day since.

"Target locked," boomed Torger, his targeting officer.

Brokk opened his eyes to stare at the screen. The six ships were now within reach. *Give it time. No need to hurry. Get them close enough for the proximity rounds too. Not just the neutronium. Deep breath.*

The enemy armada continued forward, cutting through space on the edge of the Rainbow Nebula. Hot gasses swirled around his vision. Yellow and red penetrated Brokk's viewing screen. It reminded him of Jark. His home. He would never go back no matter how desperately he wanted to.

Brokk keyed the intercom. "Fire," he ordered.

With that simple word Brokk's world forever changed. The depressing of the lever that contained the fire control for all forty guns on the port side of his ship waged a war against the Jarks that went far beyond the Kemnaut and exile. It was a permanent action that forever pitted him against the people he grew up with, served with, strove with, and fought with. In the dense soupy mixture of ultra-hot gas and extreme radiation, the ship rocked as forty neutronium rounds raced from their resting places towards the lead battleship.

"Reload with proximity," Brokk ordered.

"Loaded!" Came the response from Torger less than a half second later.

"Fire!" Brokk shouted again to feel the ship rock once more.

"Terre, break around the planet," he shouted. "Marauders, drop in elevation, re-engage."

"Tubes loaded with neutronium," Torger shouted again.

"Fire on the far destroyer!" Brokk ordered.

He watched his screen. In less than six seconds Brokk's crew had released over one hundred and twenty rounds at two separate targets. His fleet released another eighty at the last destroyer.

"Hit," shouted his intelligence officer. "Hits on targets one, five, and three. One and three are dead in space. Five is still moving."

"Bring us up and about," Brokk ordered, "they know we're here. No need to play it quiet."

Brokk watched his screen. Two ships were free-floating, the others had pivoted towards the nebula.

"Incoming," shouted Torger.

Brokk grabbed the arms of his chair just in time to feel the Juggernaut shudder under a volley of enemy rounds. Explosions rippled through the cloud as the Juggernaut's own countermeasures deployed, destroying incoming rounds. "Come starboard," Brokk ordered his pilot who was diving hard through the dense nebula to avoid incoming rounds. "Lock on destroyer five again," he shouted.

The Juggernaut lurched and groaned as thrusters fired to bring the ship about. Through his forward facing viewing screen, he could see rounds snap past the ship as they halted just in time.

"Locked," responded Torger.

"Fire," Brokk ordered again.

The Juggernaut rocked and his pilot once again accelerated, pinning Brokk's head into the back of his chair as they churned through the nebula. Brokk looked at his screen. Five of his marauders remained. The others, no longer images on his holographic display had either been disabled or completely destroyed by incoming fire.

"Hits," shouted Torger.

"One Battleship and one Destroyer remain operational," his intelligence officer chimed in. A third destroyer has been disabled but is still shooting. It looks like we've hit their targeting and navigation systems."

Suddenly, Brokk felt his own ship vibrate violently. "Drop and report!" he ordered, hoping the round that struck their hull was not a vital hit.

"Direct hit to the aft ammo hold," responded one of his men. "Seals are holding, no secondary explosions."

Brokk cursed. "That's a quarter of our stock." The Juggernaut rumbled again as countermeasures exploded around him. Light flashed and danced through the main cabin, changing the colors of his crew and disorienting his pilot. Fighting from the nebula was exhausting, but it was working. They had reduced the Third Fleet to two vessels, but suddenly, they disappeared from his map.

"They've entered the nebula," shouted Torger. "I can't find them."

"Shut the engines down," responded Brokk. "Change our load to proximity rounds on both sides, depleted neutronium facing forward."

His pilot dropped a lever and suddenly all was silent. He was alone now. The last of his marauders had run out of ammo and were either destroyed or retreating back to the planet. It would take Terre too long to find them in the Nebula, and Brokk secretly hoped Terre wouldn't come. He couldn't bear losing Terre like he had lost Lago. From his viewing screen, Brokk watched scrap metal float past his ship, a Jark body in a gray suit followed. One of his from the ammo bay. His struggle was over; Brokk hoped it had been quick.

The colors swirled and as soon as the objects passed his screen, the nebula looked as if there hadn't been a battle there at all. A bead of sweat rolled down Brokk's golden brow and he wiped it with his hand. His crew faced him.

"What next?" asked Torger.

CHAPTER TWENTY-FOUR

"My friends," exclaimed Atworth Kierce from a large steel podium overlooking the gardens in the government district, "this is a truly great day."

The crowd cheered and Atworth raised his hands in the air to settle them down. Working a crowd was what he did best and how he ever fell from favor with the people long enough to let the Iralene take over, Tamara could not say. His dark skin contrasted with a red ornate robe and glistening jewelry in a way that insisted he be taken seriously as both a wise man and rightful king.

Against Canis' wishes, Tamara decided she would attend the ceremony. "It's not safe," he protested. "You must always be the sorceress to them, their beacon of freedom and hope."

"How can I not go," she argued back. "Am I not also one of the slaves who was freed? Is this ceremony not for me too?"

He huffed when he saw he could not change her mind and went away. *His loss,* she thought, knowing that the Jark in him would scoff at such a comment.

Where she came as a slave five years ago, she walked into the city now as a free woman, and not just a free woman but a pivotal player in the uprising that would promise to free all slaves. Tamara was proud, but her heart still yearned for more. It yearned for Red and it yearned for Brokk.

"This is a great day because today, this very day, we shed the travesty of Iralene rule!" Atworth continued, his voice echoing from the tall steel and glass buildings that bracketed the gardens on all sides. "This is a great day because today, this very day, all those living on Charoth are free! Free to choose the direction of their lives, free to come and go as they please, free to find jobs, and to make money. Free to go home." The crowd once again erupted in applause and as Tamara surveyed the masses, she found many more people with scars on their heads than those without. Part of her wondered what would happen to those without, but then she lost her concern. They had been the problem. They mattered not.

Atworth, however, was not yet done with his sale. "My friends, I have waited in hiding for a day where the people could rise up once more. Now, I have seen this day and I have something to ask of each of you. The direction that Charoth takes is up to you. We have the ability to prosper here, to mine rare minerals and sell goods to all the fleets of the galaxy; but I need your help. I cannot do this alone. I ask each of you to consider how you can contribute to making Charoth an epicenter of legitimate trade. An epicenter of freedom and prosperity. If we do not," he warned, lowering his voice to a fearful whisper. "If we do not stay, this place will sink back into its old ways. You might escape, but what about your sons or daughters? What about others?"

He paused, letting the crowd hear his words. Tamara was listening too, weighing the prospect of leaving the place that caused so much pain; but for what? Perhaps her place was here, working alongside Atworth and his government.

"There is a battle being waged above us, my friends." Tamara's heart fluttered at his words. In the joy of conquering the city, she had forgotten the danger above. Atworth pointed to the ever-present nebula that glowed above them in the bright blue sky. "There is a battle being waged against our slavers. There is a legitimate warship defending us from those that would do us harm. From those that would put us back under their thumbs and force us into a life of servitude for a purpose that we will never understand nor support!" The crowd was silent as Atworth's voice boomed beyond the plants of the garden. "We are but a small and humble planet. But we can be great if we support those that support us. If we encourage those that encourage us. If we lure those to us that will prosper us."

Gunfire could be heard in the distance as Atworth closed his speech. It was the final members of the Iralene party resisting to the end, just as the guards did to Tamara in front of the government building. *Foolish loyalty to die for the Iralene.* "In the coming days," he continued, "I will present my plan to jump-start our legitimate economy. I desperately hope that you will consider being a part of it."

Atworth left the stage and climbed past the gardens to an Iralene statue of Kostia, the green skinned despot that ruled their land. He was a coward in the end. *Nothing like Red. Red would not have run.* Along with three others, Atworth stepped behind it and pushed, toppling the stone over and shattering it on the ground below. "To a new age!" Atworth shouted as the crowd roared.

People left but Tamara remained, sitting on a bench in the center of the garden with her hood pulled tight over her head. She wanted to be alone. A gentle breeze blew in as the crowd dispersed. Vines and branches swung and the rich scent of Tarib and Schalf permeated her nostrils. The flowers were all around her; they should have been beautiful. To Tamara, they felt dull.

Since Brokk departed her senses had dimmed, not from lack of power but from something deep inside her. She wanted to experience the joy that came with the freedom they now had but all she felt was worry, worry for Brokk and the men that fought with him in the stars. In his absence, life was drab and colorless.

The silent footsteps of an old Jark crept behind her. His bones ached and ligaments popped inside their hardened shells. "I sensed you the whole time," Tamara said without turning, feeling sorry for the old warrior that lurked in the shadows and dealt silently with his pain.

"You've become much more aware," responded Canis with an approving growl. "But I would not have had to get this close to kill you. You've made yourself a target now, Tamara. You are the great sorceress, the one that must die before Atworth can be overthrown."

"I don't work for Atworth," she hissed, guilt pouring over her as soon as the words slipped from her mouth. He didn't move. His heart beat steady. Tamara rapped the stone bench with her metal fingertips and then padded the seat with the palm of her hand. "Please, Canis, sit by me."

"What is wrong," he asked, coming in front of her and resting on all fours. He wasn't concerned, she knew him well enough to know that. His curiosity instead stemmed from a desire to understand her deeper. His breathing was steady and his graying eyes unshakable.

"Brokk fights for us above," she said. "Against how many?"

"The Third Fleet," was Canis' response. "Four Jark destroyers and two Jark Battleships. Hundreds of fighters waiting to descend on us if Brokk fails. Commander Szega is his enemy. He is a driven and brilliant tactician. A man I fought with many times before being transferred to Brokk's fleet for the invasion of Tassi. He was a good man. I respected him. But now he is my enemy."

Tamara crawled over Canis' words as he spoke them, trying to discern what emotions lurked behind his words and what feelings were in his thoughts. It was impossible for her to tell. He feared nothing and spoke his thoughts with dry accuracy. "Is he better than Brokk?" she asked. She had to know and as soon as she asked the question she felt more fear than she ever had before. More dread in her stomach than she ever got at Orno's. Tamara suddenly realized she would rather spend a thousand tortured nights as a slave on the farm than watch Brokk's mighty Juggernaut fall from the sky. She could not bear it.

"It doesn't matter," responded Canis. He took a deep breath into strained lungs and exhaled a heavy sigh. His age was ever-present in their discussions and Tamara sensed the pain he felt more than ever. "Battles in space are rarely decided by a captain's skill aboard his ship," he continued. "They are decided by thrust and velocity. The ability of a person to shoot and maneuver. A stray round is unforgiving and inevitable. There are always stray rounds," he said with a tired sigh.

Tamara could feel herself tremble and tapped the bench seat again nervously. "Please Canis, you are tired from the campaign. Sit by me."

This time the old warrior obliged and pulled himself over from his knuckles and onto the bench.

"I'm old," he grunted, for the first time acknowledging his age and weakness.

"What will you do?" she asked.

"I've been thinking about those mountains since we arrived," he responded, pointing to the north. "Perhaps Brokk will give me leave to explore them."

CHAPTER TWENTY-FIVE

The silence was deafening. The Rainbow Nebula was blinding. Brokk stared intently at his sensors, but Commander Szega's battleship could not be found.

"He's turned off his engines," Brokk finally told his crew. "Terre won't be able to find him unless we force his hand." *They think they'll hunt me in here.*

"So what do you want to do, commander?" Torger asked again.

Brokk was a man of action and had never once allowed himself to become prey. Win or lose they would go out fighting. If Szega survived the fight, he would go back with more scars than he had skin to wear them on. "Flush them out," he said at last. "Fire proximity rounds from port and starboard then maximum thrust. Drop us deeper into the nebula where the gasses are hotter and shut us down again. I want to fire and disappear until we find this clown."

Torger nodded and swung his chair around to face his terminal, littered with fire commands, ammunition types, and ranges. "Firing proximity rounds," he announced, depressing his lever to prime the shells.

The battleship rocked and hummed as the artillery launched from their tubes and ripped through the poison gas surrounding their vessel. Before they could burst his pilot fired their engines, plummeting the ship downward, deeper into the toxic plumes that drifted aimlessly through the nebula. Explosions roared above them, sending shrapnel into a million places; but no battleship could be seen.

The lower they descended, the more the gasses changed color from light orange to a deep purple and rich blue. Green splashed against the dual-pronged points of his ship and latched on, attracted to the silver and gold that crowned the points of the Juggernaut's glory. As the gravity increased, so did the speed of the swirling hot mass of hydrogen and helium surrounding his hull. It was dizzying, disorienting, and unsettling. But they had no choice. This would end here.

"Fire another salvo," Brokk ordered, feeling his ship rock once more against the sheer power of the weapons contained within his ship. More explosions scattered the free-floating gasses, tearing through their airy bodies only for them to heal once more as if no explosion had occurred at all.

Brokk watched the sensors once more, expectantly, eagerly, and desperately. *It had to work.*

"Engines!" shouted his intelligence officer as the hologram of a destroyer flickered onto his screen. "Destroyer almost directly above us."

Brokk's heart leapt. *Hope.* "Pursue," ordered Brokk, instantly being pinned to his seat as the powerful engines thrust the ship forward to climb the crest of the nebula. "Reload proximity and fire."

Torger nodded and sent another eighty rounds exploding in a circle around their vessel. The next load would be the neutronium and Torger didn't need to be told what to do. The Jark destroyer, thrusting through the soup of the Rainbow Nebula, climbed—its crew aware of Brokk in pursuit and desperate to avoid the Juggernaut's wrath.

Torger fired a volley of three kinetic energy shells across the destroyer's bow only to have the ship bank and roll and deploy countermeasures. "Ineffective," shouted Torger at the pilot. "We need a clean lock."

"Hit them with…" Brokk stopped. *Trap*. His mind screamed. Don't get lured in. *Too late. Get out*. "Drop the thrust," he shouted instead. His pilot obeyed just in time to see a volley of light flash past the hull of their ship and explode in red clouds beyond. Suddenly, massive engines roared to life; the crown of the Third Fleet. Szega's mighty battleship lurched forward out of the gas, firing another Salvo at Brokk that ricocheted off his hull and rattled his teeth.

"Pivot right," Brokk shouted over the noise. "Deploy smoke and mines." More rounds snapped past his hull as the behemoth battleships maneuvered past each other while avoiding their enemies targeting sensors. Engines roared, the hull groaned, creaking under the weight of the gravity of the nebula and the force of their thrusters. Cannons fired and rounds ripped past each ship, their crew fighting against the centrifugal force exerted on their bodies as the massive machines flew through space. Volley after volley exploded around the two commanders that were fighting for honor and supremacy and maybe even peace.

Let the pilot and gunner fight the ship, Brokk reminded himself. *You focus on the fleet*. Brokk strained to see his computer against the gravity swings caused by his ship violently attacking his foe. The Destroyer was pivoting now and turning to re-engage the Juggernaut. *Two against one. Not a fair fight*.

"Terre," Brokk shouted over his radio. "Where are you?"

* * *

Brokk's desperate calls could do nothing to influence Terre. The Kemnaut and its crew were already racing towards the Rainbow

Nebula as fast as he could go. On his battle map, Terre could see what was transpiring and his heart raced as he worried he wouldn't get to the nebula in time. The lone Juggernaut had lured the remnants of the Third Fleet into the nebula and was facing off against both Szega's battleship and a destroyer.

"Target the destroyer," Terre ordered. "We've got to even up the fight and then we'll tackle the battleship together."

The Kemnaut, the fourth vessel to enter the radioactive cloud, charged forward towards the clueless destroyer that had committed itself into a downward assault against Brokk's Juggernaut. All eyes were on Brokk, it was time for Terre to strike.

"Locked," shouted a member of his crew operating the gunner's station. He didn't even know the man's name yet and would have to trust that he knew what he was doing. *At least he is a Jark,* Terre thought, glancing around his crew of mixed races and wondering how they would fare against an enemy equal to them. *The Kemnaut, a cobbled together crew of slaves and merchant pilots who would be the pivotal factor in ending this battle.* Terre secretly wished that the Jark Empire would know by whose hand they were dealt this embarrassing defeat.

Terre checked his computers. Still out of range. *Ten more seconds. Maybe.* He looked at the map and watched Brokk's ship continue to circle the battleship, dropping and rising in elevation as he attempted to out-maneuver Szega's cannon fire while returning volley after volley of his own. *How long could a crew fight like this?* Terre wondered, suddenly realizing the answer had everything to do with the looming threat above, in the form of a second destroyer diving like a predator towards its prey. Realizing that Brokk's plan for surviving this battle rested fully on Terre's ability to reach the destroyer before it reached Brokk.

"Five seconds," screamed his pilot, whom Terre also did not know. This one wasn't a Jark, he was pale and skinny. A merchant pilot from somewhere. *Doesn't matter.*

"In range," the man shouted again.

"Fire," ordered Terre, feeling the ship rock back against the hot gasses that engulfed the Kemnaut as a dozen neutronium rounds raced towards the descending destroyer.

The Kemnaut pushed hard through a final green cloud of toxic gas just in time to see the Jark destroyer alter its course to avoid his salvo. Lasers and proximity shells burst around the ship as it pivoted to avoid Terre's attack and abandon its descent in order to address the new threat.

"Loaded," shouted his gunner.

"Fire," Terre screamed again. His voice crackled and his palms sweat. His face was hot and his stomach churned. Everything rested on his ability to get rid of the threat. To save Brokk. To save his crew. Another twelve rounds launched from their tubes towards the pivoting enemy. Fire erupted outward and burned against a green helium cloud that had drifted too close as one of the shells struck the aft of the ship. Its engines flickered and then flashed as massive flames shot from the rear of the destroyer.

"Good hit!" Terre roared with excitement. "Give them another."

"Loaded," responded his gunner again.

"Finish it off," Terre bellowed, speaking over the noise of the engines and the sounds of counter fire exploding around them.

The Jark destroyer was attempting to turn upwards where it could return fire, but the engine had failed them and instead, the ship spun in circles from back to belly as it fought against the uneven thrust of damaged engines. The Kemnaut rocked and shuddered as another salvo sped from its chambers towards the wounded destroyer. This time, Terre hit center and the ship splintered, sending a hiss of oxygen and metal outward followed by flames and the bodies of her crew.

Terre had no time to spare. No time to soak in the victory he had achieved. Already the Szega's battleship had identified the new threat and was adjusting its tactics. Brokk continued to circle, but Szega was now thrusting backward and piloting his ship away from the battle, bracketing Brokk's movements with proximity mines and funneling his attack by firing wildly on Brokk's flank.

"Pilot," Terre ordered. "Get us above him. Find us another angle."

The dense, soupy mixture made it nearly impossible to maneuver quickly. His pilot, an amateur at war, struggled to control the giant vessel that had to be masterfully maneuvered to gain the effect he desired. His hands shook and sweat covered his controls.

"Climb!" Terre shouted over the loud engines as they worked overtime to gain speed in the nebula.

Terre turned his attention to his targeting officer, who managed to acquire a lock on the battleship just in time for Szega to pivot down or up and obstruct their view with the Juggernaut.

His actions frustrated Brokk, who fired wildly at the ship, trying to anticipate the Jark's moves and failing each time to do so.

Suddenly, the ship disappeared. He'd escaped the nebula.

Brokk's voice came over the radio. "He's gone. Jumped back to the Empire." His voice was labored, exhausted.

"Coward," responded Terre. "Should we pursue?"

"No." Was the response. The radio cracked and Brokk's voice returned. "He has no fleet. He was defeated. We're in no shape to fight whoever is waiting for us at the other side. Head back to the spaceport. It's time to rebuild."

CHAPTER TWENTY-SIX

Birds chirped and wings fluttered as Brokk and Tamara pushed through the final row of trees that lined cliffs overlooking the dark side of the planet. As they reached the clearing, Tamara let out a gasp. Crystallized rock and solid ice peppered the desolate landscape that hid from the light of the sun and was forever winter. A thin layer of white fog hovered just above the ground, a thermocline where the warm air dared not descend any further.

"It's truly inspiring," Tamara exclaimed, finding a place to sit from the safety of the forest.

"Is it everything you imagined it would be?" Brokk asked, sitting next to her, fixing his eyes on the dreadful landscape beyond.

"For five years I stared at these mountains. For five years I sat on that farm and waited for the perfect moment to escape. For five years I swore to myself that I wasn't just a coward, that I was being smart and patient and biding my time. For five years, Brokk," she said looking at him. Tears welled in her eyes and ran down her cheeks. "For five years I told myself that tomorrow I would leave and find Red."

She sobbed. "I never did."

Brokk grabbed her shoulder and pulled her close to him. He knew what she was feeling. The pain of losing a close friend and comrade. The guilt that welled within a person when they knew there was something more that they could do but failed to do so. Self-preservation mixed with courage and fear and everything else that a person felt in the heat of the moment. Brokk felt it. Even now, looking out over the cold dead landscape that would destroy their bodies as fast as deep space, Brokk felt it. *Lago,* his mind called out.

Brokk couldn't put into words the desperation he felt for Lago and the sorrow he now felt for Tamara. It was unspeakable and yet he desperately wanted to tell her. Tears suddenly welled in his own eyes and for the first time since he was young, he let them fall. *Lost. Desperate. Alone.* But he wasn't. He had Tamara. And Tamara had him.

They sat in silence for a while, gazing out over the darkened landscape. Animals howled behind them. Packs of dogs like the monsters that attacked Tamara and Canis. Finally, he turned to look at her. "I'm glad I found you," he said.

She smiled back at him through tear soaked eyes. "I'm glad you found me too."

"What's next?" he asked. "Will you keep looking for Red?"

"I'm not sure," she mulled, picking up a gray rock and turning it in her hands. "Atworth found records but there was no mention of Red. I haven't looked through them yet." She paused, spinning the rock in her fingers and finally flinging it over the edge. Brokk listened but couldn't hear it drop. "Do you think he might have escaped?"

Brokk wanted to give her hope. He was desperate to and cared less about the truth or the circumstances surrounding Red and more about Tamara and what she needed to be able to press forward. *Hope.* "I think it's possible he escaped." Then Brokk chuckled. "Heck, if he's anything close to the way you say he is, he probably pulled the collar out of his head on day one and stole a ship."

Tamara rolled her head back and laughed. She wiped the tears from her eyes and smiled big, looking up at the Rainbow Nebula that reigned brightly in the night sky. "He's probably up there right now screaming at someone to work harder," she joked. Her smile faded and returned to Brokk. "What about you? What's next?"

"I can't stay," Brokk muttered. "They'll come looking for me. The Third Fleet won't give up; Commander Szega won't give up. I'll be hunted by more than just the Jarks. By the Tassians and the Mateens too." He sighed and kicked a cluster of loose pebbles over the ledge. "We're refueling our ships and working around the clock to fabricate new fighters. I've taken on a full crew again and Canis has replenished his ranks."

"I want to come with you," Tamara said. "I want to go where you go. I have no home here."

Brokk smiled. "I would love for you to join me."

BEYOND THE JUMP

"Gemini!" Casika screamed, running and wrapping her arms around his large gray neck. Gemini returned the hug and then pulled her away to examine her.

"You look wonderful," he finally said with an approving wink. "Have they been treating you well here?"

She smiled and twisted her body to show off her desk. The crystal glistened in the sunlight and radiated all the glory of the dual suns overhead. Casika's hair sparkled and her skin beamed with a golden glow. "They keep me busy," she giggled, "but I love what I'm doing. Everything changed after the invasion, we're rebuilding the society from the ground up."

"And what about Cale?" he asked, following her to the large crystal window that overlooked their sparkling bay. Blue waves crashed against a white sand beach where children played and adults sat. Colorful kites soared in the wind and masts of sailing ships bracketed the horizon. *Peace*, Gemini thought, letting out a heavy sigh, burdened with a heavy message.

"Cale trains almost constantly. He is certain we'll find his father and he wants to be ready. He's been promoted to the rank of Brigadier." She said, gleaming with pride.

"But how is he?" Gemini asked again.

"He's good," she insisted touching his warm gray hand and turning to face him. "He really is good."

Gemini couldn't stand the small talk any longer. "I have news for you and Cale," he blurted. "Where is he?"

* * *

The drive along the marsh brought back painful memories for Gemini. Where the city stopped, weeds and briers grew up, feeding on the waste that was pumped in droves from the city center to the badlands. The smell of sewage and standing water blew into his face and caused his eyes to water. When they stopped, Gemini instantly recognized the spot. The final battle where Remmel stood his ground against a Jark infantry brigade. The final battle that Remmel was last seen alive; missing. Taken by Brokk and his wicked army of conquerors.

Trench lines dug months ago were now either filled in or covered in grass and weeds. This was where Gemini had left Arden as well. Only a memory now, but a collective one buried in the forests of Rodam. "He comes out here often?" Gemini asked, walking alongside Casika towards an old green tent that buckled under a constant breeze.

"Every day," she admitted. "He's looking for clues. Maybe he thinks he'll even find his body."

Gemini was perplexed. "Elaborate."

"He doesn't think his father would have surrendered. Says he would have died fighting."

"It's madness," Gemini responded. "Where is Cale?"

"You'd call looking for your father madness?" a voice boomed from behind.

Gemini spun around to see Cale climbing a nearby hill. He wouldn't be put on the defensive. "You should be looking up there," Gemini shouted back pointing to the sky above. "Your father is with them, not rotting in the marsh."

"Proof Gemini," Cale said approaching them. "Proof. Then I will join you to bring him home."

Gemini reached his thick gray hand out and touched Cale's shoulder. He wanted to smile but he knew the gravity of the news he brought with him. A smile accompanied by an invitation for battle was baseless. "We've found him." He said at last, looking into Cale's brown eyes.

Cale stuttered. "You what? Who? My father?"

"No. Brokk. We've found Brokk."

"You're certain?" Casika asked, her golden eyes sparkling in the ever-present sun.

"I'm certain. He has been pirating ships and capturing people and goods. Of all the governments, the Jarks confronted him with a fleet but were ambushed and lost the battle. Only one ship survived."

"Who?" Cale asked leaning forward and eager.

"Commander Szega is the man's name. He has sworn to return to bring Brokk to justice. The Mateens have offered to join them as part of a galactic coalition. I assume you will come as well?" Gemini asked, hoping the answer would be *no* but certain it would be *yes*.

"Of course," he responded looking at Casika. "And you?"

"I wouldn't miss the chance to bring Brokk down," she said.

End of Book Two

ACKNOWLEDGMENTS

A big thank you to Sarah Keller for the beautiful book design. Thank you to Sarah Keller, Andrea Keller, Eilene Campsey, and Elke Ringl for taking time to read through and critique my work - over and over again.

Thanks to all of my readers, especially those that that take the time to review my work on Amazon and Goodreads. I read through every review posted and I'm eternally grateful for the opportunity I get to correspond with my fans.

ABOUT THE AUTHOR

Thane is a graduate of the Virginia Military Institute with a degree in psychology and a minor in English. Following college, Thane married his high school sweetheart Sarah and started his career as a cavalryman in the United States Army. Over the course of his career, he has deployed to both Iraq and Afghanistan where he was personally engaged in ground combat. His service has thus far earned him two Bronze Stars and numerous other awards and decorations.

Relying on his psychology background, military experience, and Christian faith, Thane writes novels that seek to explore human nature under dire circumstances, the reality of pain and suffering, and the resilience of individuals to accomplish superhuman feats. Thane's hopes are that as readers experience his character's journey through the gift of reading, they will be greater equipped to endure the inevitable ups and downs in life itself and dream to accomplish grander things.

In addition to his wife Sarah, Thane is blessed to have four wonderful children that do all they can to keep him from pursuing his love of writing.

PREVIEW THE NOVEL: DOOMSAYER

What's next for Brokk and his Rogue Fleet? Find out in the sequel *Doomsayer*!

Available on Amazon and at your local book stores

BEFORE THE JUMP

Sun-scorched clouds streaked a crimson sky. Night was falling, and with it, a blanket of sulfur-infused dew coated and chilled the inhabitants of the valley.

Jark, the planet of a thousand volcanoes, had finally started to cool for the wintertime. With the season of ash behind them and the monsoons ahead, Jaki'el enjoyed the crispness of the air now more than ever before. Still, he felt under-dressed for the sudden cold that pushed past his priestly red robes and through his summer fur.

"Bring her up," said Jaki'el. "We haven't any time to spare." He was tall and slender. Patches of gray intertwined with thick black hair that covered most of his body and showed his age. Unlike many of the younger male Jarks, Jaki'el preferred to remain on all fours. He thought it felt more natural and was more honorable to the Jark way. The newer generation had forgotten this. He had not. Perhaps, he told himself, they would remember one day soon.

Jaki'el's back curved forward as he looked behind him. "Hurry now, bring her up," he hissed once more.

Elongated shadows stretched across the volcanic landscape like harbingers for an omen not yet revealed. There were those who searched for a sign. Jaki'el did not. His fate was certain and his future sealed.

Shadows shrunk as two Jark males huffed quickly up the darkened cliff, their figures a mere mirage against the crimson landscape beyond. Their journey neared an end. They were close now, he could feel it, but their sacrifice had fought them every step of the way.

"Move it," grunted one of his helpers, shoving a wooden walking stick into the back of their sacrifice.

She yelped in pain and snapped her teeth at the stick but continued to move upwards. *Was it fear that caused her to react in such a way or was she willingly rejecting her people?* Jaki'el wondered.

"Don't bruise our sacrifice," Jaki'el bellowed at his helpers. "My child," he said, eyeing the girl and rising off his hands to stand above her on two feet, "there is nothing to fear. Why do you fight us so?"

The young female stopped. Her handlers didn't drive her forward. Instead, they waited impatiently to hear a response as if it would provide vindication for their extra work along the journey. Her eyes were a fiery orange and her fangs a bright white. Her hips curved outward and supported muscular legs. *She would have been a terrific specimen for breeding had she not been so beautiful,* Jaki'el thought. *But the best is for the Gods.*

"Do not act like you don't know why I resist you," she jeered.

She flexed her voice to mask her fear, but Jaki'el sensed it. "My dear, your parents have given you to the gods. It is not you or even me who can intercede now. Do you forget all that you've learned? Do you forget the danger in avoiding this glorious fate?"

She dropped her eyes to the ground. No. She hadn't forgotten. It was merely fear of the unknown, he surmised.

"Only because you gave them no choice," she finally grumbled.

He smiled at her, showing yellow fangs through parsed lips. "My dear," he whispered, "none of us have a choice in this but you will make all of us better for what you go to do."

She glanced up just long enough to search his face before returning to the ground. "What will it be like?" she asked.

"You won't feel a thing," Jaki'el assured her, placing a hand on her shoulder and allowing it to linger longer than was necessary. He took a certain pleasure from it but that too would be for the gods. "We must move," he quickly asserted. "Only a few more steps is all. Hurry."

The band of four continued their march along the rocky ridge, stopping only to catch their breath before scurrying along the narrow trail. A red moon rose high above them before Jaki'el finally spotted the offering field. A silver lake shone red in the distance. The blood moon danced brilliantly off the liquid mercury within. Fog rolled down from the higher hills as if all of nature had gathered together for this glorious sacrifice. Tonight was the night.

The girl stopped when she saw it. Her knees trembled. "Don't let her fall," Jaki'el hissed at his companions. "We must let nothing harm her here. She has to be without blemish."

"I can't," she muttered. Her arms shook as the larger Jarks grabbed her. Her face turned from red to ashen gray. Her lips trembled but she would not cry. No, the Jarks were too tough for that. Jaki'el felt pride surge within him.

"You must continue," he hissed. "They've seen us now. The lake has sensed our warmth. You must."

The rest of the walk was silent except for the dragging of his sacrifice's toes against the ground below. She had gone limp, and he did not blame her. Many sacrifices failed before this final step. None were saved.

At the bank, he paused once more. Silver mercury swirled and bubbled in the lake just beyond his feet. The ground was soft and moist. The girl shuddered behind him. She knew her time was coming to an end. Jaki'el shifted his weight back onto his hind legs and felt his belt with his hands. The knife was still there. Its blade jagged and cold.

On two legs he turned, pulling the knife from his belt and holding it high in his hand. "Bring her down to the shore," he ordered.

She squirmed but dared not cry out. No. Here even the soon to be dead dared not awaken all the creatures that lay in the lake. Her sacrifice had to be good, even she knew that.

Her handlers grunted and tugged her to the shore. Six figures now emerged from the shadowy cliffs beyond. They, like Jaki'el, wore robes, but unlike his white ones that signified his sect, these men wore robes of gold. They were priests of the highest order.

They hummed as they emerged. It was a familiar tune. The beat of invisible drums matched their footsteps and pushed the ceremony onward.

Few knew the words of the song they sang, but its effect permeated the ignorant just the same. His sacrifice stopped her struggling, she was calm. Her knees were now submerged in the silvery slime, and like a mirror, the mercury reflected her face onto the moon above. The timing was perfect. The night was ordained.

Fingers rose to the surface of the lake. Slime-covered fingers soon became hands and pulled on the girl as she submitted herself to them. The priests chanted louder. Bubbles formed out of the deep. Her handlers escaped to higher ground. The surface boiled. Jaki'el stepped towards her, blade high above his head.

She closed her eyes and let out the faintest whimper before he drove the blade deep into her neck.

Jaki'el turned before her body hit the silver pool. He didn't need to see what would happen next. Suddenly, the priests were silent. Their shadows danced between the rocks from whence they came. He was alone.

They had accepted his sacrifice. The future of the Jark Empire was secure.

***

"I didn't think you were going to show up."

Gemini smiled and took a seat next to his favorite councilwoman. She was tall and slender for a Mateen, and her light gray skin complimented her muscular physique. Long black hair fell against her shoulders and down her back. Dark eyes that drifted from his face to his torso and back to the speaker of the convention were thoughtful and precise. He had loved her once. Maybe he still did. But those were thoughts for another time, another world perhaps.

"You could say I'm curious," he smirked, sinking into the deep cream-colored chair, built for comfort, long meetings, and even some dozing. "Besides, I thought I should say goodbye before I head to Rodam."

He was taller than her by two feet. His gray and black robe with gold shoulder boards across the front was reserved for space fleet commanders. It was an impressive title and would have caused anyone other than Noura to shrink down in inferiority. Not Noura though, she had known him too long and could respect Gemini only as much as a brother, perhaps even a little brother.

Noura returned her eyes to his and locked his stare with her own. Her eyes flickered gold as she tried to read his thoughts. He wouldn't let her in though, not this time. His thoughts were a mystery even to him, no need to confuse the matter.

"You continue to frustrate me, Gemini," she said at last. "But I'm glad you came to say goodbye. I know how important your yearly trips to Rodam are. I know what they mean to your fleet."

They are important, he thought to her but was again overcome with a flurry of emotions. The desire to stay, to leave the fleet behind. To avoid another three years hunting smugglers and preventing real enemies from breaching their defenses. *If there are any real enemies left.* He smiled at her again and turned his attention to the old man at the front.

He had dark gray skin wrinkled from age and weathered by the sun. Thick glasses complimenting an even thicker brow concealed a big brain. Bigger than his anyway. Their chief scientist asked to address the Galactic Order on implications of the merge. That's what they called it anyway. Two galaxies on a crash course. What would happen was anyone's guess, and there were plenty of guesses.

He was large in stature, but he was dwarfed by the size of the stage. Light wood cibron floors native to Hestos complimented bright white walls. Lights as powerful as ship engines illuminated the stage and beamed into the old scientist's eyes. The real focus, however, was in front of him. Blue and green, the colors of a hologram swirled in front, forming the shapes of two spiral galaxies that hovered in mid-air above the stage. One was clearly theirs and had planets, star systems, and homeworlds highlighted within the image. The other galaxy was dark. A mystery to everyone who examined it. Gemini was relieved as the hologram showed the collision of the two galaxies over and over again. Mateen was safely nestled in its star system on the far end. At least this current model showed it was safe. Who knew how things would change when the merge got closer.

"It's hard to tell," the man was saying. "No one has ever been able to travel outside our galaxy because of the sheer power of the forces at play. Magnetism, gravity, dark energy, dark matter, radiation. This list goes on. There is, after all, a reason that galaxies stick together."

"Yes, yes, yes," said a fat Hestonian man wearing a flowing white cape over a black suit. "We know all that. What I'm asking is, what will happen during the merge? Do those qualities disappear, making it possible to explore the new galaxy?"

The doctor was perplexed. Gemini shot Noura a look. She returned it and leaned in. "The order is concerned about a cataclysmic event, and all this councilman can do is think about exploiting the next galaxy over. He should keep his mouth shut," she hissed.

"He's asking the same question I have," Gemini responded with a patient rebuke. "But while he wants to exploit the galaxy, my fear is that something on the other side is waiting to exploit us."

Noura placed her hand on his leg and patted it. "There is the one I've come to adore," she said smiling. "Always concerned about the future before the present has had a chance to run its course."

He grunted but chose not to respond. People who hadn't experienced war rarely possessed the paranoia that Gemini and others like him felt. He couldn't fault her for it, only constantly remind her that threats existed beyond the ones they could see with their eyes.

"We cannot say," the scientist continued. "It is impossible to see beyond our galaxy with any clarity. We don't know yet whether the gravity fields will merge and open a transitway or whether the two black holes at the center will simply tear everything apart."

The scientist pushed a button on a remote and suddenly the galaxies disappeared, showing a small research craft flying through a wormhole in the holographic space. "This," he said pointing at the vessel, "was a robotic exploration craft we sent a few weeks ago. Some of us suspected we could make some alterations to our wormhole engines to allow it to cross the void and gain some real, tangible observations of the galaxy."

Gemini watched expectantly as the video played. As soon as the craft entered intergalactic space the wormhole collapsed, and the ship imploded. The hologram returned to the image of the two galaxies, each spinning clockwise as they raced towards each other at incomprehensible speeds. "I show this video to highlight the difficulty we've had in exploring this event."

The Hestonian crossed his arms and leaned back in his chair. Gemini sensed he was frustrated but couldn't understand why. *Couldn't he see that the Galactic Order was doing its best to research the event?* A second Hestonian, the man's partner, answered Gemini's question.

"Then why are we even here?" the Hestonian protested. He was slender with blond hair and wore the traditional white robe many governing members from Hestos wore when they conducted official business. "This meeting was supposed to provide answers. Has the Galactic Order determined anything about this event at all?"

If the scientist could blush, he would have. Instead, he cleared his throat and leaned his heavy gray hands on the podium. There was a thick silence in the room, broken only by a smothered cough from a member of the audience. A lesser species would have pushed the question off to the ruling council seated in the first row. After all, these were the leaders who composed the council and made decisions. The Mateen scientist was merely an expert witness, a messenger paid to conduct research and explain where he was in the scientific process. To be angry with the scientist was foolishness, but this was not a lesser species. He was a Mateen. Before he opened his mouth, Gemini swelled with pride for the member of his own species.

"I can tell you this," he said, at last, pointing to the rotating hologram on the stage in front of him. "Every world must be prepared for the worst. This event will be upon us in ten galactic years. There is the possibility that the merge will cause such a gravitational distortion that the two galaxies will eject entire star systems from orbit and send them into the cold void of space alone. If that occurs, I implore the Galactic Order to be ready to receive billions of refugees and to evacuate the affected systems. This will cost money. As members of the order, my plea is that all systems contribute.

"It is also possible that nothing will happen, that our galaxies will simply merge, and a bridge will be opened. I suspect," he said, clearing his throat, "we will get a combination of both. The nearest planets and stars will collide, and the gravitational disturbance will eject the weaker systems, but we are lucky that our current galactic rotation saves all of the inhabited planets during that collision. The closest species, the Jarks, are still hundreds of light years from the merge event. Following the merge, a bridge will be opened, and we should rely on the order to help control the competing systems that are vying for positions to explore the new galaxy."

He paused to survey the crowd, then pulled his glasses down from his face and set them on the podium. "I would caution all of you to consider one last thing. We don't know who or what is on the other side, eager to pour into our galaxy as well."

The Mateen scientist left the stage to a silent crowd and was replaced by the President of the Galactic Council, head of the Galactic Order. He was a tall, handsome Hestonian. He wore a golden crown to signify his position, and with him, he carried the book of the laws the council swore by. He was a patient man and remained silent to allow the scientist to leave the stage before opening the floor for questions.

Gemini looked at Noura and smiled. "I am relying on you to make sure our fleets are well funded. As he said, nobody knows what will happen or who is on the other side. They might be even more advanced than we are."

She sighed. He suspected she wanted to say more than she did, but that too was for a different time, an earlier, less complicated time. A time when he wasn't a fleet commander, and she wasn't busy as a councilwoman to the order. "I will always advocate for the fleet," she responded. "Worry about nothing while you are away. The collective has always supported your cause."

Gemini rose to his feet and pulled Noura to hers, giving her a hug. "I'll see you in a few years," he said, backing away from her.

"What?" she responded with a wink. "You don't plan to stay for the discussion? Your Hestonian friends will surely have more to say on the subject.

Gemini chuckled as he backpedaled towards the exit. "What do we pay you for if I have to stay?"

Noura laughed. "That was a cheap shot," she complained. "You know you really just pay me to wine and dine out here with diplomats."

Gemini smiled warmly. "There is one more thing," he whispered.

"There is talk that I will be ordered to quell the rebels. I hope our people pursue every diplomatic effort before risking my fleet."

Noura nodded. *I will pursue peace if only for you,* she thought to him.

Gemini turned from her. Sunlight nearly blinded him as he pushed through the doors of the Galactic Order's headquarters on Hestos. The massive planet had become the seat of galactic law and order and the host to a handful of species that shared their desires for governance within the galaxy. Despite the wealth of Hestos, Gemini was eager to return to his own system and his own people. He assumed Noura felt the same way.

Blinking through the light, Gemini's eyes finally adjusted and were able to look to the north of the city. Cresting the sky was the biggest ship in their fleet. Gemini's gray battleship, a two-thousand-meter-long behemoth ready to do battle on behalf of the Mateen people.

"Bring the crew in from port call," Gemini ordered his fleet's executive officer over the radio. "It's time for us to head to Rodam."

CHAPTER ONE

A battleship and destroyer were closing fast. Pure white light from the Tassian sun bombarded his vision. "Get out!" Brokk screamed into his own mind. It was too late. Everyone knew it. Lago's battleship was too damaged to escape and while Lago accepted his fate, Brokk, sharing his mind, refused it. For Brokk, fate was for the weak. Destiny was for those that lacked the courage to control their lives.

An explosion tore through his hull and knocked him off balance. Intense pressure crushed inward against his chest as oxygen rushed from his ship and into the void. Emergency systems that should have come on were absent and the same pressure that seized him at first now squeezed him on all sides. His ears popped, and his lungs screamed. A second explosion threw him to the floor. Desperate for air, Lago gasped and replenished his lungs with … nothing. The pain was too great. He had to let go, but Brokk wouldn't let him.

"Get out of my mind!" Lago screamed. His last breath. Lungs collapsed in the vacuum. His body was weightless. All went black.

Brokk woke with a gasp. His lungs ached, and his chest hurt. He had been dreaming again, reliving the moment that Lago died. The moment that changed everything. Brokk wiped the sweat from his cold damp forehead. The room was dark, but, as he began to move, the light in his cabin brightened. He looked out of his window. Blackness. The cold space beyond his pane called to him. Lago was out there somewhere. A frozen body floating through his enemy's star system.

He would never get back to sleep. Not with a dream like that. Not after experiencing Lago's death as he had the day it occurred. The day he tested out the experimental Jark communication system that fused his mind with the minds of his fleet commanders.

Mistakes. That's all it was. His side made more of them than the Mateens. Part of Brokk refused to believe this. His training had been superior. His crew was ready.

Intervention. That was the real problem. Brokk had achieved his mission in record time, sweeping away the defenses of Tassi and dismantling their government ... until the Mateen intervened.

Betrayal. That was the root of it. Betrayed by his people. Outnumbered by an enemy that should never have been allowed to enter the fight. Hatred and sorrow surged within him, a toxic mix of ingredients that threatened to tear him apart from the inside out. No, he wouldn't get back to sleep now.

Swinging his legs over the side of his bed, Brokk felt the cold black floor until his feet touched his boots. The light in his room was growing brighter now, gradually increasing in intensity until his eyes had fully adjusted to a waking light. It was still early; his day shift wouldn't be awake for another few hours. *A good chance to grab some food in peace,* Brokk thought to himself, pulling his red and black one-piece jumpsuit over his shoulders and heading towards the door.

The hallways were dark. Quiet. Asleep. Lights flickered on and then shut off as he strode down them, passing ancient battle scenes that were hung years ago to motivate his men in battle. "Remember your past," he would tell them. "Remember the honor of our ancestors." Antique weapons decorated other walls. A jagged ax with a handle made from volcanic rock glistened as the light above it beamed down on a still-sharpened blade.

As he reached the dining hall, he could feel his sorceress pulling at the back of his mind, leading his steps forward as if invisible hands were pulling on his own, bringing him ever closer for some unknown purpose. Two silver doors opened as he approached them, and he saw her leaning in a chair against the far wall. *Tamara.* She didn't flinch when the doors opened but he knew she sensed him. She had called him here, he knew that now.

She still wore the same gold, hooded trench coat he had gifted her on Charoth. Tamara looked like one of his priests, except she had eyes and a tongue. A hand, curled up against her jaw, displayed gilded claws and shined emeralds and rubies. They sparkled brightly against the light coming from the ceiling above. They were beautiful, but they were also deadly he reminded himself.

Tamara was meditating. Staring out of the window into the dead of space. Beautiful brown hair tumbled down her shoulders and rested against the middle of her back.

Without turning, her gentle voice shattered the silence. "I was hoping you would join me this morning, Brokk."

He grunted. "I couldn't sleep," he responded suspiciously. "Did you have something to do with that?" Her voice may have been gentle, but Brokk remained wary of her. She could do incredible things, and her power seemed to grow immeasurably with each passing day. He had to be careful.

"You know I wouldn't make you relive Lago's death," she said flatly, gentleness fading and being replaced by strength and confidence. Brokk snorted and sat in the chair across from her. On the table in the middle, a cup of taka'e root tea waited for him. Steam still rose from the brown mug's opening.

"And yet you have prepared a place for me," he growled. She toyed with him far too often. Perhaps he would have to remind her that there was a limit to his patience and his hospitality.

"Call it a hunch," she reassured him, hostility retreating from her voice. Her eyes flared with a green flame before returning to a docile mossy hue. *Far too often.* "Have we not conquered together?" she asked rhetorically. "Do I not deserve greater trust than you offer now?"

During the day she trained with him and his marines. When the official training ended, she remained, practicing hand-to-hand combat and learning how to use weapons. She studied their tactics to learn where she could best be employed during a battle. She exploited her skills against dummy foes and was quickly growing to an overly intimidating force within his crew. It worried Brokk. He never considered her a threat during the day, but at night, they would sometimes sit and talk, and Brokk found himself wondering. *Paranoia,* his mind would insist. He wasn't sure.

"The closer we get to Jark, the more intense my dreams become," he admitted quietly. "I relive them constantly as if I were there. I feel the cold. The breathless, airless cold that tugs on Lago's body in his final moments. They are my final moments." Brokk paused, wondering how much he should reveal, but Tamara's eyes were still docile. Still sympathetic. So, he continued. "I believe I feel this way because I am to blame. I was the one who insisted on our doomed campaign. Now, I live with my guilt as if it were yesterday."

"If it is your fault," she asked, "why is it we drift towards Jark?"

He considered playing the game they had played the last three months where she would convince him to blame others over himself. He considered conceding once more, agreeing she was right, that it was really the Jark Empire or the Mateen that had killed Lago. Not Brokk. But he wouldn't. Not tonight. "We drift towards Jark because I believe I will feel better after I kill the man who betrayed us. But after I kill the emperor, I know this will haunt me still."

"And yet you still aim to kill him?" she asked simply.

Brokk nodded and turned his eyes towards the empty space beyond. A light flickered above him.

"Don't you see," she quickly responded as if he had fallen into her trap once more. "He is the one who didn't send reinforcements. He is the one who left your fleet to fight a hopeless battle against multiple enemies. You know this to be true."

"You're right," he responded honestly. "But Lago didn't die because we were betrayed by our empire. Lago died because I foolishly sent him to defend our doomed campaign. I could have evacuated the planet. I could have pushed our defenses beyond the Tassian asteroid belt. Better yet, I could have shed my pride before leaving Jark. Perhaps I would have seen the campaign for what it was. Instead, I ordered him to fight to the death. I was blind. I bear that guilt. Not the emperor."

Tamara returned her gaze to the window and tapped her clawed fingers against the armrest of her chair. Brokk too stared into the abyss. Finally, she looked back at him and smiled. "If you want it to be your fault, it can be your fault, but I will never believe it."

Brokk grunted but didn't have anything else to say. She noticed his silence and dropped her smile for something else. "Something you just said, Brokk. Why did you suggest you could have seen the campaign for what it was?"

Brokk hesitated. Her eyes were no longer docile. The soft hazel green had been replaced with a lantern. It was not yet a full blaze, but he had caught her attention. Piqued her interest. "I believe the emperor sent me to Tassi to get rid of me. I believe my popularity with the people had him concerned."

Tamara's face remained flat. Her eyes were narrow. The fire in them brewed beneath the docile green that shined on the surface. She mulled over his statement, compared it with what she thought she knew about the golden-skinned man and the prophecy. Tamara lifted her jeweled fingers to her head and pushed the hair back from her ears. Brokk realized she wanted to say more. Something strange and unfamiliar. *She's been plotting.*

"Why is it that you are awake?" he asked. "What have you been thinking? Why did you pull me here?" Accusation boiled off his words. Paranoia steamed from his lips.

Her eyes went from a simmer to a blaze and then faded to nothing in an instant. Tamara cupped her hands in her lap and for a moment, Brokk suspected they were actually trembling. "Something has been brewing inside me," she said at last.

"What do you mean?" he asked, perplexed at the sudden change in her tone.

She paused, and a sly smile curved at the edges of her mouth. "What if you are the chosen one?"

Brokk hesitated to answer. His mind swirled. He had not only buried the prospect of becoming a king, but he had also buried the prophecy. It was as dead to him as the priests who proclaimed it over his body when he was just a child and executed in his fury after losing the battle of Tassi.

The golden child. The man with the golden skin. It was this belief that had led him to such a foolish mission to conquer Tassi. It was this belief that blinded him to the real purpose of his conquest: their emperor's desire to see Brokk destroyed.

"Why do you mutter such nonsense?" he grumbled at last.

Tamara didn't blink. Her eyes remained fixated on his. An eerie green fire brewed beneath the surface and reflected off her golden claws. "Why is it that we drift toward Jark?" she asked a second time, her innocence faded, replaced with a toxic idea he had yet to hear.

Brokk knew better and became aggravated. Behind her fierce green eyes burned a fire that implored him to answer it once more. He didn't want to take the bait but something inside him forced him to speak. "We've been through this," he growled. "I'm going to kill the emperor."

She smiled. "So, you'll rush in like a fool then? What happens next?

You wait for the army to execute you in the square?" She paused to stare him in the eyes and challenge his gaze. "You and Red are the same. That's why I like you both so much," she chuckled, "but the truth is, if you rush to Jark, you are a fool."

"Then what should I do?" Brokk blurted, his face hot with blood. Since the battle of Tassi he had barely kept his head afloat, instead merely doing what he thought best. There had been no suggestions and no advice. Brokk strove alone, constantly judged by his crew for any decision he made. Constantly concerned about a rebellion or a coup that would allow them to turn him over as a prisoner to the Jark Empire in exchange for their freedom.

"You should kill him," she said calmly. "But you need to do it smartly. I'm not suggesting the prophecy is true or false, Brokk. I'm merely suggesting that it is true in the eyes of the people."

"What do you mean?" He pushed his anger down into his chest yet ready to call it up once more if he so desired.

"You still have the grootslang eggs?" she asked.

"I do."

"Send me then. Send me to be your messenger, to be your prophet. I will proclaim the demise of Jark due to its wickedness. I will proclaim a message of repentance and a new era for its people. Once we gather a following, we will summon the grootslang from the ground to bring terror to the capital and overthrow the government. That will be the sign before your coming and convince the remaining skeptics of my legitimacy."

Brokk was silent. Could it work? Could she convince the people to follow him? To forsake the Emperor of Jark? Could he become the legitimate ruler of Jark and end the banishment of his crew?

"They would defeat the grootslang," Brokk challenged.

"It is merely a sign," Tamara retorted with a flare of fire in her eye sockets that sent a chill down Brokk's spine. "The people believed you were the fulfillment of prophecy too. Do you not remember? Your crew believed you were the fulfillment of prophecy. Is that not why they followed you? Make it come true, Brokk. We need to change the prophecy. You can still be the chosen one," she said with a gleaming smile. "Maybe you were merely chosen to rule Jark before you exact your revenge on Tassi."

Brokk turned his gaze from his sorceress to the window. There was only blackness beyond. His head spun and twirled with strategy and motive. Punches and counter-punches surrounded him as he fought an invisible battle in his mind. She was right. She was smarter than him, and suddenly, he wondered not only about the chance of victory on Jark but also the loyalty of his sorceress.

It could work. His crew would revel at the chance to once again believe he was chosen by the gods. They would rejoice in the opportunity to return to their home, not as outcasts or prisoners but as the elite guard of their new emperor. She was right.

As if she had sensed his thoughts, Tamara rose and pulled her hood back over her head. "I'll leave you alone," she whispered, dragging a golden claw across his shoulder as she departed.

CHAPTER TWO

"Three months Gemini!" Cale was irate. "Three months since you came to me with news about my father. Three months since we shook hands and agreed to hunt the fugitive Brokk and his crew. What do we have to show for it? What have we done in three months?"

The gray-skinned Mateen remained motionless. Silent. There was nothing for him to say. No rebuttal prepared to calm Cale's nerves. Cale had a right to be angry. There was no progress. There was no federation formed to hunt the fugitive. Galactic politics had once again failed. Tassi was alone in their grief. Cale was alone in his hate.

When Cale saw no response, he answered the questions for himself. "We've done nothing, Gemini. Your words mean nothing. I will get my father myself."

For a Tassian, Cale was a handsome man. Tall and tan with golden-white hair that was cropped short to his head. He sat behind a large crystal desk in the crystal government building they fought together to free. A brilliant array of colors penetrated the crystal walls and danced all around Gemini. Even in the beautiful white light that bathed the room, Gemini could see Cale's anger. The man would leave to find his father, and nothing could stop him.

"That's not a good idea," Gemini protested. Cale still hadn't offered him a seat in his office, and the Mateen was suddenly relieved. The conversation was going nowhere, but he wouldn't back down from providing his counsel. Cale deserved as much. He had a lot on his shoulders since his father had been kidnapped, and there were few wise counselors in any government. "You are still rebuilding your fleet and your pilots are inexperienced. Brokk is seasoned. His armada has already defeated the Third Jarkian space fleet. It is dangerous. You should wait for a coalition to be formed."

Cale waived his pale hand flippantly at Gemini. "I've been busy. We've been building faster than you realize," he said, letting a grin appear where a scowl once sat. Pride seeped from his features.

"Yes," Gemini admitted. "I've been made aware of the Tassian ambitions. The Hestonians too, they're nervous about the newfound sense of nationalism on Tassi."

Cale threw his head back and boomed with laughter. The sound echoed around their crystal office and vibrated the papers that had been strewn across Cale's desk. Gemini suspected Cale wanted to startle him. It wouldn't work. "As if the Mateens have any right to protest," he muttered bitterly. "You've been safe in your little corner. No one looks at your homeworld with a desire to conquer it. You've built your weapons and your ships and now you try to speak on behalf of the Galactic Council as if they have any right to dictate the course of my people."

Gemini grunted, but Cale wasn't finished. "The Hestonians are greedy. Tassian military strength would challenge their economy."

Gemini let out a visible sigh. Cale returned a cold stare, dared him to continue the argument. Gemini suspected any attempt to reason with him would only cement the young commander's resolve. "I fought by your father's side when the council forbade it," Gemini responded softly. "My people have never relied upon our membership with the galactic council for security, but to cut yourself off from them completely is madness." Cale's stare softened momentarily. He was deep in thought. "A lot of Mateen blood was shed defending your planet." Gemini continued, "I would love to come with you to bring Brokk to justice, but—"

Cale laughed cutting Gemini off. "There's always a but," he said flatly, letting the laughter echo from the clear crystal walls as he twisted out of his chair. "Come out with it already. Why are you here?"

"Our fleet has been redirected. It is no secret." He paused to validate his assumption. "You know the struggles the Mateen are having with its separatists right now. I've received orders to quell the rebellion."

Cale shrugged. Gemini suspected that not even Cale in his anger would blame the Mateen for trying to bring peace to the violent rebellion that left a black eye on the galactic community. "And what about the Hestonians?" he asked. "Have they lost their nerve without Mateen supervision?"

Gemini sighed. "The galactic merge is upon us, Cale. Magnetic fields are mixing. Soon, the two galaxies will become one. Wormhole travel will be opened between galaxies. The Hestonians want to exploit the new galaxy as soon as possible but traveling halfway across our galaxy to the fringe will take months and they argue that they cannot spare the ships to hunt down a criminal."

Cale's anger returned to his face. "The greedy fools are going exploring instead of honoring their commitment to peace?"

Gemini held back a smirk, instead, he tried to reflect the sorrow he truly felt for Cale. The young leader had lost too much and now the burden was upon him to bring justice to his people.

"And the Jarks?" Cale asked. "What is their plan?"

Gemini caught the sudden change in tone. "What are the Jarks to you, Cale?"

"Surely you know I am bringing charges against them at the Galactic Council. They are my enemy," he responded. "We both know Brokk wasn't rogue. The Jarks wanted our world. We won't let that happen again."

"They will send Commander Szega and the Third Fleet to the fringe as well," Gemini replied, realizing his error but already engrossed in the truth. "They are worried about the Galactic Merge and want to ensure there is no enemy preparing to cross into our galaxy."

Cale smiled. "The enemy is within our galaxy," he hissed. "I'm headed to Charoth to inquire about Brokk, and I won't wait a moment longer."

Cale gestured towards the door. Gemini didn't budge. His crimson eyes stared hard into Cale's golden ones. Cale's face remained flat. Emotionless. What could he do? Had Cale just hinted at war with the Jarks? Was it Gemini's job to prevent it if he had? "Where will the Tassian fleet go, Cale?" Gemini asked.

Cale motioned again towards the door. "You can petition my government to learn the details of Tassian fleet operations."

"What about Casika?" Gemini asked, softer this time. "Is she safe?"

"She is on Hestos, doing what I lack the patience to do," Cale replied. "She is safe. Now really, I must be going." He motioned towards the door once more.

Gemini nodded and left the crystal office for his shuttle on the roof of the building. After ascending the stairs and exiting the clear door, he was bombarded even more fiercely by the pure white light that shone down upon him from the dual helium stars above. From the roof, he could see the pristine blue ocean, more radiant than anything from his homeworld. On the horizon, his gray battleship waited. It was a weapon of war, and, against the backdrop of the beautiful blue water and hundreds of Tassians flying kites on the beach,

Gemini wished the battleship didn't exist at all; and yet, that same tool of death above had brought freedom to Cale's world.

***

Cale watched Gemini ascend the crystal steps before leaving his own office and heading down. Since the Jark invasion, a lot of work had been done to renovate and repair their capitol building. At the time, Cale believed his father and the government were foolish. They had set their trust upon the Galactic Order for security and were abandoned in the face of war. Cale would not make the same mistake.

As he descended the steps, a brilliant spectrum of light danced around him. The crystal city had been returned to its former glory. For that, he was grateful. Improvements were made as well. The clear wading pool that once existed at the bottom of the building was no more. Instead, Cale had built science labs, dedicated to the research of Jark magic and advancement of Tassian military technologies.

The war had been good for something. Hundreds of Jark fighters had crashed on Tassi. Thousands of Jark soldiers had been killed. An opportunity suddenly existed to exploit the equipment and develop them for Tassian use.

Money once used to enhance the tourism industry was rerouted, instead, massive fabricators and industrial machines were built. Fleets were being produced in record number, all based on Jark and Mateen technology that had crashed on their planet during the battle. Soon, the entire galaxy would recognize their error. Tassi would be viewed as a sleeping giant, one who had just been awakened.

Cale reached the bottom of the steps and paused. The memory of a stun grenade flashed before his eyes. He saw his soldiers scattered. Casika was terrified and the giant beast that was summoned from another world rose above his head. They were distant memories now, but he couldn't help but feel panic surge within him as if they had happened merely yesterday.

Cale lowered his face to a retina scanner and two metal doors slowly opened, revealing sterile white hallways and Tassian scientists dressed in white robes and long blue gloves. The crystal ceiling had been replaced with steel and concrete. The dual suns could not penetrate here. Unlike his father's government, this new Tassian government ended transparency where national defense began. Cale ran on a platform of nationalism, pride, and fear. The people didn't hesitate to give him the support he required.

Cale strode down the white-walled hallway briskly. The hour was almost upon them, and Gemini's surprise visit risked him missing the show. At the end of the hallway, Cale turned left and entered the Biotech wing. A man wearing glasses and a white lab coat greeted him.

"Cale," the man said warmly. "I'm glad you made it." The doctor was old, perhaps twenty years older than Cale and had lost his hair years ago. His bald head shined in the bright fluorescent light above, and thick black glasses accented his face. If Cale hadn't known him, he would have judged him as a school teacher or librarian. Instead, this was his chief scientist, and he had been busy.

"Good to see you again, Chayyim. Did I miss anything?" Cale asked, trying to hide his excitement.

"No, you're right on time. Shall we get right to it then?"

Cale nodded, and the two walked another few paces to a white door. It slid open at the request of a green key card and closed behind the two. Chayyim handed Cale a white bodysuit and a face mask, which Cale donned and then followed Chayyim through another set of doors. Oxygen hissed as the doors opened and closed. He could feel his mask squeeze his face. The pressure was different here, he was in a vacuum meant to replicate space.

When the doors opened again, Cale found himself in a massive chamber standing on the top of a perforated steel platform with railing on either side. Below were three segmented worlds, separated by heavy glass and steel. The first room was dark. Dim red light shone down from the ceiling. The atmosphere was hot and dry. Cale could almost taste the sulfur in his mouth. As he looked at the sensors recording the room on a dial on the railing, he noticed the gravity was almost four times as dense as it was on Tassi.

"It's remarkable how closely you were able to mimic the environment," he said to Chayyim.

The man nodded. "Yes, as you know we were given a lot of information from the Jark soldiers who surrendered," he said. "We even tested the atmosphere on a few of the prisoners just to make sure."

"I think it's perfect," Cale said. He smiled at Chayyim from behind his mask before remembering the scientist wouldn't be able to see it.

Cale looked down once more to see Jark prisoners from the battle leaning against the glass corners of their new prison. Black soup gurgled up from the ground below, and silver mercury bubbled in round little pools. A block of glass and steal separated the room from an empty space and then a third chamber beyond.

"This represents Tassi," Chayyim said, motioning Cale towards the final chamber. "As you know, we've replicated each environment quite specifically to ensure our tests are as accurate as possible.

Cale looked down to see another Jark soldier resting on all fours. His black hair and scarred face angered Cale. There was superiority and audacity in the Jark's features. It was a certainty that drove Cale mad.

"So, he is infected?" Cale intuited.

The doctor nodded. "Yes, yes. Because we knew when you were coming, we took the liberty of infecting him two days ago. This way you can see how quickly the agent spreads once a host becomes infected. The struggle that we have is timing a biological agent with a government's rate of detection. If you allow an agent to kill its host too soon, you risk not infecting a large enough population. If you allow the agent to linger for too long, someone will be able to treat it before it becomes a pandemic."

He paused, eyeing Cale as if there was something he had forgotten. "And you know," he continued, "that while anyone can catch this biological agent, it has been fine-tuned to Jark biology."

Cale nodded. "And you managed to actually solve the problem of transporting living organisms through wormholes?"

"Not without losing a few," Chayyim said slowly, "but, yes, we have a mostly stable method to send the prisoners home."

"Show me."

Without hesitation, the doctor pulled a computer out from the railing and pressed some keys on the pad. "These bulky suits make it impossible to use current technology," he muttered under his breath.

Cale ignored him and watched the simulated Tassian homeworld below. What started as a small black dot hovering to the right of the prisoner expanded into a wavy circle that the Jark could fit through. Startled, the Jark prisoner backed into the far corner of the glass. Blackness suddenly turned to a reddish hue, and a similarly amorphous circle opened into the simulated Jark chamber.

"Prisoner," the doctor ordered through a microphone beside the computer, "enter the portal."

The Jark remained frozen in place. Cale delighted at the fearful expression on his face. He deserved as much.

"Prisoner," the doctor ordered again, "enter the chamber or be executed."

The Jark looked up for a moment and then slowly crawled on all fours into the portal. Instantly he disappeared and reappeared on the far side. Cale was astonished to see him not only still alive, but apparently unaffected.

The Jark seemed just as confused, but upon seeing two other Jark prisoners, he ran to them and embraced them.

"In the interest of your time," the doctor said, "I won't make you wait here another two days. The biological agent has already spread to the others."

"Just like that?" Cale wondered.

He nodded and entered a second code into the computer. Seconds later, the three men below grabbed their stomachs and gagged. Screaming for help, they fell to the floor and choked to death.

"At its heart, this is a blister agent. They are drowning in their own fluids as liquid sacks build up in their throats and lungs."

"Have you made history?" Cale asked with a smile.

The scientist looked perplexed before answering. "Of course not, you are aware there are many blister agents that have been employed."

"No, no, no," Cale responded through his suit. What I mean is, this is the first time anyone has transported a person through a wormhole, right?"

"Ah," Chayyim gleefully exclaimed. "It is just too bad that no one will be able to know about this."

Cale nodded and then returned his eyes to the simulated Jark world below, studying them until the three Jarks below no longer moved. His father would be proud.

I hope you've enjoyed this preview. You can buy Doomsayer on Amazon or at your local bookstore today!